MEDICINE OF THE WHITE OWL

Wendy Padilla and Donna Simko

MEDICINE OF THE WHITE OWL

© 2008 by Wendy Padilla and Donna Simko

U.S. Copyright Office 101 Independence Ave. S.E. Washington, D.C. 20559-6000 (202) 707-3000

This book is a work of fiction, and its characters are fictional. Any resemblance to any person living or dead is unintended. The institutions, organizations, businesses, publications, broadcasts, and places that appear in the text are fictional or are used fictionally.

Published by Lulu

ISBN: 978-0-615-25510-1

To all of you who find your selves
Arriving at the point of no return,
Your feet now firmly on the path.
May you, too, imagine and discover
The wonders of creativity.

A Special thanks to Michael Simko for both his computer expertise and his creative designs for the impressive book cover!

MEDICINE OF THE WHITE OWL

Contents

CHAPTER 1

THE MASSACRE

THE MASSACRE

The lizard stared back at Carlotta. Both reptile and child froze in their tracks just as, the moment before, each had scampered unaware on its own side of the adobe wall. Carlotta held her breath. The lizard blinked but did not move. The shiny black eyes revealed nothing beneath the reptilian skin, which seemed as old as the New Mexico terrain that camouflaged its very existence.

The eight-year-old studied the subtle gray, and sand-colored scales that had also managed to capture an overlay of a tangible slice of the blue sky. The eye-to-eye chance meeting was an opportunity not to be missed, and Carlotta resisted the impulse to brush back a wayward lock of hair that hung tormentingly across her nose. The ancient desert sentry appraised his challenger and, choosing his own moment in time, finally conceded the small shady area on top of the wall. Carlotta climbed quickly into the lizard's vacated spot and, folding her legs neatly beneath her, adopted the reptile's demeanor. This was the child's intimate way of learning about the world around her, already a quiet practice of observation and identification that had largely circumvented a need to communicate with the mission friars.

Each afternoon, since the summer's sun had returned to the Sangre de Cristo Mountains, Carlotta had managed to steal away from the other children to seek the solitude of the decaying adobe blocks at the end of the wall. The hidden alcove was a place where order was not determined by the bells or Friar Alcazar and to a degree meant freedom. The mission's courtyard enclosed an arid patch of land, an incongruous repetition of the terrain outside the mission's gates. The only exceptions were the small garden kept for the needs of the kitchen and the corrals that housed sheep, goats, and the friar's horses. On three sides of the courtyard ran long dark walkways sheltered by the extended roof. From Carlotta's secluded corner, the walk's cool adobe bricks spread out in a diminishing pattern, turning at their vertex and trailing off behind several willows, which concealed the mission gates.

Carlotta watched as the lizard scurried off and mounted a large boulder. There he perched absorbing the energy of the day's collected sun. She envied the lizard's ability to remain rooted, invisible to the life around it. The day was warm and still, except for the drone of bees flitting from blossom to blossom in the hot sun and a rush of wings as several birds swooped under the heavy roof beams to care for new hatchlings. From her secret vantage point, Carlotta viewed uninterrupted life in the courtyard.

This was the time of day, after the noon meal, when the children were expected to be quiet. It was understood that the wrath of Friar Alcazar would descend on them if any rowdiness disturbed his siesta. The youngest would sleep, while others would amuse themselves or study. The oldest were frequently sent out to work as apprentices to the people of the town. It was here, in the dark reaches of earthen walls, Carlotta spent as much time as possible by herself, separate from the other mission orphans. Though her years were few, she had already come to realize the pleasure of privacy and the idle hours spent considering her own uniqueness and the world's.

Carlotta had brought two books with her, one a primer suitable for children her age and their expected ability, and another, which she now carefully opened. Friar Serna had not wanted to consider any but the primer when he had excused her from the common room, but Carlotta had begged for a more interesting book, hopefully the one with the engravings depicting other times and places. The child's pleas had finally won over the friar and he allowed the book to leave the room, a highly unusual circumstance.

Friar Serna would have been more than mildly surprised to learn how well Carlotta had progressed with her reading, particularly because there was little emphasis in the mission on the education of children who were largely made up of the uncivilized.

It was not just the pen-and-ink drawings spaced randomly throughout the book that fascinated the child. The few lessons she had absorbed, reinforced by the answers to the nagging questions she continually asked her older brother Diego and others his age had given her all the impetus needed.

Carlotta's nose was buried in the old volume when from the corner of her eye she glimpsed a movement. Not twenty paces down the corridor, Friar Alcazar exited a doorway. He placed one foot warily onto the adobe brick and cautiously looked to the left and right. Seemingly satisfied, he entered the corridor accompanied by another man.

Carlotta caught her breath. She had not been seen, and she knew intuitively that it was best she was not. Friar Alcazar was an intimidating presence under normal circumstances and the children did their best to avoid him. The friar's handsome face bore a dark countenance and his mouth appeared cruel. Carlotta examined his robes, which hung ominously from his tall frame - almost as if they were hiding something evil, she thought. Not at all like Friar Serna, whose plump, awkward figure bustled about the mission, drawing involuntary giggles from the children.

Friar Alcazar was a strict disciplinarian, frequently demonstrating a sinister desire to belittle and humiliate his wards, but it was the friar's furtive actions that now gave Carlotta reason to suspect her own danger. She watched, not daring to move a muscle.

The second man turned in Carlotta's direction and the hood of the cape that, curiously, he was wearing on this hot summer day, fell to his shoulders revealing his face. The child recognized him at once as Tito Sanchez. Alarmed, she identified the notorious bandit who had terrorized the town and neighboring pueblos.

"Then you will make the arrangements immediately?" Sanchez asked, as he ceremoniously handed over a small tied bag to the friar.

Alcazar received the bag somewhat distastefully but replied, "Yes, the children will be sent within the hour."

There were no other words, not even in departure. Sanchez drew the hood around his head and left just as quickly as he had appeared. Carlotta could barely hear the sound of his boots as his steps receded on the brick walkway, and though she listened carefully she did not hear the heavy iron gates unlatch.

Friar Alcazar stood vigil for several minutes. In mock death his shadow fell eerily behind him, sending tendrils in search of the adobe wall. Carlotta listened, fearful her own pounding heart would betray her, but Alcazar turned abruptly and withdrew through the doorway.

Though the day was warm, Carlotta shivered. She held her position on the wall several minutes longer in the event the friar would return. Finally, assured he must have other business to attend, the child moved into the sunlight. She rested one small hand on the wall beside her, her palm absorbing the sun's warmth. She felt comforted.

It was inconceivable that Friar Alcazar and Tito Sanchez had reason to meet. One represented God and the other the devil. The thought did not find fertile ground to grow in Carlotta's mind. Her youthful instruction in the mission had allowed only a black-and- white perception of morality, and until now there had been little reason to suspect a contradiction. As the moment's fear retreated, the child felt an unreasonable anger fill its void. Shaken and bewildered by her own emotion, she raised an innocent face to a blue perfect sky in an intuitive effort to erase the previous scene.

Carlotta took a deep breath of air. The fragrance of sun-warmed pines, which grew on the outskirts of the village in scattered patterns, had traveled the wind's currents down the mountain slope.

"I was looking for you, Carlotta!" Diego had come up the walk from the other direction.

The eleven-year-old boy stood before his sister in an exaggerated stance that only hinted of the man he would become.

Diego's feigned authority amused Carlotta and she laughed gaily. "I thought you had left for the blacksmith?" she questioned.

Both Carlotta and her brother had the fine-chiseled features of their Spanish heritage. Their heavily lashed dark eyes, too, revealed a relationship to the woman who had hurriedly arrived with them five years ago in the horse-drawn coach. Contessa de la Montoya's stay had been brief, her purpose to find sanctuary for her children. It was Friar Alcazar who would later recall the resemblance, as the arrangements, which had promised handsome payment for the care of the children, had been an intense, private affair.

Diego was three years older than Carlotta and rapidly growing tall. The pants that had fit him at the beginning of summer barely covered his brown calves and his gangling limbs protruded in exaggeration. Carlotta knew better than to point out the reason for her laughter.

"Maria wants your help. Some of los niños are leaving for Blue Mesa."

Carlotta's heart jumped. Blue Mesa was her favorite place to play. Over millenniums, layers of rock formation had built a huge but accessible mountain top. Its flat table-like surface was an open offering to the blue sky and an enticing place for the children's games. All of the children loved to play on the mesa, but none so much as Carlotta. The missed opportunity was too much for the child and her eyes swam with tears.

"Why can't I go?" she asked.

"I don't know, little sister. Friar Alcazar read names from a list and they were the children allowed to go. Don't look at me like that. I wasn't called either, and there were others who have to work in the village today," he admonished. The maturity Diego had only affected a moment ago became genuine. The boy placed an arm around his sister, hugging her to him.

"We'll go another time, but right now you had better hurry to the cocina, or Maria will be angry."

***

In the center of the room where Maria cooked there was a long ruggedly built wooden table. Aside from locally built benches, this was one of the few pieces of furniture belonging to the mission. It had only been in the last few years that the trading routes had become secure, and eastern furniture was beginning to make its way west. The usual seating, as well as storage shelves, was built into the adobe walls. These were nestled nooks, frequently the assigned places for those who were sent to help prepare the food, and as Carlotta pushed aside the blanket covering the doorway, Maria pointed to one with a wooden spoon.

Several children were already at work. Virginia, a mute ten-year-old girl, was sitting in the designated alcove grinding corn, while Two Bears sat at her feet shelling beans. The Indian boy was from one of the local Pueblo tribes, and to Carlotta's delight had promised to one day take her with him when he returned.

Carefully setting her books beside her, Carlotta joined Two Bears at the huge basket of beans. This staple of the orphans' diet required continual toil, from planting and cultivating, to harvesting, shelling, and the eventual preparation in a black-iron pot that hung in the recessed fireplace.

Two Bears smiled shyly at Carlotta, a new expression on his otherwise somber face. He had told Carlotta only yesterday that in the pueblo's culture it was not the custom for boys his age to be toiling at women's work. He had seen thirteen winters and his place should be at the side of other boys his age, learning the particular secret ceremonies and responsibilities relating to his clan.

But this was the mission and all of the children had learned to abandon individual culture, just as life had precipitated their abandonment. Though the children had come from many walks of life, collaboration determined by their common situation had prompted innovative measures.

Each child brought his or her native language to the mission. The languages of the Comanche, Apache, Navaho and Pueblo tribes, besides French, Spanish, and English had eventually melded together to form a hodgepodge dialect, which meant communication for children desperate to be understood. Out of necessity, the language of birth was the first forfeiture, along with their given names that only reminded the priests of their heathen dress and customs.

Alcazar was determined to forge Christians from the survivors of tragedy. The salvation of heathen souls and the occasional assets the children provided in physical labor were worth the consequence of lost cultures.

Carlotta watched Pilar hobble to the table. This child, Carlotta's own age, was one of the few who were handicapped from birth and not through the difficulties imposed by life on the western frontier. A withered, underdeveloped leg dragged behind the Mexican peasant girl serving to support her while the working leg made the next step. Pilar had conquered the art of balance, and though an unequal gait threatened her stability she fairly ran from one place to the next. She was a slight child, who had suffered from malnutrition and would never recover from her stunted growth, even though Maria had seen that she was given more than the allowed meager portion of food.

Maria handed a small bowl of masa to Pilar and directed her to the wall bench where she would sit and make tortillas for the evening meal. Pilar's adept hands gathered a small ball of masa and quickly began patting the dough into shape.

"Where is Felicia?" Maria's eyes quickly searched the room. The three-year-old was not there.

"Did you see her when you came in, Carlotta?"

"No, Señora," Carlotta answered. "Maybe she followed the others ... to Blue Mesa?" she offered. She never imagined the answer to her prayers that followed.

"Go quickly! Find her before she becomes lost. The others may be far ahead by now!"

"Yes ma'am." Carlotta stole a look at Two Bears and shrugged her small shoulders, but left before Maria decided to send an older child.

***

Carlotta felt the gate's latch fall in place before she remembered the books, carelessly ... disrespectfully ... left behind on the floor of the cocina. There was nothing to do now, of course, because she, too, was concerned for the safety of Felicia. Though the climb up to the mesa was safe enough for the older children, one so young might get into trouble.

She hadn't been more than three herself when she wandered away from the mission and the village one warm spring day. The surrounding mountains had beckoned with a promise of adventure. Miraculously, Carlotta had found Blue Mesa without getting lost in the nearby caves, or toppling over one of the steep ledges along the worn trail.

When her weary little legs had, at last, brought her over the rise, it had all been worth it. It was heaven, she was certain. The immense blue sky had introduced her to a new concept forever. Carlotta had run across the flat mesa, arms open wide, hoping to somehow capture eternity. She had played alone on the mesa for most of the day, finally collapsing with exhaustion.

Friar Alcazar had found her fast asleep, lying prone, her angelic face lifted to the sky. When Alcazar gazed on the small body on the mesa, appearing for all the world like a sacrifice to a pagan god, the obvious parallel to his own motives had naggingly perturbed him. There was consolation in finding his charge alive, not because he had any particular benevolent feelings about the child, but because she was the better half of a sizeable investment. He had gathered her limp little body and carried her down the mountain.

***

Carlotta ran quickly up the trail, picking her way around rocks recently washed down from the gorge. She looked to her right and remembered times she and Diego had explored the arroyo's rugged terrain of boulders and brush.

One autumn day they had watched a startled jackrabbit leave the trail. The rabbit seemed to know exactly where it was going, veering silently around large rocks and bounding easily over smaller ones. The children had followed the gradual slope of the ravine, soon mesmerized by the rabbit's effortless escape. When they had reached the arroyo's upper end they found the creature's secret world of low-hanging piñon branches and dense thickets.

Carlotta read the evidence of flattened grasses and broken brush, just as Two Bears had taught her, and proudly pointed to Diego the nests and homes of rabbits, deer, and other wildlife.

Feeling very wise and much older than her years, Carlotta confidently pushed aside a scrub pine branch and entered a world of sudden darkness. For a moment she was bewildered. The sun was eclipsed by some strange force, and she and Diego, who had joined her, stood disoriented in inky blackness. Before their eyes adjusted to the absence of light, other senses reported on a strange environment. Carlotta felt the cool depth of the space around her. A hollow feeling accompanied the distant sound of trickling water and the echoing fall of faraway pebbles. As murky shadows replaced the night, the children realized they had entered a large cave. On future occasions they discovered it was one of several.

Another time Carlotta would have found the caves irresistible as a respite from the hot sun, but today she hoped for time to play on her beloved mesa. She envisioned the sea of wild flowers that would greet her at the top, blue and violet bells bobbing gently in the constant breeze that swept the mesa. This vision obscured the fresh tracks of horses beneath Carlotta's feet, but as she drew closer the voices of adults intruded on her vision. Instinctively, she took cover behind a boulder and listened intently.

Carlotta's curiosity pressed her to raise her head and peer over the ridge of the mesa. Angry voices drew her attention to a half dozen men on horseback who were circling the children, restricting their movements. Several wore the uniforms of Union soldiers and others, the worn and sweaty clothing of the Comanchero. Closer to Carlotta, Felicia had just come over the rise. Laughing with delight at the sight of what appeared to be a wonderful game, the three-year-old ran to greet her friends. The little Mexican girl was not ten feet from her destination when a large hand reached down and brutally snatched her from the ground. Felicia screamed in fright as the soldier roughly slung her over his saddle.

"No!" cried the boy closest to the soldier's horse. "You are hurting her. Let her go!" he demanded and immediately tried to pull the child free. The same large hand, this time made into a fist, swung down hard on the side of the boy's face. The boy went sprawling into the dirt, his nose bleeding profusely.

Angry and defiant, the boy scrambled to his feet and spat with remarkably good aim into the soldier's face. For a brief moment there was silence while the children and the soldiers and even Carlotta, who remained out of sight, witnessed the soldier's face turn livid red and then a fearful shade of purple. The soldier withdrew a revolver, and pointing it deliberately at the boy, fired.

The boy fell in a bloody heap, as those around him gasped in horror. Tentatively, fearfully attempting to put as much distance between the men and themselves as possible, the children slowly backed away. The horses nervously broke position, circling in the dust, while their tense riders pulled up reins and attempted to regain control.

Felicia, who had been frozen in fear, began to pull away from her captor. Squirming and crying, she managed to free one small wrist and then another, only to fall from his grasp. Her movement startled the soldier's restless mount and the horse reared. The children screamed and bolted at the sight of Felicia's body rolling under the horse's trampling hooves. They ran, screaming, frantically searching for the trail that would lead to safety. The mesa became pandemonium. In the dust and confusion an order was called out, and Carlotta's eyes were drawn to the leader dressed in black. It was Tito Sanchez.

"Stop them, they mustn't return!"

Gun shots rang out. Carlotta watched incredulously as the children ran along the plateau and one by one their small bodies fell, swallowed up in the swaying field of wild flowers.

As the horses approached, the sound of pounding hooves filled the air. Carlotta turned and fled down the trail, burning tears blinding her vision as she ran. Unprepared for the rocks that obstructed her path, she stumbled. Carlotta screamed in anguish as a foot caught on a rock, sending her tumbling painfully to the ground. Her fall ended abruptly at the base of a large bush.

Carlotta's heart pounded in panic. She looked up the ascending arroyo, and seeing a rabbit bound ahead, thought of the cave's safety. Lifting herself from the ground, oblivious to her bleeding knees, she hobbled up the gully, forging a path through the brush.

At the canyon wall a piñon gnarled protectively around the cave's opening. Carlotta pushed aside the brush and sought the known refuge of night. Crawling across the rock floor, the child felt the cool stone soothe her cuts and bruises, as the quietness soothed her spirit.

She drew herself along the dark recesses of a wall she only knew tactually. Her small hand explored the smooth surface, finding serenity in the curves and valleys of its ancient carving. Carlotta's mind shut out the nightmare on the mesa and focused only on her sense of touch. Lying close to the wall, Carlotta pulled her legs up to her chest, finding succor in the fetal position. Her fingers slid idly into the shallow indentations that matched the shape of her hand, and merciful sleep soon engulfed her body.

CHAPTER 2

THE BURIAL

THE BURIAL

Alcazar sat before the massive desk, his prized possession, and admired the intricately carved wood. He had paid dearly for this sole representation of a better life, a life he had come to covet in spite of his vows to the Church. The friar leaned back in the roughly hewn chair. It would have to do as the desk's accompaniment. He smoothed back his straight black hair and placed both of his large hands caressingly on the desk's surface. The Old World beckoned, with its refined, sophisticated society and other creature comforts, and here in Alcazar's humble rectory he visualized with renewed hope the possibilities opening before him. The Americans would help him make it happen. Indeed, they already were doing so.

While the village of San Ramon was under Spanish and then Mexican rule, Alcazar's authority had been undisputed. There had been no interference from Mexico or the Church. Why would there be? Once it had been determined that there was no gold in the area, the only concern had been for the souls of the local peasants and a foothold in the New World. In this vacuum, this absence of outside influence, Alcazar had lived comfortably.

The good citizens of San Ramon had served his needs well, willingly bringing to the Church a portion of their earnings as payment to their protector. Their mission, their God, their Father Alcazar would watch over them, blessing their crops, christening their babies, and praying over their dead, and all the while forgiving their sins, which the villagers were destined to repeat over and over again; a circle of life that never deviated in its monotony, but was mercifully accepted by the Church as human nature.

Alcazar's benefits were limited to the meager pleasures the village could offer, and he had tasted them all. For most of his adult life he had held the sovereignty of San Ramon within his hands. Now, at the age of fifty-two, Alcazar's power was absolute. A handsome and virile man, the friar had sought and found devious ways to satisfy his own desires and lusts and yet preserve his irreproachable position as father to his people.

Through the years of this unquestioned reign, Alcazar had strayed far from his original relationship with God, but only he knew how fragile the relationship had been.

There had come a time when Alcazar's greed had demanded more. Certainly, with the appointment of the new American governor to the New Mexico Territory, he felt his ambitions slipping through his fingers. The Mexican governor and he had exchanged many favors over the years. The news of his replacement had first shocked and then angered Alcazar. Opportunity for his growing influence was squelched when word came from Washington that John Maxwell would be the new governor, to be seated at the Plaza of Governors in the heart of Santa Fe. Alcazar had held his bitterness in check, and in the meantime explored the possibilities that the newly opened trade routes might offer him.

It had been an unpalatable necessity dealing with Tito Sanchez, the rude, coarse leader of a band of renegade traders, but perhaps the Comanchero's recent legal recognition would work to Alcazar's advantage. The American government could no longer ignore the need for commerce on the long trail west, and it licensed the innovative community of renegade traders. Already, the Comanchero's questionable, but profitable, dealings had drawn the interest of those American soldiers who were greedy to supplement their meager pay. From the East, spilling across the Plains, flowed a stream of goods. A thirst for the finer products of civilization, along with the discovery of gold in California, had helped to carve a trail that would profit those who had something to offer in trade.

Alcazar's fine walnut desk had come west with the last caravan of covered wagons, along with blacksmiths' tools, bolts of fine cloth, seed for planting, and the new rifles, their destination the army post in Santa Fe. For his part, Alcazar had been able to pay in silver, a rarity among mission priests. Regardless of the assault on his sensibilities his new relationship with Sanchez had generated, it had become undeniably profitable.

Sanchez had presented the scheme when he had reported on a terrible mining accident in the largest silver mine in northern Mexico. Hundreds of workers had been killed when a huge tunnel collapsed. There was a need for replacements -- slave workers -- as few others would willingly sacrifice their lives in exchange for the harsh treatment and bare sustenance the owners of the mine provided. The leader of the Comancheros knew the only asset or coin the mission had to offer was its children. He was also aware of the small value attached to these young lives by the friar himself. The children's souls might be worth saving, but their lives were a drain on the stores of the mission. The children were expendable, and so Tito Sanchez had proposed a trade for silver. He had even offered the young, ambitious lieutenant, James McGiver, a role in his plan.

The assistance of the military in Sanchez's more dubious dealings was not common, but not without precedent. There had always been soldiers unhappy with their lot. Lt. McGiver, however, had been noticeably aggressive in his desire to better himself financially. This lent artfully to the Comanchero's long-range plan to abduct the unwanted or the unaccounted children of neighboring Indian tribes and mission orphans, while supplying the labor needs of the silver mines.

Alcazar smiled with satisfaction. He felt comfortable with his new associates, and the knowledge of where the balance of power truly lay. The friar's own intelligence, and years of political influence, would continue to work to his advantage. Neither a scurrilous trader nor greedy young military officer was any match.

Alcazar's thoughts were interrupted with the sudden sound of boots in the courtyard. Knuckles pounded impatiently on the door to his quarters. The friar granted permission to enter.

The subjects of his recent thoughts entered noisily, blustering incomprehensible words that overran each other's sentences. The lieutenant stood before him, his face shiny, red, and swollen above the collar of his military uniform. Immediately the officer swept his dusty hat off his head, the only contradiction to a self-imposed dress code. The soldier's eyes darted wildly around the room and Alcazar recognized the look of a trapped animal.

"We have bad news," the lieutenant managed to expel.

"We? Dios mio!" Tito Sanchez slapped his hand with emphasis against his stained leather leggings. He made no apology for his expletive and his black eyes flashed in anger.

"Your stupidity has cost us! Big man! You military jackass!" The Comanchero was furious and his sarcasm was aimed like venom at the young lieutenant.

Lt. McGiver was striving hard to regain composure. Knowing instinctively that his only advantage was in his Union uniform, he brushed nervously at his jacket and pants.

"There isn't one man among you, you..." The lieutenant sought frantically for the word that would express his contempt for the filthy Mexicans and Indians who made up the band of Sanchez's men. At the same time he sensed, correctly, that the wrong word might seriously escalate the argument. "... your *company* ... who understands the meaning of discipline!" Unhappily he chose the weak definition, and then no longer able to contain his defiance, snarled, "The children would be *alive* if your *men* would have told them to stop in their own language!"

Alcazar's eyes widened. "What are you saying?" he demanded. The friar had remained seated until now, watching the curious exposure of vulnerability the two were displaying, but now his interest was genuine.

"What about the children?" he thundered. As Alcazar rose from his chair, his full height rising several inches above the heads of Sanchez and McGiver, his looming black robes accentuated his appearance.

The bickering between the two antagonists ended abruptly. To his credit the lieutenant faced his accuser and said, "They're dead, sir. They are all dead." He felt Alcazar's eyes burn through his own. His head fell in shame, and in fear of the expected retribution stared miserably at the floor.

"How did this happen?" Alcazar's voice had fallen to a hoarse whisper, more frightening than the tone of his first question, and he turned to Sanchez, as if expecting the older of the two men to have a plausible answer.

The leader of the Comancheros began again to attack the lieutenant with accusations. Feeling the friar's eyes now boring a hole through him, he turned and said, "There was a scuffle, and a boy spat in one of *his* men's eyes ... and he *shot* him!" Sanchez was genuinely incredulous.

"Yes!" the lieutenant answered recklessly. "And this man yelled out an order for all the others to be killed!"

Calmly, patiently, Alcazar began to ask questions. The story unfolded. It had been a massacre on Blue Mesa. All fifteen children, those sent and paid for ... those who would be turned over to work in the silver mines, were dead. "You are certain they are all dead?" asked the friar. "And you weren't seen?" Alcazar's cool, pertinent questions had an immediate affect on the two men. Sanchez's anger subsided and he reported the events at Blue Mesa in a matter-of-fact manner. He had not personalized the affair beyond his monetary loss. The children were only chattel, property he had received and for which he had been paid. Now, because of the Union soldier's bungling, the Comanchero was out his investment. His interest in arguing was to justify compensation, hoping for an opportunity to recover at least a part of his loss.

"That is why we could not allow los niños to return! How would it be, if they reported the actions of your private, huh?" Sanchez directed his question to the lieutenant, who cringed at the obvious reference to his company's lack of discipline.

The friar sat back down in his chair and studied the two men before him. Tito Sanchez's motives, as immoral as they were, were easily read. His greed was indisputable and he made no apologies for his actions. The lieutenant, on the other hand, was a concern to Alcazar. The man had a nervous conscience, a very dangerous attribute, in light of their dealings. The lieutenant's reaction to Sanchez's words hinted at his vulnerability and the friar seized the opportunity to explore this weakness.

"An unfortunate affair," Alcazar said, shaking his head somberly. It was essential that he not grant moral sanction. "Sanchez is correct, of course. Your military career will be over when today's events are revealed. A tragedy really."

It was equally important the friar lay blame where it belonged, and he watched Lt. McGiver's face carefully for an expression beyond the obvious guilt, and felt encouraged when he read the primal fear familiar to one who gives refuge to human souls.

The lieutenant remained silent and Alcazar allowed the moment its proper recognition before he continued.

"A massacre of orphans." Alcazar took one more opportunity to name and imprint forever the day's transgressions on the minds, if not the souls, of his companions.

"You are absolutely certain you weren't seen?"

Both men nodded solemnly.

"We have returned immediately. You are the only one, Father." Sanchez replied. He, too, seemed humbled by the presence of God's judgment.

"All right. Listen carefully," the friar spoke gently, but with precise articulation. "Lieutenant, your company came upon this tragedy on your way back to the fort. Your men discovered the dead and dying children, and the evidence that confirmed an Indian attack ... an Apache attack. You gave chase to no avail, and then you correctly came to the mission to inform me."

Alcazar leaned back in his primitive chair, and with his arms behind his head, addressed the men as if he saw an entirely different scene than the one from which the men had just returned. Through the father's eyes, Sanchez and McGiver could almost believe it was the truth. Blue Mesa was painted over. The impulsive reactions that had seemed unalterable mistakes back on the Mesa were carefully eased from their minds. Their souls were soothed, and history was rewritten in the process. Effortlessly, details were offered to fill in the picture and amend the disparities in their story.

"You will bury the children immediately. A proper burial, one in which I will attend and hold a service. Then, Lieutenant McGiver, tomorrow you and I will ride to Santa Fe and report to your Captain Sedlow."

Tito Sanchez left the priest, feeling relieved. The immediate problem had been resolved. Alcazar would make it clear to the townspeople and the Union soldiers that the children had been killed by Indians. This was no skin off Sanchez's back. In fact, it would serve his bigger plan to raid the American and Pueblo settlements for more children. Now all eyes would be on the enemy, the Apache. Sanchez could see this serving everyone's interests. It was obvious the soldiers needed an enemy, but he thought even the Indians of the more peaceful pueblos would be happy to have the marauding Apaches under attack. Certainly the ranchers in the area would focus their wrath on the more aggressive Indians, and that would divert their attention from the Comancheros' activities.

The half-breed leaped onto his horse easily from the rear and slapped the pinto's rump. Taking the reins, Sanchez dug his spurs into his pony's flanks, and hurriedly departed from the mission with his men before the Comancheros drew unwanted attention. He had cautioned his men to keep a low profile in the brush, and wait several hundred yards from the mission's walls, while he met with Alcazar. He hadn't been as foolish ... as had been Lt. McGiver and his men ... as to place his trust in the temporary partnership of the three.

Tito Sanchez's Mexican and Indian parentage was a continual reminder that no alliance was permanent in a world where race was everything. His own mixed blood had determined Sanchez's role as outcast. Never having been fully accepted by his Apache mother's people or his Mexican father, Tito had learned early in life to be resourceful.

Though the meeting had ended in a satisfactory manner, there was still the matter of the silver. The Comancheros were out their pay on this bungled deal. Sanchez knew who owed him, but he also knew there would be a more appropriate place and time to collect payment.

***

The sun was setting when Lt. McGiver, his company, and Father Alcazar left for the mesa with picks and shovels from the mission. The lanterns had been brought from the sacristy, where they were kept with the sacred vessels used during Mass. McGiver's men had followed, subdued, since they had only been addressed regarding their assigned burial detail. Each man still feared the punishment for his own part in what had amounted to the massacre of innocent children. Their minds were busy imagining the possible consequences.

It had been for this reason McGiver had ushered the soldiers into the courtyard, ordering their mounts to be corralled until after his meeting with Alcazar. Whatever the outcome, McGiver was determined it would be the same justice dealt to all.

James McGiver thought of the finesse Alcazar had displayed in answering the anxious questions of Friar Serna. The father had appeared at the door to Alcazar's quarters just as they were leaving. He was concerned that the children had not returned for dinner.

Friar Alcazar told him the terrible news. In his recounting of the story, which he had supposedly just heard from the lieutenant, Alcazar appeared to labor for control. The children had all been slaughtered by Apaches. An Indian uprising now threatened the mission and town.

He stressed the fact that he would have to rely on Father Serna to stay with the other children, keep them calm, and care for them. Alcazar must administer the last Holy Rites and assure himself these poor orphans' souls would ascend to heaven and not linger in purgatory.

The friar's plump form paraded before them, nervously pacing in anticipation of Father Alcazar's guidance. Serna began weeping uncontrollably and Alcazar put a protective arm around his shoulders.

"We must be strong for the children's sake" Alcazar cajoled.

"Oh yes," moaned Serna, "but how will I ever tell them?"

Friar Serna realized the personal task that lay ahead. And then he thought of Carlotta's brother.

"Diego? I don't know that he will be able to handle this. He and his sister were so close!" Serna shook his head, unable to accept the future.

"Carlotta was one of the children?" Alcazar asked, startled.

"Yes, she was sent by Maria to find Felicia. The child had run off to play with the others."

It was only at this moment that Alcazar's composure seemed to slip. Lt. McGiver thought he saw the friar's face twitch as he clenched and unclenched the muscles in his jaw.

The procession rode up the trail, and in the last blue light of day, the men were stark silhouettes against the sky.

In silence, Alcazar reviewed the startling information given to him in the last hour. There had been fifteen children sent to Blue Mesa. And now he was told there were two more among the dead. Felicia, the child belonging to the cook Maria was of little concern to the friar, but Carlotta Montoya de Medina was an investment lost. The arrangement for her care and her brother's had been made six years ago. The frightened Contessa de la Montoya de Medina had arrived by carriage with her two small children and had pleaded with Father Alcazar to take her son and daughter. She was running from her cruel and influential husband. Her own future had been uncertain, but her family's power and wealth were absolute and she had guaranteed a handsome reward for the children's upbringing.

Alcazar's knowledge of the Montoya family in Spain, their land and many holdings, left no doubt in his mind that the contessa's claims were valid, and the children's lives would mean his own fortune.

Payment had come regularly from Spain through Mexico. Once a year a letter would arrive from an uncle who was obviously their benefactor. On fine parchment he would reiterate their agreement, reminding Alcazar that there would be a time when the children would presumably be sent to Spain for the finishing of their education. At that time the larger balance of payment, in gold, would be delivered to Alcazar for his faithful act of Christian charity.

There had never been any intention to place the two Medina children in harm's way. Alcazar had always seen to their care personally, though Diego, the older of the two, had protectively assumed the responsibility for his sister, even to the point of annoyingly challenging the friar. But now the child Carlotta was presumably dead.

All of these facts ran through Alcazar's head, and yet he knew he was superior in his ability to turn misfortune into fortune. While the others succumbed to panic, he would remain calm and pluck the opportunity their vulnerability presented.

As they neared the summit and the edge of the mesa, darkness descended, and Lt. McGiver instructed two of his men to light the lanterns and begin the search for the bodies in the high grass. Three others began digging a large grave. A gruesome detail forked out on the plateau, the light from their swinging lanterns throwing irregular shapes eerily across the landscape. The men picked their way gingerly. No one made a sound, which only emphasized the quiet. Not a bird or frog had sought to reclaim the mesa.

A yelp came from the first man to discover the trail of death. Involuntarily, the young private reacted as the toe of his boot stumbled on the small form lying on the ground. He reached down and, groping in the blackness, hollered for more light as his lantern's wick flickered a last effort. Without the stationary light of the moon, the young man's eyes played tricks. He watched frozen in place as a shadow rose from the tall grass. Finally his voice found his throat and he screamed.

His blood-curdling scream spanned the horizon, reaching with icy fingers into the bodies of those who were already uncomfortable with the task before them. McGiver felt his scalp crawl and a chill shudder down his spine. The lieutenant fought for control over his body, convinced his men would flee in panic if he did not regain immediate authority.

"Hanson, bring the lantern over here and give Martin a hand." His voice was husky but strong.

The two were joined by a third and began the task of locating the dead. Again, the others hefted their picks to their shoulders, swinging them forcefully toward the earth, and for a long time the only sound was the swish of picks cutting through the night air and the dull thud of metal against sod. An unnerving twang vibrated as an occasional pick or shovel hit a stone.

One by one the soldiers lifted the lifeless bodies and brought them to the edge of the large mass grave. There, Alcazar stood authoritatively, appearing in his vigil as if he was presiding over a pagan sacrifice.

Alcazar counted each corpse, knowing the full count must be seventeen; the fifteen who were sent, plus Felicia and Carlotta. When Private Hanson claimed that was all, Alcazar demanded they search again. In the black night the lieutenant and his five men swept the mesa, thoroughly seeking every possible place, yet certain the children had fallen in their path of flight. All had to be accounted.

Finally, Alcazar had to accept the inevitable. There was a missing child, and another complication in putting an end to this mismanaged affair. He had to proceed with the funeral and deal with this later. The evidence of foul play had to be buried.

The children were lowered into the grave and though the soldiers were petrified with fear laboring at such a task in the dark, they were thankful not to look on the children's individual faces. Alcazar stood with the one working lantern, and as each child passed before him he attempted to reveal their identity. Innocent faces framed with matted hair radiated an incandescent blue above blood-soaked clothing.

Not one of the soldiers could look on their victims. Hurriedly, they shoveled dirt into the pit. They were anxious now to leave this site. Whatever awaited them in reprisal for their deeds was preferable to facing the dead children. But they were not to be let off that easily. Alcazar spoke a long prayer in Latin, unintelligible to the Cavalry's men of common heritage, and just when they had concluded the friar was through and they might leave this terrifying place, he addressed them in English.

"Your Lieutenant McGiver will report to Captain Sedlow tomorrow. He will be certain to relate your heroism in tracking the murderous Indians who have spilled innocent blood here today."

Even in the black night, each man could feel Alcazar's eyes on him, and swore the truth had been forcibly seared and buried in his heart forever. A white owl, with silent wings, swooped out of the north. The huge owl descended, flying low over their heads, while the men cowered under its giant wingspan. Without a sound, the owl soared off the mesa, taking their secret with it.

CHAPTER 3

THE OWL AND THE CAVE

THE OWL AND THE CAVE

Carlotta had slept fitfully, retreating in and out of consciousness, fighting the demons of the day. In the cave, with its absence of light, hours passed with no recording. She still lay, knees drawn to her chest, as close to the wall as her small body could manage. Her hand, fallen by her side, no longer sought human comfort in the stone and carving of an ancient peer.

From deep in the cave the clear and bell-like sound of water dripping rang resonant. Repetitive and hypnotic, the sound beckoned Carlotta back to Blue Mesa. Bewildered, she brushed back her hair and looked up into the nodding faces of blue and violet prairie flowers that seemed to be watching her. The sound of voices roused her, and Carlotta struggled to rise above the sleeping blossoms. Propping herself on one elbow, she turned in the direction of the laughter. The children, her friends, were running gaily toward her. Light-heartedly they called to her with their arms open wide. Carlotta's initial fear diminished as they drew closer and she saw how alive and vibrant they were.

There was no recognition on their faces, however, as they continued running past her and on to greet some unknown destiny. Creeping fear gnawed at the edges of Carlotta's heart. Confused and frantic, she waved her arms hoping to be seen. Carlotta would not give up and she hurriedly rose to follow. The children had advanced quickly and she called in sudden panic that they might leave her alone, again. Far ahead, she saw the last of the children turn and motion her to follow.

Again, Carlotta heard the hollow sounds of the cave, the plopping drip, drip of water falling on smooth rock. Then she was back in the cave, facing the entrance with anticipation. In the faint starlight streaming through its portal, a magnificent bird appeared. Black against the sky, its silhouette grew larger as the giant bird swooped through the portal and rushed toward Carlotta on silent wings. She felt the air stir above her head as the bird continued its flight past her, and now she could see it was a giant white owl. It flew into the dark depths of the cave, and just like the dream-child, beckoned her to follow.

***

"Wake up! I need your help."

Carlotta woke suddenly and was surprised to find she was not alone. Several inches from her face sat a mouse staring at her. She turned to find the source of the voice, but could see nothing in the dark. Her eyes came back to the mouse, who did not seem at all afraid, but tilted his head quizzically. There was nothing particularly remarkable about the mouse, who seemed to Carlotta like all the others she had seen scampering through the mission, unless this one had really spoken.

"What?" Carlotta asked.

"Come with me. You need my help," the mouse contradicted himself.

In the middle of darkness the mouse was brightly illuminated, as if it carried around its own small sun trained to shine on it. Carlotta sat up and rubbed her eyes and stared. The mouse had no patience and again urged her to get up.

There didn't seem to be anything else to do. Carlotta obeyed, and getting to her feet, brushed her tattered and dirty frock. She stood tall before the small tyrant hoping to impress him with her size. But the mouse seemed indifferent to her implied power and even ignored the difference in their species. The creature turned and looked back once, to confirm his instructions were being followed, and then retreated. The light, which cast a dim, silvery glow along the cave's walls, followed the rodent. Rather than remain alone in the dark, Carlotta obediently followed them both.

The cave's passage became more prominent as Carlotta progressed. There was a sense of growing space, a tunnel whose circumference was expanding. The walls echoed a larger area and the air felt cooler. Carlotta had never imagined the depths of the cave, and without the mouse to light the way, knew she wouldn't have dared to explore it alone. As she was drawn farther into its recesses, turning where the mouse turned, following his direction at frequent crossroads, she began to realize that she would never make it back without him. Carlotta hurried to keep up with the scurrying rodent.

They had traveled for some time before their path began a steady incline. Carlotta's field of vision grew and was illuminated to include various plants. The foliage here was unlike any the child had known: various shades of silver and gray, a botanical opaque world without color. The plants seemed to sprout mysteriously from the cave's floor and walls. Large fronds of lily pad shape hovered horizontally between delicate ferns. Carlotta wanted to stop and admire their beauty, but the mouse brooked no hesitation in its mission.

A light in the far distance promised an exit and Carlotta pushed on expectantly. As they drew nearer she saw there was indeed an opening and pure and sparkling sunlight streamed through the hole's circumference. Carlotta stopped, mesmerized by the golden light flowing around her, and watched flecks of dust dance in the sun's rays. Standing in the rays she felt the dust particles float in a spiral pattern, swirling around her body, pulling her toward the cave's mouth.

Inside, the child felt a stirring as her soul stretched in yearning for the light's comfort. For the first time since she had left her brother, Carlotta felt complete trust. She allowed herself to be pulled up and through the opening, and then she was suddenly standing on the other side.

***

Ahead darted the mouse in erratic patterns.

"Watch out!" he called. "Keep your eyes open and learn." His last remarks faded as he disappeared from view.

Carlotta rubbed her eyes. Color, rich and vibrant filled the world. She wasn't sure where the exit had placed her, whether on the other side of a gorge or a mountain, but it was daytime. Before her spread a meadow, green and rich with grasses that rippled in the wind. Carlotta watched the white owl soar off over the field and out of sight. Two stallions, rearing on hind legs rose above the blowing grass, their long manes tangled in the same wind currents. One horse was coal black with eyes like fire that rolled wildly in their sockets. The other was the white of an egg shell, vaguely iridescent. His eyes, too, were wild with fright, but the color of turquoise.

The horses were at war in an intense battle of wills, and close enough to Carlotta that she could hear their brays and heavy breathing. Their bodies were lathered with white foam that flew, flecks even reaching Carlotta as they rose, forelegs pawing in the air. Again, they came crashing down and the earth shook under their weight.

The child hadn't had time to wonder about the mouse who now reappeared and was darting for the cover of a rock ledge. The mouse seemed quite ordinary, no longer intent on giving Carlotta directions. Just as Carlotta thought this might be a more normal world after all, a lizard came from under the rock to challenge the mouse's presence.

"I am dreaming of the future here within these shadows. Do not bother me," said the lizard.

"But, I must remain here so as to properly see and record each detail!" Mouse protested.

Carlotta was puzzling over this matter, when wild raucous laughter drew her attention to another rock closer at hand.

A tan and gray coyote was perched on top of a stone outcropping, the ledge projecting from a small earth mound. The amused coyote sat attentively watching the two stallions at war on the meadow. Carlotta thought the scene reminded her of the arena seating she had seen at the plaza in Santa Fe. The coyote laughed again, a high-pitched, staccato like noise that hurt her ears. Incongruously, the wild dog was actually enjoying the events taking place on the meadow.

Unafraid, the coyote turned to face Carlotta, as if to invite her own show of appreciation. The child was bewildered. Certainly the coyotes she had heard on the outskirts of town were shy and secretive, and even though they lived close by were seldom seen. Not at all like this brash dog who encouraged the horses to fight and laughed hideously when they inflicted wounds on one another.

And there were wounds. Rivulets of scarlet red rolled down and over the strong-muscled flank of the white horse and each thrashing of the stallions' body sprayed blood droplets, which flew and mingled with the white lather. The black stallion, too, glistened under the blood bath that now poured from the two magnificent creatures.

Carlotta stood horrified while the coyote mocked their death battle. His laughter grew louder until the sound filled the meadow. The noise magnified, levitating to boundaries from which the pitch reverberated as if the meadow was caught within a drum. Carlotta thought her head would burst as the vibration coursed through her body, but just then the waves of sound began to fall and the blinding light that had accompanied them subsided. When she could see clearly again the horses were gone and so was coyote.

In coyote's place was a wolf, larger than the coyote and exhibiting a grizzled reddish-brown coat tipped with frost. The wolf had salivated and his spittle hung in frozen icicles from his slack jaw. Carlotta felt pity for the poor creature and thought he must be close to death. Despite the animal's size, he was obviously half starved and sat, weakened with hunger, gazing at the meadow.

Carlotta's eyes followed the wolf's gaze to the snow-covered field. The meadow was unrecognizable now that snow drifts had leveled and smoothed its terrain. Here and there were clumps of dried reeds lying bent and broken. Several winter birds scavenged for grass seed.

The wolf addressed Carlotta, "Many will die in the time of winter. Like the raven, take courage. The raven will deliver your message."

The child listened attentively but without understanding. To her left, far in the distance across the field, a speck hung on the western horizon. It grew in size as it moved closer and Carlotta quickly recognized it as the black horse. The majestic animal approached her and said, "Ride with me upon my back. Go with me into the dark void where the answer lives."

Carlotta backed away in fear. Restlessly, the horse pawed the frozen ground, awaiting her reply. As the child cowered before the black horse's authority, from out of the East came the giant white owl. The same owl Carlotta had seen fly into the cave. Immediately she felt comforted. The owl came to rest on a bleached white cottonwood limb, its downy feathers draping softly about its form. Turning its head to look down on Carlotta, the owl spoke in a woman's voice.

"Do not fear, child. I will go with you into the night and light the dark."

The owl swooped down, plucking Carlotta gently from the ground, and in one swift movement deposited the girl on the back of the black horse.

Seated bareback, Carlotta felt the animal call on its great strength. The black horse lunged forward, thrusting one mighty leg ahead of another, hurling them in the direction from which he had come. Carlotta seized handsful of coal black mane and clung, fearful she might be thrown. As they plunged on and into the west, the owl flying just above Carlotta's right-hand shoulder, night soon overcame them.

The blackness was complete, and all that Carlotta knew was the steed's rippling body beneath her and the very real but unseen presence of the white owl.

As they thundered through the dark she heard the howling of other animals. Human cries soon joined them, becoming a cacophony of approaching death. Voices, overlaying one soulful sound on to another, called out their mournful pleas for mercy, and Carlotta felt as though her heart was being torn from her body.

White owl, at her shoulder, whispered, "Know that you are safe, and with that knowledge allow your heart to see ..."

The day returned, a blue and brilliant backdrop to a frozen white landscape. Carlotta and her mount were flying over the countryside, the horse's hooves barely touching snow and ice, skimming the winter landscape. In the drifts were fallen bodies, slumped figures that had perished in the cold. As they passed, Carlotta knew that hunger had ravaged a people. Tears came to her eyes and formed drops of ice as they fell, but the child did not turn away. She wanted to know the reason. She needed to know the cause.

They pushed on until they saw a herd of antelope. The leader of the antelope came forward and spoke to Carlotta.

"Look down on your steed," he instructed.

Carlotta did as she was told. She saw that her fists were wound tightly around the flowing mane of the white horse, and her tears, where they had fallen, shone like clear crystals in the sunlight.

"What happened to the black horse?" she asked of white owl.

"You have faced your fears," she answered. "Now you are free to find the answers."

The antelope, lithe and yet stoic, stepped forward and spoke again. "I am here to serve. It is my gift ... that the children may live."

"Thank you," Carlotta said humbly.

A raven dropped suddenly from the sky, settling his black wings on the snow. In his beak was one golden kernel of corn. "I, too, offer my services. Watch for me in the smoke."

They left as they had come, this time the white stallion carried the child into the north. Again Carlotta felt the presence of the white owl and lifted her head. With wonder she felt the certainty of her blessing and the offering of her power.

Across the plain they rode. The cold wind blew through Carlotta's hair, twisting the tendrils of the white horse's mane and rushing past them. She felt the white horse change direction, as they were propelled gloriously into the Eastern sky. She was vaguely aware of her mount stumbling and then felt herself airborne, sailing from the white horse's back.

With the softest of thuds Carlotta was thrust back into her own future.

***

The air was cool and clammy, and in the darkness it was several moments before Carlotta realized she was once more in the cave. An overwhelming sense of abandonment settled on the child and she huddled with her knees drawn to her chin, tears, only of salt, falling once more.

A sudden rush of air brought the wings of the owl swooping down on her. Great expansive wings of gentle feathers fell around Carlotta's shoulders and with remarkable strength clasped her. The owl had come back with her! In the dark Carlotta heard her speak again.

"You have sought me, child. Owl Woman's medicine is yours."

Cloaked in a feather cocoon the exhausted child fell asleep. Carlotta slept deeply and untroubled, enfolded within the strong arms of a young Indian woman.

***

Hours later the woman gently roused Carlotta, and taking her by the hand, led her out of the cave and into the night. A burro stood tethered to a piñon tree, his large ears silhouetted against the starry sky. The animal brayed his welcome, and patiently allowed the child and Owl Woman to mount.

Carlotta soon fell asleep again in the comfortable rocking motion of the burro's gait with Owl Woman's protective arms warmly embracing her body. They traveled through the night, far across the hills without stopping, until they reached the pueblo.

***

The sky was still bluish black, stars the only light, when Owl Woman arrived with the sleeping child. Only one had seen her leave just after dark, and now all, except he, were sleeping. Sak-mo-i-si, the Sun Watcher, would never interfere with the decisions of Owl Woman as he respected her medicine and influence in the tribe, but he had been concerned for her safety and so had waited patiently in the night air for her return. Upon seeing her ascend the hill, Sak-mo-i-si discreetly returned to his dwelling, disappearing through its T-shaped doorway.

Owl Woman and Carlotta left the burro in the corral just outside the pueblo and began climbing the stone steps to the third terrace. The child obediently followed Owl Woman as she descended a ladder into her own dwelling. Glowing coals from the room's corner fireplace cast a warm, cheery light off the white-washed walls.

From a hanging horizontal pole, the Indian woman took down the necessary bedding. Owl Woman eyed the sleepy child; she would have no difficulty encouraging her to return to sleep. In a short time she heard Carlotta's even breathing and left her side to tend the fire.

There would be no sleep for Owl Woman tonight, and she stared into the fire recounting the events that had led her to the sacred cave. She thought of the years when she and her sisters lived in the cave. Ostracized from the tribe for practicing witchcraft, the three had sought sanctuary in the only natural shelter known for miles. There was no contact with the community that had interacted with them, heretofore, on a daily basis. The loneliness weighed heavily on their lives, but none more so than on Owl Woman's.

***

In those days her name had been Blue Corn. Owl Woman remembered with sadness her name and those of her sisters, which were never to be spoken again. This was the way of the people of her tribe; so the eldest girl re-named the three. Owl Woman, the youngest, was the only one innocent of the accused crime. It was assumed she had been with her sisters when they entered the sacred ceremonial kiva. Women and children were forbidden entrance into this large underground room reserved for the practice of religious ceremonies, and the few exceptions made were with the explicit consent of Sak-mo-i-si.

On that fateful day most of the people of the village had either participated in or attended as spectators the racing games. Outside of the pueblo, below the mesa, were the fields that required hand watering in this desert climate. The races were a means to encourage the very real task of covering long distances in the shortest time. Blue Corn's sisters, staying behind, had remained hidden, instructing her to do likewise. Leaving Blue Corn to stand watch at the rooftop opening of the kiva, the two sisters had brazenly descended into the large room. The girls, intrigued by that which was prohibited, began to explore the Kachina house ... a niche in the wall where ceremonial masks were kept.

Several silver chalices, vessels that had been in the tribe since the coming of the Spanish, were kept within this cache. Worked metal was a fascination to the Indians and so the pieces were held in honor, along with their own tribe's sacred objects. The temptation was too great and the two older sisters each stole a chalice, swearing Blue Corn to secrecy. Blue Corn had been too frightened to protest. At the age of fourteen she recognized the danger in their venture. Her worst fears materialized when the elders returned, several days later, to find that the objects were missing.

It was a simple matter, to review and conclude who had been absent at the games. The three sisters were brought into the plaza, and with no living relatives to plead their defense, stood trembling before the council. It was argued that their act of betrayal of The People would bring bad medicine. Several years of drought had made the elders fearful, and witchcraft was strongly suspected.

Blue Corn stood beside her two weeping sisters as they were mourned by The People. Banished from the pueblo, they were told to gather their belongings, food for two days' journey and depart with one burro. Only the eldest two girls knew the silver pieces were wrapped in a blanket, stored in a shallow hole off the mesa. The sisters retrieved the chalices on their journey into exile.

That was eleven years ago, and when Owl Woman looked back on her life in the cave that first year, she still wondered how she and her sisters had survived. In their absence, the old Sun Watcher had died and Sak-mo-i-si, the new Sun Watcher, Owl Woman's friend, now guided the people. Sak-mo-i-si assumed the sisters had died during the first winter.

That particular winter was not harsh, but as the elders had predicted, the drought continued and there was little salvaged from the corn fields at harvest time. But it was not agriculture that brought the three outcasts through the winter, nor the succeeding four winters.

During the first summer they had dug for wild yams, sought the berries and roots of the high-desert country, and managed to keep their stomachs quiet. One late-summer day, the three girls were gathering their meager stores to prepare against the winter when riders approached. Startled, the girls first thought to run, but realizing there was no place to hide decided to face the tired, dirty band of men. The men were looking for water, and in this dry, barren land that need consumed them, taking precedence over any other.

The oldest girl led them to a spring the sisters had found, but wisely kept their cave a secret. They learned the men were Comancheros, traders of goods between the Americans, Mexicans and the Indians. The girls also discovered the men thought of them as witches, because there was no visible sign of a family or tribe to support them. The sisters did nothing to clear up the mystery, and instead fed the men's superstitious natures with an offer to tell fortunes.

Thus began the trade of prophecy and magic potions for food stores and firewood. The two older girls entered into other arrangements, as well. Frequently, one or the other of Owl Woman's sisters would be gone for a day or more, returning on the back of a Comanchero's horse. Laughing and flirting, the girl would slide down from the Comanchero's saddle, encouraging his return … with more provisions, of course.

Owl Woman had been protected from this form of payment, in the beginning because of her youth, but later because of her disposition. She was silent during much of the time when the girls were together. Her interests were peculiar and solitary. She would do her part of work and more, but she found the time to gather herbs, somehow knowing the correct ones to use for the various ailments afflicting the Comancheros. This particular talent enhanced her reputation as a healer, but it was her exploration of the cave that made even her sisters respectful of her power.

Visions were Owl Woman's medicine. Her shaman's journey was both physical and spiritual, revealing secrets within the dark depths of another world. Within the first year the older girls learned not to press Owl Woman on any matters, and in fact named her for the night bird that flew into the cave and familiarly perched itself on her shoulder, screeching a terrible warning if they came too close.

***

The coals were reduced to embers, and Owl Woman rose to fetch more wood. This all-night vigil was unusual, but so had been her vision.

***

CHAPTER 4

OWL WOMAN AND THE PUEBLO

OWL WOMAN AND THE PUEBLO

They were sitting on a terraced hill, the highest of four concentric levels of dwellings. Owl Woman and Carlotta had come from the last room at the end of the half circle, seemingly the most isolated in the community, to seek the warmth of the morning sun. Two small girls came running toward them, their brown skin lightly clad and their feet bare. They called out in delight when they saw Owl Woman, and approached curiously to learn more about the girl in ragged clothing. Owl Woman spoke to them in her language, and Carlotta found many of the words and phrases to be familiar. She understood her own introduction as the One Who Traveled Far, and corrected her.

"My name is Carlotta Medina," she said.

These were the first words the child had spoken, and Owl Woman was surprised and pleased to learn that she had some comprehension of The People's language.

"One Who Traveled Far, your name was spoken in reverence. Please excuse our rudeness." Owl Woman smiled gently, and Carlotta was aware that her caretaker was very beautiful, her black eyes shining bright in anticipation.

"It seems you understand our words, Car-lot-ta?" She labored with the syllables.

"Yes. I have ... had friends at the mission. Some of the children are Indian. One spoke like you ... Two Bears was his name." The memories of yesterday momentarily flooded Carlotta's mind with paralyzing grief. She fell quiet as she thought of friends that were gone, some dead and others still alive but gone from her life. Would she see her brother or Two Bears ever again?

"Two Bears? You were at the mission with Two Bears?" asked Owl Woman. But the child hadn't heard. The bowl of mush she had been holding dropped and broke, a clear, bell-like sound that echoed on the terraced mesa.

The Indian children watched as the Spanish child, in apparent pain, raised trembling hands to cover her ears. The screams of yesterday rang through Carlotta's head, and in anguish she tried to block the sound of gunfire.

Owl Woman placed her hands on the girl's shoulders and gently pushed her to the ground. She then pressed one hand on Carlotta's forehead and the other at the nape of her neck. Whispering softly, her voice fell into a repetitive rhythm and then, in a low chant, Owl Woman hummed the words that soothed.

The pressure subsided, the memories retreated, and Carlotta turned and buried her face in Owl Woman's blouse, allowing her tears to dry, hidden from the eyes of the Indian children.

"It is over. It is over," Owl Woman said. There was no reproach in the woman's voice as she instructed the two children to leave them alone.

They were silent for awhile, both listening to the sounds of a waking village. When the child had recovered, Owl Woman took her shoulders, holding her out at arm's distance, and spoke to her at eye level.

"Two Bears is the son of our Sun Watcher. We must know, is he safe?"

"He was in the cocina when I left the mission. He didn't go to Blue Mesa to play ... with the others." Carlotta hesitated, "He is alive then?"

"Yes, as you are, child. And you must live to bear witness. There are many things for you to learn now. The most important of which is to know the truth. With time you will come to recognize the vision's signs as they make themselves known in your life. For now, it is sufficient that you know you have the medicine of the owl. This powerful medicine will enable you to silently observe. You will not be deceived if you listen with your heart."

"Owl is my medicine, as well. That is why I was directed to the sacred cave. The white owl is an old friend of mine and he has shown me many things. He brought me the vision on the mesa ... and your journey to his cave. But this is enough for now. Everything in its time."

Owl Woman pointed to the central plaza and smiled. "This is a special time for The People and you will share it with us. The Kachinas will depart soon for their home in the mountains and there will be a ceremony to send them."

The mysterious trek through last night's darkness was now unveiled. The pueblo's setting was that of a city suspended above the desert floor. The contrast was breathtaking. Carlotta watched as the first rays of light crossed the mesa, lighting one pueblo wall and then another. The sun brought immediate warmth to the East-facing village, which rose above the surrounding plain. The child's world had changed so quickly in such a short time: from her life at the mission, to the terror of Blue Mesa, to the lonely darkness of the cave and the remarkable journey within, which still begged comprehension.

From her seat on the wall Carlotta looked up at the hawk, whose circled flight mirrored the shape of the pueblo's plaza. She looked out at the many rooms of the pueblo with their sharp angles and long shadows. Her eyes swept across the plaza to the distant majestic red mesas, and she knew herself to be part of the people who floated above the earth.

Carlotta thought of that earlier moment when she had first opened her eyes. The sun had penetrated the room's keyhole opening and fell on her closed eyelids, steering her consciousness away from the world of dreams and gently nudging her into the new day. The golden fuzzy light filtered through her drowsy eyelids and revealed the stark, clear objects of Owl Woman's room. Several bowls and baskets lined the wall near the entrance, each filled to the brim with their dazzling yields of recent harvests. A few were spilling over with lustrous ears of corn, some the familiar yellow maize, and others a blue that reminded Carlotta of the first blue of nightfall. In sharp, colorful contrast the other vessels contained beans, squash, and melons.

The child's first thought was that she had somehow managed to bring back with her the color, the life and the vitality of her journey into the depths of the cave. She found herself lying on the floor of a small room, a heavy buffalo robe between her and the rock floor and a lighter-weight blanket made from sheep's wool pulled up close to her chin. Carlotta was comfortably warm, though the morning air was cold enough to see her own breath. As she came fully awake, she realized she wasn't alone. There were voices outside, children's laughter and the clear, breathy flute music Carlotta had heard before she fell asleep.

Last night. The child still remembered the strange night that followed a day of horror, but it no longer pained her in the direct way it had before Owl Woman had found her. She still felt her protective arms around her, as light and yet as strong as the feathered wings of the owl. Though she knew she was alone in the room, she no longer felt lonely.

Owl Woman appeared in the doorway, confirming Carlotta's feelings of security. The young Indian woman carried an armload of juniper wood for the fireplace. She entered quietly and crossed to the corner of the room, stacking the wood by the fire. She turned and smiled modestly and asked Carlotta if she would like something to eat.

The child jumped to her feet, eagerly hoping to be part of the morning ritual. Owl Woman stirred a pot of mush and with a small bowl scooped out servings for Carlotta and herself. Carlotta followed, bowl in hand, as Owl Woman went outside and sat in front of the sun-warmed wall.

For a time they sat preoccupied with their thoughts, content in each other's silent presence. Owl Woman finally rose from the terrace, beckoning Carlotta to come with her. Climbing down a ladder, the two descended to the next level where the Indian children were watching an old woman make pottery. Carlotta was introduced to the little girls' grandmother, who was patiently instructing the children in her craft.

"I must go to meet with our Sun Watcher. You will stay with the girls until I return," said Owl Woman.

Carlotta's fascination with the pot making allowed for the quiet retreat of Owl Woman. The work was intriguing and captivated the child's attention. The old woman's hands slid caressingly over the wet clay, shaping a new form over the outside of a finished bowl. Taking coils of clay, she pinched them into place on the base along the edge of the mold, and with subtle pressure and manipulative fingers controlled its evolving shape, increasing the height of the vessel walls. She then began the task of scraping, thinning the vessel walls with a gourd rind, ultimately obliterating the coils.

Seemingly satisfied with her accomplishment, the grandmother set aside the unfinished bowl and began to work on another that had been set to dry. Dipping a smooth pebble in water, she rubbed the bowl's surface until it became quite shiny.

While the grandmother applied herself to serious work, the two little girls attempted smaller replicas of the larger bowl. Their efforts, though less artful, became pretty miniatures that delighted Carlotta.

The old woman, finally satisfied with her bowl's completion, turned to the children.

"I have no more of the yellow clay. Go down to the stream, to the place I showed you, and bring some back to me." She motioned to Carlotta to accompany them.

There was excited chatter between the girls, which indicated that this would be a pleasurable chore. Carlotta felt happy to be included in their assigned task.

Before they left the pueblo, the eldest of the girls asked Carlotta to wait while they went inside their dwelling to retrieve something. Carlotta waited patiently on the roof while the girls disappeared down the ladder. When they returned, they each had a piece of cloth and a wooden replica of a clothed figure in their hands.

Carlotta had never seen a doll and looked curiously at these colorful scaled-down versions of humans who seemed to be disguised as animals. She would have liked to hold one, to study it more closely, but the girls were eager to be on their way and called for her to follow.

Retracing some of the steps Carlotta had made during the night, the girls skipped along the path, delighted with their new freedom. The path forked and they took the trail, unfamiliar to Carlotta, which curved back horizontally hugging the side of the mesa. Gradually the rocky path descended to the base of the mountain where a stream flowed, sparkling with reflected sunlight and the clear blue of a cloudless sky. A stand of cottonwoods grew by the stream, their rustling leaves mimicking the sound of water cascading over rocks.

It was a cool, enchanting place and the Indian girls pranced over the hard sandstone, their feet following the distinct footprints of children who had lived and played there in the past. Carlotta joined in their game of tag, gaily abandoning the restrained, quiet behavior expected in the grandmother's presence. Setting their wooden dolls and the bundled cloth on the bank, the girls splashed in the shallow water, their laughter echoing down the arroyo. For a moment Carlotta looked back longingly at the dolls, then with carefree exuberance ran off to join the others in their chase. The girls' small hands smacked the water, sending a flurry of spray flying behind them. Carlotta responded, kicking the water in their direction. The girls' boisterous behavior was quickly subdued when they suddenly realized they were not alone.

Several industrious Indian boys playing upstream were launching small boats made of bark and broken twigs. Each group of children had played contentedly, involved totally in their own game, but now were equally surprised to discover they were not alone. The boys' crafts floated merrily by the girls, some capsizing in the current, while others swept on to a longer journey. The boys waded noisily downstream in search of boats caught in the perilous reeds that grew at the turn in the creek. They freed one miniature barge, then another, intent on ignoring the girls and displaying their masculine concern for more serious matters.

Irruptive giggles soon broke the silence and the pretense. The girls' game became a half-hearted simulation of their previous rough-water play. The boys, too, self-consciously feigned an interest in the game that had brought them to the water. Carlotta, in the meantime, having no comprehension of the children's shy glances or blushing faces, soon began to lose interest in a game in which she found herself the only player. Wading back to the bank, Carlotta sat down beside the small treasures, the wooden dolls.

There had never been anything like these Indian dolls in Carlotta's experience at the mission. Toys were not crafted objects. The poor children of the mission resorted to imagination in their play. It simply had never occurred to her or the other girls to make a wooden pretend friend when in their games they could become one another's playmate, adopting the role of mother, father, or child, acting out a life only imagined by orphans. Carlotta gently touched the costume of one of the dolls. Soft feathers were fastened meticulously in place, forming a cloak over the shoulders of the figure. A headdress sat dramatically on the doll's birdlike head. Attentive detail had been given to designs painted in vibrant colors. The total effect was overwhelming to Carlotta. This miniature figure was representative of a glorious, larger-than-life human being, and it miraculously could be held in her hands. Carlotta gingerly picked up the doll, her eyes wide in conscious appreciation. It was only natural to hold the figure close, protectively. "Who are you, little person?" Carlotta asked in a whisper. Knowing full well this inanimate, yet convincingly real, piece of wood could not answer her, she gave the doll her own words and its own life.

Oblivious to the sounds from the creek, Carlotta withdrew into a magical world. She began a conversation with the two wooden dolls, giving them their own distinct voices. Here she dared to ask the questions adults had always silenced, and she found the imagined answers, articulated with tangible words that had only floated about abstractly in her head. Carlotta's gestures were gentle and maternal, and though the figures represented grown men, she offered them the unequivocal adoration she herself had never known as a child.

The play was soothing and reassuring to a child who had found no way to express the terror she had just survived. Time went by and Carlotta's inner wounds began to heal.

When the girls tired of the boys' attention, and the exciting prospect of meeting had been reduced to the reality of teasing, they joined Carlotta at the water's edge. Reluctantly, Carlotta gave back the magical possessions and sadly watched as others cared for her charges.

The older of the two Indian girls finally reminded them of their mission and they all went to an area where the yellow clay was abundant. They scooped out clumps of the clay from the banks of the dry wash with a stick, and wrapped them in the rags. The girls looped the cloth, tying the ends together, and swung them over their shoulders. Then, much to Carlotta's delight, they asked if she would carry the two dolls back to the pueblo.

***

The sun was lowering in the sky as Owl Woman left the kiva. She looked out across the mesa to the distant mountains, whose flanks were black with pines, and inhaled the beauty of her world. Slowly her breath escaped, a measured return of appreciation. The woman had worked this afternoon, cleaning and preparing the kiva for the sacred ceremonies that would begin this evening.

Though Owl Woman's role in the pueblo's community allowed her entrance to the kiva as an exception to the exclusivity of the tribe's men, she also willingly labored beside those of her own gender.

Owl Woman felt good, a joy that had mysteriously become more pronounced after her meeting with Sak-mo-i-si this morning. She had gone to him for two reasons, and neither had seemed a clue to these good feelings that she carried home with her.

The Sun Watcher had been expecting her, as he had made his final determination regarding the timing of the Kachina ceremony. It was the Sun Watcher's duty to determine the alignment of the sun, moon, and stars in order to plan the tribe's ceremonies, which were significantly tied to the winter and summer solstices as well as the vernal and autumnal equinoxes. His observations were made through strategic openings in the ceiling of the kiva. Sak-mo-i-si had confirmed the alignment, and told Owl Woman of his authorization for the event. But her personal reason for going to him had been more urgent. She went to tell him of her trip to the cave and of the child she had brought back with her. Owl Woman had not known of Sak-mo-i-si's late-night vigil, awaiting her return to the pueblo, and so had been mildly surprised at his remark.

"I am glad to see you have returned safely," he said. Sak-mo-i-si's calm composure was strangely disquieting, and Owl Woman's eyes sought his face to read the reason. There was nothing in his demeanor to feed her awakening hope for more. The Sun Watcher stood tall and straight. He appeared extremely handsome, she thought. Owl Woman turned her eyes away quickly, lest he observe her unsettled feelings.

"Yes," she explained, "I was directed by my power to return to the cave of the white owl, the home of my sisters and my childhood. White owl showed me a vision, a terrible vision of dying children and their murderers. I was not the only witness. This child I have brought back, a child of the mission, has been called by white owl. She has told me that Two Bears was not one of the children killed on the mesa, and so I am reasonably certain that your son is safe. There is still so much I do not understand" Owl Woman's voice had turned soft and distant, and the Sun Watcher recognized the Tuhikya's ability to fathom other dimensions, but also her struggle to relate what she had seen.

"Do not be overly concerned. You will come to understand, as you have at other times." Sak-mo-i-si was eager to ease her mind.

"I do not wish to bring the White Man's holy men here looking for her, but the child is not well yet, and it may be unwise to allow her to return until she has mastered her feelings and can carefully choose her words." Owl Woman looked steadily into the eyes of the tribal leader. "May she stay with The People through the Kachina ceremony?"

"It is not for me to determine, nor would I deny any child your medicine, Owl Woman." Sun Watcher's voice dropped huskily, caught in a moment of emotion. He reached out and placed his strong brown hand over hers, emphasizing his choice to abdicate the decision.

During Owl Woman's walk back to the dwelling, she thought about this new feeling of heightened clarity, and wondered how it could also bring such happy confusion. Owl Woman climbed the many steps up the east face of the pueblo's walls. This was a new look at an old friend, she thought.

CHAPTER 5

THE KACHINAS
AND THE PEOPLE WHO FLOATED
ABOVE THE EARTH

THE KACHINAS AND THE PEOPLE WHO FLOATED ABOVE THE EARTH

"What is a Kachina?" Carlotta asked. The excitement was contagious, and the child's question had already been ignored twice, as the Indian children bantered back and forth. Carlotta had been content being the observer until now, but this word Kachina was on everyone's lips and her curiosity was peaked.

"What is a Kachina?" she pressed.

"They are the spirit people who have come to promote and insure the life of all living things." Owl Woman, watching the children, was moved by the child's intense but respectful insistence on answers.

"The Kachinas will be leaving our village now, returning to the mountains where they live. It is the ceremony sending them off for which The People now prepare."

"What do they look like? Have I seen a Kachina?" Carlotta could not imagine missing some of the remarkable Spirit People the children talked about. Older children had described the marvelous attire worn by these spirit creatures, and yet Owl Woman said the Kachinas were living here in the village!

"They will make themselves visible when the ceremonies begin tomorrow," Owl Woman acknowledged, "but now you ask too many questions and it interferes with your corn grinding. See?"

Carlotta looked down dismally, and the two little girls, her new friends, giggled knowingly. It was true. She and Owl Woman had been sitting side by side, behind the wooden trough containing the metates. These were the milling stones used to grind the corn. Her own metate was the smoothest of the three, made of sandstone. The manos tool, which she rubbed up and down over the stone was supposed to produce the finished fine flour. Carlotta saw that she had not added much flour to the waiting bowl and tried harder to concentrate on her work.

She thought of the piki room she had visited earlier, where Owl Woman and her relatives had gone to bake the special paper-thin bread. The stove dominated this small room with its hooded chimney and long, flat tablet stone, which served as a griddle to cook the piki. Carlotta had been with the women when they began the slow process of stoking the fire. Owl Woman had explained the necessity of controlling the temperature so that the tablet would not crack, finally running off Carlotta and the other laughing children in fear that it might.

The women would be making piki bread today for the Kachinas, who would give it to the spectators at tomorrow's events. Carlotta couldn't help but feel the excitement of The People, as every facet of village life turned its focus on the Kachina ceremony, and so she put new strength into her shoulders as she firmly rubbed the manos over the corn.

A large commotion just outside drew the attention of the girls and Owl Woman away from their work. Children were screaming and it took a moment to realize that their voices were expressing delight. They were apparently greeting someone whose presence had surprised them.

"Two Bears! Two Bears!" called the children.

Carlotta looked up at Owl Woman and smiled brightly. Owl Woman and the girls rushed outside to peer over the ledge. Below, they saw two boys cross the plaza to meet with Sak-mo-i-si.

"Diego!" cried Carlotta. With no explanation, Carlotta tore down the terrace, scrambling down the ladders to the lower levels. The others watched, as the child from the mission ran across the plaza.

"Diego! Two Bears!"

The boys recognized her at once and waved their arms.

"She is alive! I told you Two Bears, I knew my sister was all right!"

Carlotta flew into the arms of her brother and The People began to gather on the plaza, interested in this demonstration of emotion.

"We were afraid for you, little sister. Many of our friends have died on Blue Mesa. Friar Alcazar told us that the Apache are responsible." Diego gazed appreciably at his sister's well being.

"No, Diego, it was not the Apache!" Carlotta's words were lost as Sak-mo-i-si stepped forward, and placing both hands on Two Bear's shoulders welcomed his return.

"Hakomi?" Sak-mo-i-si asked, turning to face Diego and Carlotta.

"Pardon me, Father. This is Diego, brother of Carlotta. They are my friends from the mission." Two Bears' voice was solemn and calm though his face was flushed from their travels.

Diego extended his hand courteously to the tribal Sun Watcher, who clasped it in warm recognition of the boy's respectful manner.

Owl Woman approached the throng, the two little Indian girls hovering about her skirts. Two Bears came forward to greet the girls and openly embraced Owl Woman. Carlotta watched, surprised at this evidence of a previous relationship.

"Tell me, my son. How is it that Apache have killed little children?" Sak-mo-i-si asked, incredulously.

"No!" Carlotta loudly interjected. "It was the soldiers and the Comancheros who killed the children! I was there and saw them shoot our friends, Two Bears. I saw them shoot *all* of them!"

Men and women looked at one another. The people of the tribe were taken back by the strength in the child's words. It was not in the Indian way for a child to speak so forwardly. Though no one actually moved, there was a sense of physical retreat, a feeling that the clan had stepped back in acquiescence. In this void Sak-mo-i-si's voice boomed.

"Is this true?"

Owl Woman, raising her hand said, "One Who Traveled Far – Carlotta - has seen the truth, as you know. It is time for the elders to call the council and give The People the direction of their wisdom. The child and your nieces can see to the nourishment of Two Bears and the boy," said Owl Woman.

Sak-mo-i-si nodded his approval, and the children eagerly departed.

With the children gone, the crowd began to disperse, returning to their preparations for the next day's ceremony. The plaza cleared until there remained only those men and women who, with age and wisdom, had earned the title of the elders.

A graying old man, who wore his blanket close to ward off an imagined chill, was the first to speak.

"The words of the boy do not ring true. Never in my days have I heard of the Apache killing, unprovoked. Children ...

humph!" The old man expressed his disbelief, his words trailing off in a guttural exclamation.

"Remember what Two Bears said," reminded Owl Woman. "The White Man's priest told him it was the Apache."

"It would be like the White Man not to know one Indian from another," an elder volunteered.

" ... or, an Indian from a Mexican!" stated a wrinkled old grandmother.

Sak-mo-i-si considered these possibilities and thought of the most likely candidates, those who traded on horseback. The Comancheros had become the Indians' agent in the trade of their goods. The villagers supplied cornmeal, bread, and the fruits of their recent harvests, in exchange for sugar, bolts of cloth, and other goods. Sak-mo-i-si had studied the Comancheros and their ways.

"The Comancheros have no regard for life or little else, unless there is a profit to be made. Tito Sanchez might be involved ..." Sak-mo-i-si offered.

"Perhaps this is how we have lost children working in the corn fields," said Owl Woman.

"One does not kill those who are valuable as slaves. And the soldiers ... the girl spoke of soldiers!" Sak-mo-i-si was perplexed.

The People explored all that they knew of the massacre, and each was now left to his or her imagination. It was not sufficient to make a judgment, but enough to present an advisable warning.

Sak-mo-i-si had an added concern. His son was learning the white man's language at the mission, an arrangement that gratified the wishes of the mission's men of God and, in turn, insured the clan's autonomy.

Alcazar had been satisfied with Sak-mo-i-si's decision to send Two Bears to live at the mission part of the year. It was very important to these priests that everyone worship the White Man's god. Sak-mo-i-si saw no reason to believe his son was at risk. Certainly, this teaching of theirs was an investment they would be willing to protect.

In the meantime, his son was initiated in the Squash Society. The Sun Watcher was confident of Two Bears loyalty to The People and of his physical ability, as well. The children of the Spaniards were not ignorant, either. Counseling the children to watch quietly was the surest way to guarantee the safety of all three. From time to time, in a manner that would not draw attention to themselves, they would return to the pueblo, and then The People would learn of their observations.

***

"Didn't Maria give you and Two Bears anything to eat for your journey?" asked Carlotta.

She and the girls sat mesmerized at the sight of her brother and Two Bears greedily sating their appetites. With the pride of approaching womanhood, Carlotta and the Indian girls had busily served the simple meal. Small round loaves of bread made of corn and the fruit of the prickly pear quickly disappeared, while the girls looked on, amazed. Diego raised his head and smiled.

"Yes, Maria prepared food for us, though she cried and begged us not to go. It has been very hard on her ... losing Felicia." Diego's countenance darkened.

"We finally convinced her that we must warn Two Bears' people and swore her to secrecy, at least until after we had left, so that no one would stop us.

"But, thank you sister. We were very hungry!" Again, Diego's smile lit up his face. Carlotta gazed adoringly at her brother, and realized how much she had missed his resiliency. Diego's face could change as swiftly as a fast-moving storm, first dark and thundering, and then just as quickly the sun would break through claiming a bright new day. As a reminder, Diego's eyes narrowed when he questioned Carlotta about Blue Mesa.

"Tell me how you managed to survive, little sister."

"Maria sent me to find Felicia, Diego ..." Carlotta's voice fell to a whisper as she recalled her trip to Blue Mesa.

When she had finished her account of the massacre and her run for safety, Carlotta sensed a need to keep private the mysterious events deep within the cave, and ended her story abruptly.

"Owl Woman found me that night and brought me here."

Two Bears was relishing the last few crumbs of his loaf of bread, when the mention of the cave caught his attention.

"Owl Woman found you there?" he asked.

"Yes," Carlotta answered, wistful memories returning.

"That is where Owl Woman took me and healed me." Two Bears said.

The children studied the son of Sak-mo-i-si, and waited anxiously for him to continue.

"When I was very small, I was thrown from my pony," he said. "My leg was badly broken and I could not move. A woman found me in a gully off the trail to Blue Mesa, in an area where I was not supposed to ride. She carried me to the cave, where she lived.

"There, she gave me her medicine and nursed me until she thought I could travel. The woman spoke my language, and in talking to me learned that Sun Watcher was my father. When it was time, she prepared a travois and dragged me the long distance back to the pueblo. My father was very grateful for my return and impressed with the woman's courage and strength. That was when I learned her name was Owl Woman.

"Later, my father told me the story of the Tuhikya, the woman who healed others. When she was young, long before she was named Owl Woman, she and her two older sisters had been banished from the tribe. The elders had accused them of being Powaqas, or witches. When they saw the evidence of Owl Woman's ability to heal, they talked among themselves. Admitting the decree had been a bad ruling, they offered her a home with The People.

"The People have never regretted their decision. Owl Woman has been the healer of many Indian children, and has clear visions that have helped to lead our people wisely. To me, Owl Woman is like the mother I lost when I was born."

Carlotta recognized the same feelings within herself, and instead of jealousy she felt a kinship with Two Bears she had not known. Their eyes connected in a moment of understanding.

Was there more that Two Bears was not telling? Carlotta wondered. Had he gone deep within the cave and found the enchanted world of color and animals that she had seen? Had he brought back the power of white owl? Or, like the rabbit who ran, driven by his own fear, had he disappeared before he entered the cave and never learned the wonder of its inner world? Carlotta kept her thoughts to herself. Two Bears said no more, and instead asked Diego if he had enough to eat.

***

The People spent days in preparation for this last Kachina ceremony of the year. The dancers, who would impersonate the Kachinas, practiced for days the songs and the intricately choreographed dances out of doors on the plaza. A great amount of time and careful detail was spent in the making of the masks and other items that would be used for the dances. The spirits of all the invisible forces of life would be persuaded to bless the crops with the clouds and rain necessary to bring in a bountiful harvest. The Kachinas would convey the prayers and messages of The People for long and healthy lives and harmony in the universe. Afterward they would leave, returning to their homes in the mountains until the next Soyal, the winter solstice, marking the beginning of the six-month growing season.

Everyone had a role in preparation for the ceremony and felt an intricate relationship to its meaning. Men and women prepared special gifts and food. From the pueblo to their own bodies, all was made ready. Care had been taken to wash the hair of the dancers in the suds from the amole, and with the smudging of the sage smoke they performed the spiritual cleansing. This was a time of joy and optimism, each generation looking forward to its own particular pleasure.

As the soft gray of early morning gave way to a pale rose, tousled children emerged from their homes. From across the terraces and down the far side of the plaza chanting could be heard and everyone knew the Kachinas were at hand. Several women were busily sweeping their homes, while others were finishing breakfast around the outdoor pots of food. An air of anticipation rose on the smoke of the morning's fires.

Two Bears left his father's home in the first light of dawn and made his way to Owl Woman's abode. There he found her busy at work. With Owl Woman's permission, the boy entered the room and nudged Diego and Carlotta awake. Soon the two sleepy children were rubbing their eyes and stumbling behind Two Bears into the morning air. There they became part of the unfolding ceremony of Niman Kachina.

As Carlotta exited the room, she saw a group of men sitting on the roof of the highest pueblo rooms. With their backs to Carlotta, they were peering over the side of the mesa, intent on the source of chanting voices. A wind was blowing up from the desert floor and it whipped at Carlotta's dress, flattening it against her body. She shivered from a moment's chill, but began to follow, curious to find the source of the beautiful music.

"No," Two Bears warned, "Women aren't supposed to look on a Kachina without his mask ... unless they are serving food."

The children hurriedly found an area on their terraced wall to sit, and with legs dangling in nervous excitement waited for their first glimpse of the Kachinas.

A boy, close in age to Two Bears, ran swiftly on silent moccasin feet toward them. As he passed them, and went by each doorway, he called softly his announcement of the Kachinas' arrival. The sound of musical instruments preceded the appearance of the Kachinas, and a hush fell over the pueblo.

Carlotta strained to see the arrival of the much-talked-about Kachinas. She gasped excitedly as feathers and spires of headed grass appeared, seeming to float ghostlike on the desert breeze. The elaborate headdresses bobbed and swayed, delicate frameworks of wood and metal trembling in the air. Again, Two Bears explained that they were "tablitas." There was the irregular rhythm of rattles and the jingling of bells, and then suddenly the children saw the Kachinas. As the Kachinas climbed over the rocks and into view on the mesa they followed a long cotton string. Two Bears pointed out the white and yellow feather tied to the string, indicating this to be the trail that would lead them and their blessings in among The People.

"I can't see! Can we go down there?" Carlotta pointed to the children cautiously exploring the edge of the plaza. Little ones were gathering in small groups, where they sought strength in their numbers.

Diego was about to put a stop to his sister's pestering when Two Bears surprisingly agreed.

"Come, I'll find us a good place," he said.

Intent on moving inconspicuously, the three scurried quietly down ladders and weathered steps. They slipped in among the nearest children and sat cross-legged to wait.

The colorful dancers filed over the horizon led by two men. The first man dipped his hand into a small bag and scattered sacred cornmeal on the ground before the dancers.

The second held a water bowl from which he flipped drops of water with an eagle feather. Carlotta felt her breath cease while she weighed fear against awe, for the Kachinas were wearing masks, some garish and others beautiful.

The Kachinas stopped before a rock shrine and deposited grains of cornmeal, then moved forward onto the plaza. Carlotta saw that each performer wore spruce around his neck, and a white kirtle and sash. Then she discovered the source of the rhythmic clicking she had heard; there were deer hoofs and turtle shell rattles tied beneath their right knees and on their left legs they wore a strap of bells. Nearer they came in a manner that dramatized abundance, their arms laden with spruce, rattles, musical instruments, and other mysteries.

The Kachina closest to Carlotta was painted with corn smut and wore a skirt of piñon boughs. His mask was a brilliant turquoise-blue with feathers sprouting from the top and from his ears. Interlocking crescent symbols were painted on his torso and on the dancers who closely followed. The next Kachina was suddenly upon her with his frightening wolf mask, its jutting jaw lined with hideous teeth. Carlotta shrunk back against her brother's protective shoulder as the Kachinas swarmed into view.

Slowly, the dancers filed in to the center of the plaza and with each step they engaged and seduced their audience. The leader directed them in their movements and in unison the group played out his will, much like ants who abide within the group, obedient to a higher mind. Brown moccasin feet began to beat out a deliberate rhythm and painted bodies began to swing left then right. The swishing skirts entranced the audience further, adding to the hypnotic effect of the chanting.

As the Kachinas moved to and fro, Carlotta saw the front and the back of each frightful, yet beguiling mask. Forward they came, their arms outstretched with offerings. A world of color advanced, closing in on the circle's perimeter of awe-struck children. Several older boys reached out their arms, anxious to receive the gifts like those remembered from past ceremonies. With patient reverence, an arc of young and old began to form. Indian children, arms extended from their bodies, sought the manna of the spirits, and the Kachinas reached out with laden arms to complete the act of giving.

The line of converging bodies descended upon Two Bears, Diego, and Carlotta. Carlotta felt enveloped by the Kachina who stood before her. His mask, like the first, was a brilliant turquoise, and on this background stood a beautiful rainbow. The bold colors were enticing, but Carlotta had never seen a rainbow quite like this. The clear, bright colors seemed to merge into one another and dance together, creating their own sense of life. Carlotta wanted to be part of that beautiful swirling rainbow. She reached out to touch it, but the dancer moved back slowly and deliberately, letting her only savor the dancing rainbow. The beauty of the moment was broken by the dancers as the tempo increased, and soon Carlotta was joining the other children in laughter as she recognized the Kachina's burden to be gifts of miniature bows and arrows, and …

Suddenly her heart seemed to stop as she saw the small dolls carried in the Kachina's arms, just like the ones she had held in her arms only yesterday. She ached to touch and hold a doll again. Surprisingly, the Kachina approached Carlotta and gently held out a doll to her. Although Carlotta couldn't see the face under the mask, she felt the love and sense of oneness with this wonderful being, a being who cared so much for her that he would give such a gift. Tears began to well in the child's eyes, as she was overcome by her feelings. Lovingly, she reached out and the Kachina placed the doll in her hands. Time seemed to evaporate as Carlotta drew the doll to her and tenderly nestled it to her body.

In this suspension of time, Carlotta vaguely felt herself caught up in the compelling movement that swirled around her. Masks of all shapes, some elongated rectangles with black slits for eyes, and others with their elaborately formed tablita-style headdresses, swam before her. Colorful painted designs that represented clouds and rain, tinkling bits of metal that cast their magical sound into the air; all became a part of the complex spinning that filled the plaza. Underneath, the drums continued to beat out their ever-changing rhythm.

Owl Woman placed a gentle hand on Carlotta's shoulder and the reverie was broken. She smiled, acknowledging the gift Carlotta had received from the Kachina.

"You have accepted the gift of love … a necessity for one who will give love."

***

The dance was spirited on by the Kachina father as he instructed the dancers to sing louder and harder, and the People, one by one, stepped forward, to toss cornmeal on the Kachinas, blessing their efforts. Carlotta's eyes, which had been riveted on the Kachinas, lifted to take in the majestic panorama. She noticed the two spruce trees, which had not been in the plaza yesterday but, Two Bears had said, were ceremoniously planted during the night. Their clean fragrance was magnified in the heat of the day. She saw the eight maidens, wearing orange masks and beautifully attired in black mantas covered with red and white blankets, shuffle their white deerskin boots in unison. Carlotta watched as ears of corn were offered to the Kachina leader and the maidens, who then returned to the kiva, climbing down the ladder and out of sight.

Carlotta then looked up to the village's surrounding terraces. There on a rooftop a tethered eagle flapped his wings, hopelessly attempting flight, and she saw that everywhere The People stood with their eyes fixed on the ceremony.

Three more times during the day the Kachinas repeated their dance. More gifts were bestowed on the children, and during the third ceremony Carlotta was delighted to see Diego receive a colorful toy bow. Between dances the Kachinas tossed to the audience piki and the first small fruits of harvest; miniature ears of corn and tiny melons.

Those Kachinas that had descended into the recesses of the kiva came out just before sunset for their final appearance. A breeze lifted, bringing a welcome relief from the hot sun, which had beat ruthlessly on them all day. The People eagerly sought out the cool shadows, and the Kachinas began to dance for the last time. The mesa was washed red with the last rays of a sinking sun, and the brilliant purple, orange, and reds began to fade into the dusty colors, less real than the magnificence of the day.

The Kachina father delivered his farewell to the Kachinas. He prayed for the rain that would renew all life in the name of all people, animals, and plants everywhere. Finally the ceremony was over and The People came up to pluck sprigs of spruce, which they would later plant in their own fields. The dancers now filed across the plaza, their unearthly silhouettes black against the blazing sky. Sensing the imminent loss of their enchanted world, the children gathered around the departing Kachinas.

The Kachina father stepped forward and warned the children.

"No, you mustn't follow. The Spirit People must return to their home in the mountains. They are needed in their own world, as we are needed in ours."

Carlotta watched sadly as each Kachina momentarily hung suspended on the mesa's cliffs and then descended out of sight.

***

CHAPTER 6

LOS NINOS

LOS NINOS

They left at first light. Carlotta hurriedly joined the boys. She was eager to see the unknown world she and Owl Woman had traveled through three nights ago. They climbed down the rugged steps of the trail and took the path that dropped to the desert plateau. Here, they passed the horse and mule corrals and looked out at a cluster of planted geometric shapes. These were the result of The People's long efforts. Descending from the red bluffs, the children saw the green corn stalks growing randomly in one of the fields. As they drew closer, they could see the parched sand that was called on to support the corn's growth.

Two Bears pointed to the clouds gathering on the horizon and said, "The rains are overdue. We must hurry. As my father warned, the desert can be a dangerous place during a storm."

"Do you see the dry wash coursing down the mountain?" Two Bears asked.

Diego and Carlotta looked up and saw how the Indians had utilized every drop of moisture on this barren landscape. The wash had split in a myriad of directions and Carlotta could imagine the runoff racing down the hills, dividing and finally taming itself. An elaborate irrigation system waited to accept the rain, the promise of life for thirsty crops. They continued their walk and saw beans, squash, pumpkins, and even melons rising valiantly from the dry, cracked earth.

"This field is ours," Two Bears said with pride, indicating a plot on their left. "When I was very young, it was my job to keep the ravens from the fields so that they would not destroy the crops. My people hand-carried ollas from the stream and even the caches on the mesa. If I was not in school at the mission I, too, would spend my days bringing water to the plants that feed my people. And perhaps I, too, would have disappeared like some of the other children," Two Bears added.

Carlotta heard the unguarded fear in Two Bears' voice and asked, "What happened to them?"

"No one knows, but the elders have talked of witches."

The sun was rising quickly, washing the land in its golden glow. A warmth spread across the desert and protectively surrounded the children. In this safe environment it was difficult to imagine witches and the darker side of life. Carlotta could see that Two Bears would like to stay with his people, and for the first time she understood the pain he must feel in having to live away from the pueblo.

Two Bears continued, "Sometimes, when the Navaho and Apache are seen in the area, we build shelters and live by our fields to protect our harvests."

Two Bears bent over and pulled back a big leaf, revealing a large round pumpkin.

"These are my favorites." He smiled back at Diego and Carlotta.

Diego gently nudged Two Bears and said quietly, "It's time, we must go."

Carlotta knew she was going to miss the people of the pueblo, but she found herself anxious to return to the only home she had known. She clutched tightly her new friend, the gift from the Kachina.

The Kachina doll and Carlotta had been inseparable since the ceremony. She had barely noticed the food that was offered, part of the celebration that captivated the other children. She had sat apart from the others, legs tucked beneath her, carefully examining her exquisite gift. The doll was a marvel of imagination, with its brightly painted designs and soft feathered costume. Wasn't it wonderful? Carlotta thought. She had received one of the little people with a beautiful face, instead of the hideous wolf who frightened her. Carlotta told herself she would always care for this special treasure.

Behind her, the boys were discussing a serious matter, and Carlotta's joy evaporated at the mention of Father Alcazar's name.

"Father Serna and Father Alcazar will be thankful to know Carlotta has survived," said Two Bears. "But I hope they won't be too upset with us for leaving without permission."

"We are almost men now," Diego said. "It is right that we act on our own."

The high desert plateau began to slope, widening into an expansive valley. Its lush grassland swept away to meet the horizon. Carlotta was reminded of the meadow and the horses in her dream, but she had no real memory of ever before coming this far east.

When the three travelers reached the Rio Santa Fe, they found a familiar spot at the bend in the river. Choosing a site on a big rock beneath the shade of cottonwoods, they ate the food from the bundle Owl Woman had prepared for them. The cool breeze off the water brought welcome relief from the sun.

Two Bears broke a loaf of bread, giving each equal shares. There were several strips of jerky, which the children ate greedily, knowing meat to be a special treat. The meal was over all too soon, and Carlotta occupied her time wrapping the Kachina doll in the woven bundle.

Diego spoke first. "We must be careful to remember what the elders have told us Carlotta. The priests must not know about the Kachinas. The church has warned Two Bears' people not to practice the ceremonies. The Kachinas are forbidden. Many of our friends will be hurt if the priests find out."

Diego took a deep breath and looked at Two Bears. They both glanced at Carlotta who had not let the Kachina doll out of her arms.

Carlotta looked at the boys and immediately understood that she was in danger of being separated from her new friend.

"No!" she said stubbornly. Looking down at her doll, she added, "I won't give her up."

But Carlotta's voice weakened as she realized what would happen to The People if this doll was seen. Slowly she got to her feet and walked away from the boys. She needed to be alone with her new friend.

Carlotta didn't want Diego and Two Bears to boss her around about her new Kachina friend. She didn't wish to bring any harm to her pueblo friends, any more than Diego, but she must find some place safe for her doll.

Turning frantically to her brother, she said, "I will hide her in the bundle, below your shirt! No one will see her. I know of a place, behind the adobe wall in the courtyard. It is my secret place and no one will know, I promise!"

The boys looked on this small defiant girl, so resolved in her decision. What were they to do?

***

Father Serna was standing at the mission gates when the children arrived. He was struggling with a mule, cajoling the stubborn animal to leave its sanctuary. Wiping his brow, the stout padre tugged again at the mule's reins, mumbling platitudes in Spanish. Carlotta laughed with delight at the sight of this tug of war.

At the sound of the child, Serna's head jerked around, and the mule seized the opportunity to bolt back through the open gate. Serna, however, paid little attention, and with arms open wide, came running toward them.

"Gracias Dios! You are back. You are well? Ah, but you are alive!" The padre's words tumbled, one upon another, as he took Carlotta into his massive arms. Stunned by this welcome, Carlotta protested, struggling to breathe and speak at the same time.

Diego grinned and spoke first, "We found her Father. She was with Two Bears' people, safe and sound." He had remembered what Owl Woman had told him. It was better if Carlotta did not talk about what she saw on Blue Mesa. It would only bring unwanted questions.

Carlotta broke away, her smiling face streaked with dirt.

"See! I'm fine!" she said. This was remarkably easy, she thought, and they would not have to lie.

Large drops of rain began to fall from the leaden sky. Together, the children and the friar ran for shelter in the barn. When they reached the corrals the mule was standing in the barn doorway waiting for them. The group found cover just as the scattered drops turned into a downpour. A deafening torrent fell on the high roof of the barn and they decided to wait for a lull.

The smell of wet earth excited Carlotta. She had been tired from their journey, but now felt refreshed. This rain was the answer to The People's prayers, and it would bless the mission gardens, too, she thought.

The children peered out from beneath the eaves of the barn. A sheet of rain had dropped a shroud between them and the mission walls. Carlotta tugged gently at Two Bears' shirt.

"Your corn is watered," she whispered.

Father Serna shuffled restlessly from one foot to the other and finally said, "I must return to the rectory. You children can wait out the storm here. It might be best if you brought a bucket of milk back with you. I will let Father Alcazar know of your whereabouts."

Serna pulled the hood of his robe up over his head and trudged across the courtyard, his boots splashing in its many puddles.

"So far, so good," said Diego.

"Yes, but we must be careful." Two Bears looked worried, in spite of the needed rain.

"Carlotta, you must hide the Kachina, while we milk the goats." Two Bears took down two covered buckets hanging from an overhead beam and handed one to Diego.

The boys made their way to the end of the barn where four milk goats were corralled. A wooden partition divided them from their newly weaned kids, and a raucous clamor grew as the boys approached.

Carlotta could hear the hungry kid goats cry as she dashed to the mission with her bundle. Heart pounding, she walked quietly down the passageway to the end of the wall and the hidden alcove. Protected by the roof's overhanging tiles, Carlotta tenderly placed her Kachina in the wall's hollow. Lingering a moment, she spoke to her doll, reassuring her that she was loved and wouldn't be forgotten. Resigned to their separation, Carlotta picked up the woven bag and turned to walk down the corridor.

A hand reached out and roughly grabbed her shoulder. Carlotta yelped in surprise, but the hand flew over her mouth, muffling her protests.

"Hush! He's coming," the voice murmured.

It was Miguel, one of the Mexican orphans from the village. Carlotta decided to obey rather than take a chance. They both retreated behind the low wall just in time to watch Father Alcazar walk by swiftly.

Alcazar's stride was purposeful and he quickly disappeared at the end of the corridor. Miguel released his hold on Carlotta's arm and they both exhaled.

"What were you hiding?" Miguel asked.

"I can't tell you. It's a secret!" Carlotta answered, rubbing her bruised arm.

She hadn't been home an hour and already she was in danger of being found out. Carlotta had to be more careful, otherwise she would break her promise to her Kachina.

"Well, no matter, but it was obvious you didn't want Father Alcazar to see you. Right?"

Carlotta hesitated and then muttered, "Thank you."

"Where have you been? Everyone thought you were muerta! Were you with the others?" Miguel examined her earnestly, his expression genuinely confused.

"I can't answer your questions right now, Miguel. I've got to get back to Diego and Two Bears. They're in the barn waiting for me."

"They're back, too?" Miguel was unequivocally happy now and said, "Let's go!"

The children darted across the courtyard, dodging raindrops. The sun was coyly peeking out beneath a heavy streak of dark clouds when they reached the barn. As they approached, they could hear voices behind the heavy door. It was too late, Alcazar was here.

Reluctantly, they slipped inside. Father Alcazar was questioning the boys, and seeing Carlotta and Miguel, called them over. Alcazar appeared unusually friendly. Carlotta thought his voice was almost silky.

"Tell me, Carlotta, how is it that your brother and Two Bears have found you with the Indians?" Alcazar asked the child.

Carlotta looked down in silence. If she could have run ... if there had been the slightest chance she could have escaped, she knew this was the time. But the moment vanished and Carlotta saw that she could not stand frozen in front of the friar any longer. Others depended on her, and their well-being depended on her own deceit. It was an instinctive decision, only partially conscious.

Carlotta looked directly in his eyes and lied, "I was exploring ... and I ... I guess I got lost."

Alcazar was above her, and reaching down gently, he lifted her small face in his hand.

"You mean to say that Maria asked you to go to the mesa to find her little girl, and instead you decided to play?"

Shamed by the question's implication, more than her falsehood, Carlotta winced, but held his gaze.

Diego bit his tongue. He knew that if he or Two Bears offered any excuse it would only rouse suspicion. He stared at

Two Bears, willing him to remain silent. An interminable time held them all, as if they were caught in a spider's web.

Alcazar's eyes narrowed, "Have your friends or your brother told you what has happened to Felicia?" His voice had lost its velvet cover.

"Yes," said Carlotta, overcome with remorse. "She and the others were killed by Apaches!" The last word left her clenched teeth with feigned loathing.

The friar searched the child's eyes, looking for something that wasn't there. Seemingly satisfied, his hand dropped away from her face, and he turned back to the boys.

"Well, at least we won't count your sister among the dead, eh Diego?" Alcazar was smiling once again.

The tension in the air began to leave. Diego thought their answers had satisfied the friar and he turned to milk the goat waiting patiently. Carlotta, too, was relieved, and had decided to walk over to where the goat kids were playing, when Alcazar's hand reached down and seized her woven bag.

"And what might this be?" he asked.

"My brother's shirt," Carlotta answered, more confidently.

She willingly handed over the bundle that Owl Woman had given her to carry their food, but Father Alcazar seemed satisfied with Carlotta's gesture and dismissed her offer.

"Finish up your chores then, and see if Maria has something for you to eat before bedtime. I trust you will all say your prayers for the departed souls of los niños?"

In unison they nodded, anxious that the interrogation be over.

***

The four walked to the cocina, deep in their own thoughts.

There was not much reason to rejoice, Carlotta thought. True, Father Alcazar had easily concluded her actions were careless and irresponsible, but now she must appear before Maria ... the hardest judge of all. Would Maria hate her? She had been sent to bring Felicia back, such a simple task. She had returned three days later, alive and well ... and Felicia lay dead. Carlotta gulped. It was not the lie that hurt, it was the truth.

But these were feelings that had no time or place to be expressed, and Carlotta, Diego, and Two Bears parted the blanket covering the door to the cocina.

Maria was genuinely happy to see them. Her face was swollen from endless crying, and though fresh tears prevailed, they were shed with relief.

"Muchachos, mi muchachos," she said repeatedly, as she hovered over them with beans and tortillas.

The children felt Maria's need to mother them and sensed their own duty was that of submission. The boys tried to tell her of their search for Carlotta, but she brushed their explanations aside. Maria asked them no questions, content instead with the knowledge that the three were safe and sound. When she was assured they could eat no more, she retrieved the two books Carlotta had left that fateful day and placed them carefully in the child's hands. Wishing them a peaceful sleep, she sent them to bed.

***

The orphans of the mission were housed in a long room at the end of one of the three wings that bordered the courtyard. In this wing the youngest children were cared for by Maria, in a room off the kitchen where they could receive her constant supervision.

The older children's large room was casually divided, girls at one end and boys at the other. A constant rain was falling when Two Bears, Diego, and Carlotta entered the room to prepare for bed. A lone candle burned on a small table in the middle of the room and it flickered tentatively, as they closed the door behind them.

Carlotta listened to hear if anyone was still awake, as she placed her books carefully on the table. The thought of leaving her brother and sleeping alone in her own cot was not comforting. In the darkness she knew there were many empty cots and she thought of the children who had gone to Blue Mesa. She slipped out of her dress, shivering and quickly pulled the muslin nightdress over her head. Carlotta took the candle from the table and followed Diego and Two Bears to the end of the room. Lightning flashed in one of the room's high windows, sending light flickering across the floor.

"Please talk with me just a little while," Carlotta pleaded, setting the candle on the floor.

"Oh, Carlotta, go to sleep," Diego whispered. "We are all tired."

"Let her stay Diego," Two Bears said.

Thunder rumbled in the distance, and Carlotta jumped in Diego's bed, pulling his blanket up over her head. The child made no attempt to move or speak, and Diego shrugged his shoulders.

"I should let her keep the Kachina to sleep with," said Diego, hopelessly. "Better it than me!"

"You know you can't," said Two Bears.

"I don't understand Two Bears. Why is it a danger if the priests find out?"

"Do you really want to know?" asked Two Bears. "Because if you do, I'll tell you."

Diego took a blanket off the cot next to his, and spread it on the floor by the candle. He then reached under his own cot and pulled out his sole possession, his guitar. "Yes, I would like to know," Diego said, absently holding his guitar in his lap. He turned and gave his undivided attention to his friend.

Two Bears sat down beside him and took a deep breath.

"Many years ago, long before I was born, the Spanish first came to our villages. We welcomed them as friends. It was not long before we learned they were not friends but enemies."

Miguel was awake and quietly joined the storyteller, with the Comanche twins, Chano and Chuey, right behind him.

Two Bears was quiet for a moment, as he considered whether he should tell his story to the children. It was not the children who were a threat, he decided.

"At first they took food," Two Bears continued, "but they did not take only what they needed. They emptied all of our stores of food to feed their priests and soldiers. That left us with nothing and our people began to starve.

"It didn't stop there. If they saw something, they took it, even the blankets off our old people's backs. Everything they wanted, they took. The Spaniards looked around for gold and silver. They brought guns and sickness, and many of our people died."

Lightning flashed again, and the boys could see that other children had wakened and were quietly finding a place in the circle surrounding the candle. Carlotta raised her head, and letting the blanket fall, revealed an unruly mass of dark hair. Her eyes shone, wide and black, in a face made eerie blue in the lightning's sudden glare.

"But the worst was yet to come," Two Bears continued. "The Spaniards appointed a priest to govern us, and he said it was wrong for the Kachinas to come. He said we must worship his god and forget our ways."

"But ... I'm Spanish ... and I wouldn't do that!" Carlotta interrupted.

"No, but the priests would, and do!" said Two Bears.

"Hush,Carlotta! Let Two Bears talk," Diego said impatiently.

"Our people knew that without the Kachina ceremonies, the rain would not come and the corn would not grow. But the priests did not listen. When my people tried to practice the ceremonies secretly, the priests found out and killed the people. Soon the small children and the old ones began to die of starvation."

"Our priests wouldn't do that, would they Diego?" Carlotta was certain Two Bears was mistaken, and she looked for reassurance from her brother and then over to Pilar and Virginia who were sitting at the foot of the bed. No one offered an explanation. The children remained quietly solemn and waited for Two Bears to continue.

"In despair, my people secretly conducted the Niman Kachina among the cliffs, and four days later the rains came. We knew then that if we were to survive we must return to our own ways. You see ... the Spanish god could not help my people."

Carlotta listened to the steady rain falling on the roof, and thought about Two Bears' field of corn.

"We joined with the other pueblos under a powerful medicine man," said Two Bears, "and we took back our land and lives from the Spanish. At our pueblo, the priest was thrown from the mesa. His body was buried in a dry wash and cattle and sheep were driven across his grave so that the Spanish could never find any proof of his death.

"The vestments of the church were hidden in a cave along with the soldiers' armor and weapons. Then the people destroyed the church they had been forced to build. The friar had treated our people as slaves and many of us died while building that church. The Spanish were driven out and for sixteen years our people were free."

Two Bears stopped short of telling the growing group of children about the ceremonies the three had witnessed. It would not be safe for them or his people.

Jean Paul adjusted his bent, wire-rimmed glasses to his thin face.

"Did you lose your parents from the disease the Spanish brought?" he asked. As a survivor of the French settlement that had suffered the epidemic, Jean Paul felt great compassion for the plight of Two Bears' people.

"No, but my mother did not survive my birth," said Two Bears.

"All of you must promise not to tell the priests about the Kachinas," he reminded them. "It could bring great harm to my people."

The children nodded with genuine concern.

"Many of us were killed. Did you tell Carlotta about this?" asked Jean Paul.

"Yes, but it was not as it seems. It was not Apache. They were soldiers and Comancheros," said Two Bears.

"How do you know this?" asked one of the Comanche twins.

"I was there," Carlotta said simply.

"And you mustn't tell the priests this, either," Two Bears added.

"But, we must … so that they can stop them!" said Miguel.

"No!" said Carlotta. "People believe what they want to believe. Until they have proof, anyway. We must watch and learn."

The children were lost in thought, each reflecting on the stories they had just heard. Diego began to softly strum his guitar, and Carlotta felt reassured hearing the familiar melodies. Virginia, too, felt the music's solace, and finding Carlotta's hand, gently squeezed it. Not to be left alone, Pilar crawled to their end of Diego's cot and took Virginia's free hand.

Without a word, one by one, each child took the hand of the child next to him, seeking strength in their unity. Only Diego sat apart, finding his strength and comfort in the touch of the wooden frets and steel strings of his beloved guitar. Resonant chords drifted through the room as Diego began to sing softly in Spanish. His clear voice floated angelically, protectively, above the circle of los niños. The candle melted, its flame struggling for one more breath, and finally died. Reluctantly, they left one another to find their own cot.

***

CHAPTER 7

THE CALLING OF THE MEDICINE

THE CALLING OF THE MEDICINE

The empty rooms and corridors echoed with silence. More than half of the older orphans were gone, never to return. It was their voices that haunted the young survivors. A boy absorbed in play mistakenly called out the name of one of the dead, as his playmate stared, silenced with a memory summoned. The magic and imagination of play evaporated as a shadow of fear passed over and left the children cold on this summer day.

Their loss was made even harder to bear because of Father Serna, on whose warmth and love they had all counted. There were new wrinkles on his brow and his jowls hung, dejected and heavy, as he entered the school room.

Friar Serna, the children's caretaker and instructor in religion, was a dispirited man. He avoided the young questioning eyes; each child's presence brought back the pain of others lost. The friar clapped his hands for their attention.

"After morning prayers, I want those I call to leave for the following haciendas and ranches. The rest of you will stay and attend to your chores. There will not be any lessons today.

"Diego, you are to go to the Valenzuela hacienda today," he began.

Carlotta looked up from her book, as Serna called out Diego's name. She knew this pleased her brother. Diego had talked frequently about the beautiful hacienda and the magnificent herd of caballos. The horses were always on his mind ... before Blue Mesa. She was happy for him, but the day held bleak prospects for herself.

Serna proceeded to call out the names of boys and girls who were to work outside the mission. Typically, the older boys were sent to work on the ranches on the outskirts of San Ramon, and a few girls were assigned to domestic work in the more affluent villas.

"Virginia, you will work at Doctor Gentry's today. He has been asking for you for some time. I know he is pleased with your work." Father Serna managed a small smile for Virginia.

The old doctor had asked specifically for the mute girl to clean and tidy his small house and office. He was interested in this child, who had no apparent medical reason for her inability to utter a single word. The doctor was a practical man and generally knew his limitations, but he still tormented himself with the child's presence, running over and over in his mind all of the possible reasons for her silence.

The friend Carlotta hoped to work with, the one who could not ask troubling questions, left for the doctor's house, leaving her and Pilar to work in the cocina with Maria. The two girls left the school room and walked to the end of the corridor. As they drew closer to the hidden alcove, Carlotta decided against entering the cocina immediately, telling Pilar she would be along in a minute. It just wasn't possible for her to face Maria any more than was needed. The woman had been kind, but Carlotta could still see Felicia tugging on her mother's skirts, and then the other terrible scene when Felicia fell beneath the soldier and his horse.

No, she would visit her Kachina doll, secretly, of course. Carlotta climbed onto her hidden spot on the adobe wall and noticed her friend, the lizard, sitting immobile at the other end. She examined him closely. The lizard remained unruffled by her arrival, and Carlotta thought for a moment he might be dead. She reached out warily to touch his trancelike body, but quickly withdrew her hand when his eyelids slowly closed over his bulging eyes.

Carlotta heard a movement and looked up in time to see Friar Alcazar exit the rectory. She studied the father, reminded of the day she had seen him and Tito Sanchez in the corridor. She felt the old fears return with the bewildering unanswered questions. Why were the friar and the comanchero together that day? How could a man of God befriend such an evil man?

There didn't seem to be any answers that made sense, but then Carlotta remembered, for no obvious reason, how easily Alcazar had accepted her lie. She thought about the absence of the children's further explanation and the friar's willingness to believe ... what he wanted to believe. A chill shuddered through the eight-year-old's body, as she felt some piece of knowledge come menacingly close and then dissipate, leaving only fear and a tremendous need to hold her Kachina.

***

Joaquin angrily dusted the dirt from his breeches. He watched as the young stallion sought a more certain footing and lunged up the draw, a spray of rocks and pebbles flying in the air behind him. His anger turned to futility as he saw his colt disappear in a cloud of dust. The horse deposited him a good hour from the hacienda; an hour, if he ran all the way back, he admitted to himself.

His father, Luis Valenzuela, had warned him. Joaquin's face burned with humiliation when he thought of the caballeros waiting at the paddock to greet his rider-less mount. The coal black stallion was still beyond Joaquin's bareback ability, a fact he would never willingly confess to his father. But he thought, if he started now, he might arrive before his father returned from Santa Fe and his business at the bank.

Joaquin climbed up the draw, cautiously seeking a reliable foothold on loose gravel. When he reached the narrow path he ran, eyes scanning the ground ahead to avoid hazards.

The terrain on the northern slope of Volcan Mountain rarely bore the hoof prints of horses. Very few riders came in this direction to battle the rocky, uneven land and risk breaking a good horse's leg. A dense thicket of underbrush disguised the treacherous holes, which could just as easily swallow a boy's boot and ankle. The mountain, part of the Valenzuelas' holdings, blocked no one's destination and therefore was rarely trespassed. This was reason enough for Joaquin to be here. He loved the loneliness of the mountain and was content to spend a day by himself, exploring the tracks of animals. On other rides, with more reliable horses, Joaquin had discovered the path that wolves traveled. It became a passion of his, to follow the wolf pack at a distance, observing their behavior.

Joaquin was now familiar with this canine family and marveled at their newest members, pups who struggled to keep up with the pack. So far, he thought he had observed undetected, yet he was certain his scent and that of his horse made his presence known. The agile boy leaped over small earthen depressions and rocks, doing his best to avoid the fragile blossoms of tender wild flowers. Today he thought more about his return home and this morning's expected visit of Diego to the hacienda. Señor Valenzuela frequently hired Diego as a stable boy, a request that in the beginning was for labor but had now grown into a real fondness for the boy.

The successful horse rancher was a wealthy man, but also a lonely man. There were few things he valued more than his horses, but his son Joaquin was the center of his life. It was a mutual love, as the boy worshipped his father, perhaps all the more because of his mother's death.

Señora Valenzuela was thrown from her horse when Joaquin was just four years old. She had stayed, pale and still, for weeks in the large family bed upstairs, her coma finally ending in death. Gradually, Don Luis and his son sought each other's comfort, finding reason to face their future. The bond grew between them, cultivating a gentle loyalty, an unspoken communication. This so impressed the servants, they conceded to Joaquin's authority as being interchangeable with his father's. The boy, though only twelve years old, could be depended on as a just patron.

Joaquin's days were filled with the studies his father had carefully planned, and of course, with the horses. He enjoyed riding, even though he was not the natural horseman as was his father. Still, there were times Joaquin wished there was someone closer in age to share his pleasures, the riding, exploring and even his studies.

Diego came, and with him came those things neither son nor father had dared name as missing from their lives. Diego's laughter echoed through the barns, bringing life back to the hacienda. Joaquin and he became immediate friends, their personalities balancing one another's strengths and weaknesses. Joaquin's seriousness was countered by Diego's quick, wry smile. Ordinary activities became fierce competitions, bringing excitement and challenge back into their lives. Don Luis watched and approved. The influence on his son was healthy, and besides, he found he genuinely liked this boy, who bore the air of Spanish aristocracy more than as stable hand.

Fresh wolf spoor in the middle of the path caused Joaquin to extend his leg in mid-flight, bringing his foot down, easily, on the other side. The boy stopped and looked up. There, not twenty paces ahead, was the pack. The dominant male and others stood absolutely still, their grizzled coats well disguised in the mottled light streaming through the trees. The wolves' eyes darted from left to right, immediately searching for escape paths.

Joaquin found himself willing them to stay. He had no fear, only the painful, sweet wish to know and understand. He lowered his brow, but held their gaze. The moment was frozen, and Joaquin could see the scene as if from above. This was as close as he had ever been to the wolves and he was on foot. He carried no threat and no power, only the desire to commune. For moments an energy flowed between the pack and the boy. Then slowly, members on the edge of the pack sniffed the earth, searching the intangible. One by one, a restlessness awoke within each wolf, and the lull in their purpose, the time of peace, was gone.

The animals parted, retreating from the path. A concession had been made, and Joaquin knew the leader had made his decision. Not one of surrender but of tolerance.

He walked for awhile, his reason for running temporarily forgotten. Something was filling up inside of his chest. It took some time to identify these feelings as satisfying, because the surge of love and gratefulness was so encompassing. As Joaquin reflected on his own reaction, unabashed tears spilled down his cheeks, and he reached beyond this subconscious display of emotion to embrace the wolf within his soul.

***

All thoughts of embarrassment vanished. Joaquin did not notice the caballeros who waited by the corrals, relieved that he returned safely. If the men had chosen to laugh, the boy would not have known. He walked past the paddocks and straight to the barn; Joaquin was certain his colt was there.

A shaft of light streamed through the high window of the barn, barely penetrating lazy particles of dust and straw floating in the air. In the middle of this circle, Diego was grooming Joaquin's black colt. Diego looked up as Joaquin entered and smiled.

"He's got a devil in him, that one," Diego offered.

"I would have thought so, but I think there is a better explanation," Joaquin said. He walked up to the horse, and gazed curiously into his brown eyes.

"He knew you were coming and wanted to beat me back here," Joaquin said, flatly.

Diego searched Joaquin's face for a sign of jealousy, but there was none.

"This thing, you seem to have with my horse, I think I understand. But it's probably time you learned how to ride him."

Diego was stunned. This was the last thing he would have expected to hear. Joaquin and he had become good friends and because of this he was privileged to ride with him, but not on this mount. He knew the colt, El Norte, was his father's gift to Joaquin for his twelfth birthday.

"Why did you say that El Norte knew I was coming?" Diego asked.

"Oh, Diego look, for heaven's sake, my horse adores you. It is magic not to be questioned. It is a power, like, well, like something that just happened to me."

Joaquin's attitude was quite buoyant, not at all cross, as his words first indicated. Diego considered this.

"This magic, this power, do you mean the horse came to me because he *knew* I wanted him to?" This was an amazing thought. Diego looked at his friend curiously.

Joaquin proceeded to tell him about his meeting with the wolves. Diego listened, fascinated. It was the way he felt about caballos, even though he had very little experience with them. If it weren't for Joaquin and his father Don Luis, he would not have learned to ride, but more than that, he wouldn't know the animals. He would not feel the humble offering of his steed's power, as the horse patiently offered his body to carry Diego anywhere he might order. Diego could never get over this willing subservience of such a magnificent creature.

While they talked, Diego began cleaning the barn's stalls. Joaquin put his colt away and joined him with a shovel. When Diego protested this work as being beneath the son of a haciendado, Joaquin answered,

"How am I going to have time to teach you to ride El Norte, if we do not get the work done?"

***

When Señor Luis Valenzuela returned, the two boys and El Norte were in the paddock engaged in an intense riding lesson. Don Luis put his feet up on the rail and leaned back in his leather chair. On the hacienda's veranda, shaded with fragrant vines, Luis Valenzuela had an unobstructed view of his son and Diego. They could be brothers, he thought.

***

The day was grand. Diego couldn't remember another as wonderful as this. The chores in the barn were finished quickly with Joaquin's help, and they spent the entire afternoon working with the black colt. Joaquin told Diego how his father had named his horse after the country to the north. El Norte's spirit reminded him of the American spirit, which he had read about in books written by the statesman, Thomas Jefferson. Joaquin's father said the horse reminded him that freedom was a necessity.

The sun was falling fast when Diego reluctantly left the hacienda. Here, with Joaquin and his father, there was no fear, no reason to be leery. Don Luis treated him kindly. More than that, the haciendado returned the respect that Diego felt for him. Don Luis even asked Diego to play a song on his guitar before he left. The black horse ... and his music, he could never ask for more.

Diego returned through town. He walked on the narrow boardwalk in front of the businesses whenever possible, avoiding the street that horses and carts had churned into mud. While last night's storm had left the Valenzuela hacienda clean and refreshed, the small town's shopkeepers battled the mud their customers continued to track inside.

The boy crossed in front of the doctor's office, which looked forlorn with its white clapboard siding shedding old paint. Dr. Gentry's shingle creaked in the gentle breeze of early evening. The door to his office opened and Virginia came out, the gray-headed doctor behind her.

"Ah, Diego! How about you walking Virginia back to the mission like a good lad? She has my place appearing spanking new. I want you to tell Friar Alcazar, I'll be looking for the child next week."

The doctor reached into his pocket and drew out some coins, which he deposited in Virginia's hand, closing her fingers over her palm. Patting her blonde head, he urged them both to hurry back before dark.

Taking Virginia's free hand, Diego said goodbye for them. Diego, like the other children of the mission, was accustomed to watching out for Virginia. Though the children knew she understood everything that was said, Virginia was seen by most adults as simpleminded, not just because she was mute, but also because of her apparent lack of comprehension. Life with her peers was a different matter. Increasingly, when the children talked, Virginia's face would become animated.

Virginia smiled now, as Diego talked about the black horse. Diego spoke aloud, content that he could express the wonder of the day with one who understood. By the time they reached the mission's gate, the sun had set, and the sky blazed fuchsia behind the cottonwoods.

Diego rang the bell and the two waited for someone to open the gate. In the half-light Friar Alcazar admitted the children into the cloister. He stopped them and held out his hand expectantly. Virginia dropped her coins obediently, while Diego searched his pockets for the forgotten, unimportant pesos.

***

The scream cut through the black room, waking every single child. Carlotta's gasping sobs soon followed, and the startled children sighed, relieved to know that the source of the blood-curdling sound was human after all.

Diego was instantly awake. He knew the cries were those of his sister and quietly went to her bed. Carlotta's shoulders were still trembling, but her lips were pursed, holding back the sobs that still wrenched her body.

"What is the matter, Carlotta?" he asked, gently stroking her hair.

Carlotta defiantly shook her head, determined not to speak.

"All right, then. You must be quiet, you woke up everyone," said Diego.

"No!" Carlotta pleaded. "Let me sleep with you, please?"

She whispered with such intensity, Diego knew she was on the verge of panic. He looked around the room and saw several children sitting up in bed, while others retreated under blankets, escaping back to slumber.

"Come with me," Diego said, "and you can tell me about your nightmare."

Diego knew better than to think she would let this go. His sister was only eight years old, but when she made up her mind she firmly stood her ground. Carlotta dragged her trailing blanket, as she followed her brother to his bed. Miguel was sitting on the next cot, very still in the moonlight. He seemed lost in thoughts of his own.

After Diego tucked in Carlotta and was certain she felt secure, he insisted she tell him about the dream.

"I was on Blue Mesa!" Carlotta cried fearfully.

"That's all right. It was just a dream," Diego reminded her.

"There was this, this *man*. He was dressed in black and I couldn't see his face, but he was scary."

Miguel leaned forward, interested in her story.

"He had something in his hands," Carlotta said.

"What was it?" Miguel asked.

"I, I don't know. I couldn't quite. Maybe it was a bag. Yes, it was a small bag!" she said triumphantly.

"That doesn't sound so bad, Carlotta." Diego wanted to gently ease her back to sleep, but his sister sounded much too awake.

"It was bad! The children are dead, up there on Blue Mesa. You know that!" Carlotta was determined he should know her horror.

"We won't forget, Carlotta." Miguel's words were soothing.

Carlotta squinted in the dark. She saw Miguel's dark eyes and watched his eyelids slowly close. Something was familiar about the way his eyelids lazily withdrew. It was like her lizard, Carlotta thought. This somehow made Miguel's words more valid.

"So, what did the man do with the bag?" Miguel asked.

Carlotta thought hard. She envisioned the dark scene in the nightmare, and said, "He held the bag. I think someone was giving it to him." Suddenly, the dream didn't seem so frightening. Maybe Diego was right. Carlotta continued to study

Miguel, who sat so very still on his cot, reminding her more and more of the desert sentry.

"Do you have the lizard medicine?" Carlotta asked him.

"What?" Miguel asked.

"Does the lizard give you his power?" she asked again.

Her questions were unmistakable. They had heard correctly, but Diego and Miguel looked at her quizzically.

"She means, like what you told me, Diego, about the horses," said Two Bears. He was one of those sitting up in bed unable to sleep.

"Yes! That's right!" said Carlotta. "You are like the horse ... strong. And I am like the owl ... I will know the truth."

"Where did you ever hear this?" Diego asked, curious about this reference that reminded him of his earlier conversation with Joaquin.

"Owl Woman told me."

"She did?" asked Chano, one of the Comanche twins.

Chuey turned to his brother and said something in their native tongue, but Chano protested.

Two Bears interrupted them. "No, it is the same woman, but she is not a Powaqa. It is all right to speak of her. She is a healer, a Tuhikya of my tribe."

Miguel, who had sat listening to the others, asked, "The man in your dream, Carlotta ... do you know him?"

The question jolted her. She was back on Blue Mesa and the towering robed figure was real.

"I don't want to talk about it anymore," she said firmly.

"It might be important that you do," Miguel said.

All of the children had now gathered around the cot. They understood Miguel was serious.

"Miguel is right," said Jean Paul. "Maybe there is information in your dream ... some important detail. You should go over it and over it until you find it. After all, you are the only witness."

"The point is, you had to dream it," Miguel insisted. "Is it too ugly to look at when you're awake?"

Carlotta wondered, what was it the white owl had said, the one in her dreams? "Know that you are safe, and with that knowledge allow your heart to see ..."

The vision suddenly closed in on Carlotta and she saw the face of the robed figure. She also saw the man who gave him the bag. Carlotta gasped and her hand flew to cover her mouth.

"It was Friar Alcazar. He was in the courtyard with Tito Sanchez right before I was sent to Blue Mesa."

"And Sanchez gave him the bag?" Diego asked the question they were all thinking.

"He lied to us," Carlotta said with sudden certainty. "Alcazar knew who killed our friends!"

"I'll bet we'd learn more if we returned to Blue Mesa?" Jean Paul regretted his question as soon as he asked it.

"There may be clues there," Diego agreed, "but, I think it is important that Carlotta and I go alone. She would know where to look, and any more than the two of us would cause suspicion.

**

CHAPTER 8

LAUGHING COYOTE

"Pack the false bottom of the wagon yourself, Pedro. There is no reason to discuss this cargo with the men," Luis Valenzuela instructed his foreman on the loading of the crates.

The fewer who knew about the shipment of silver, the better. Don Luis' confidence was well placed with Pedro. His loyal foreman cared for the Valenzuelas and their property as if they were his own. Luis' own son would be the only other person privileged to this information.

The silver from Chihuahua would be sent to the bank in Santa Fe in the morning. Today, it was necessary Don Luis arrange for a military escort at Fort Granger to guarantee its safe arrival.

Luis Valenzuela smiled his approval. He was a handsome man, his braided riding jacket and pants flattering to his lean physique. He stood assured, his feet slightly apart, hands on his hips. A taut line drew across his high cheek bones, the only clue to the intensity he gave this last review before departing.

"Would jefé be visiting the lovely señorita?" Pedro's words were affectionately teasing.

Unabashed, Don Luis told him he fully intended to invite the new governor, John Maxwell, as well as his niece Rebecca, and many other important people of the New Mexico Territory, to his dinner party at the end of the month.

"She is lovely though, I agree," Don Luis conceded, good naturedly.

He was intrigued with this beauty, a recent arrival from America's eastern schools. They had met at the opera in Santa Fe, and he was enchanted with Rebecca's wit and astute observations. Rebecca read the local politics clearly, and found humor in those who took themselves too seriously. During the brief moments he spent with her, he vowed to pursue the relationship. Life was too short not to enjoy female companionship, he told himself.

In the past, the Valenzuelas were known for their hospitality and grand balls. The local haciendados naturally expected the reception for the new territorial governor to take place within the Valenzuelas' magnificent ballroom. So far, Don Luis managed to accommodate his neighbors' expectations, though he was rarely tempted to socialize with the young women his well-meaning friends had introduced over the last eight years.

None had compared to his sweet wife, and after her death there was only Joaquin. He thought of Joaquin now and was glad he requested Diego's return to the hacienda. The day would be lonely for his son, as his visit would require an overnight stay in Santa Fe. He knew that the combination of Joaquin, El Norte, and Diego would fill the long hours.

***

The moon lifted quickly in the sky. It was early evening, warm and filled with the hum of crickets. Carlotta was alarmed to see her shadow and Diego's trail behind them.   How were they to cross the courtyard, undetected, in a night as bright as day?

Answering the unasked question, Diego pulled Carlotta to his side, directing her to follow him down the corridor. The children hurried, urged on by the looming shadows hanging in the recesses of the cloistered walls. They willingly sprinted across the moonlit yard, completing their last challenge before escape.

Once the iron gate was safely closed behind them, Diego and Carlotta sighed with relief. A luminous landscape rolled out before them. Shrubs and cactus, bathed in the soft blue moon glow, presented a friendly invitation to join them in this alternate world. They had no problem finding their way. All things were familiar and yet remarkably different at the same time.

Carlotta saw a pair of eyes in the scrub and wondered about the small animals who inherited this land after dark. She wasn't frightened but intrigued by a world she knew only by day.

The transfixed eyes, those of a jack rabbit, turned away and the animal bounded across their path. Carlotta pointed to him, laughing.

"Look, Diego! Doesn't the rabbit remind you of Two Bears? He leaps like that when he runs, too."

It was true, Diego thought. Two Bears ran very fast, but the real reason he was always the winner in the children's races was his ability to avoid obstacles. The Indian boy's quick maneuvering saved precious time and frequently it seemed he was in the air as often as he was on the ground. Onward the two hastened, confident in their steps. The trail became steeper as the landscape dropped away.

Carlotta gazed at the stars ahead and imagined their vertical ascent leading them to the heavens. Friar Serna had once told her that the moon was a far distance from the earth, and until tonight she thought it to be true. But surely he was wrong. Carlotta could almost reach out and touch this golden sphere with its sculptured human countenance marking their progress to the mesa.

The stars lived farther away, at depths Carlotta couldn't fathom. The entire sky was three-dimensional, and it drew the child's eyes and then her mind into a new thought. For the first time she wondered if her home might be somewhere other than within the mission's walls.

When they came to the place where the arroyo intersected their path, Carlotta instinctively hesitated, looking up the draw in the direction of her cave, but Diego gently pulled on her hand, urging her onward.

They came over the rise of Blue Mesa and stopped. It was breathtaking. A gentle warm breeze flowed across the grassy field, turning the mesa into a liquid, rolling silver carpet. Waves of pewter rose and fell like tides beneath the moon. Violet and blue bell-like flowers danced upon this sea.

Diego finally broke the spell.

"Carlotta, now you must tell me everything that you saw. Start at the beginning. Where were you standing?" he asked.

Carlotta pointed to a large boulder. "There, Diego. I hid behind that large rock." She had no interest in continuing with this uncomfortable memory.

"Come on," Diego coaxed, "you must tell me what happened here. You are the only witness to that day."

Hesitantly, Carlotta recounted what she remembered. Diego listened to her, taking care not to interrupt, holding his questions for later. Ahead, simple crosses dotted the horizon, lonely silhouettes against the indigo sky. Carlotta impulsively bent down and picked a handful of the delicate wild flowers to place on the graves.

The two approached the row of fresh mounds, and Carlotta reached out to touch the bare earth, but someone had already carried out Carlotta's plan. Flowers, now wilted, had been carefully placed beneath each cross. Father Serna, she wondered? At once, she saw how futile was his gesture. The flowers of the mesa, those fragile bits of life, had died. Carlotta dropped to her knees and cried. Her friends were like the flowers, and they, too, were dead.

For moments Carlotta sobbed, unaware of her brother until a familiar sound began to filter through her misery. Children were laughing. Carlotta looked up to see the source of these magical voices, but all across the mesa, only flowers beckoned. Flowers, alive bobbing dots of color, danced across the prairie, fairly leaping into the sky.

A calm enveloped Carlotta and she smiled through her tears.

"They're not here anymore, Diego," she said, confidently pointing to the twinkling stars. "See? There they are!"

Diego's eyes followed her direction and he stepped forward, stumbling. Catching his balance, he looked down for the cause among the flowers.

"Look, Diego!" Carlotta saw it first.

Both children began to dig and pull at the piece of leather protruding from the ground. Diego yanked and finally tore it loose.

"Saddle bags. How did they get here?" Diego asked.

"I remember, they fell from the horse when he reared. They must have been trampled under his hooves."

***

They knew at that moment their mission was complete, and they hurried back, anxious to search the saddle bags. Diego winced as the door creaked open and was relieved to see the faces on the other side. Their friends had waited up, too excited to sleep.

Diego swung the horseman's belongings onto the floor and they slid to a stop, midway in the circle of waiting children. Two Bears spilled out the contents of the saddle bags, and various articles scattered across the floor. Hands pounced on the prey, greedy to discover any clue that would further explain the massacre.

The more interesting objects were grabbed quickly. Miguel took the spy glass, turning it carefully in his hands, and looked through first one end and then the other.

"Oh!" he said, backing away from its magnification.

He had little chance to try again, as Chuey and Chano wanted to see the strange sight that had startled him.

A military compass rolled directly into Virginia's lap. She held it carefully and marveled at its wavering arrow, which always pointed to her even though she moved it in circles.

Jean Paul picked up a small book, lying unnoticed. Ignoring several letters tied together with string and tucked under its cover, he began to read the first page of the book. The other children were poring over the clothing and a piece of plated tin that reflected their amused faces. No one was listening to Jean Paul, as he struggled to clear his throat.

"Listen! This is important!"

"What?" Diego finally asked.

Jean Paul pushed his ill-fitting glasses up the bridge of his nose. "This seems to be a record of some sort. A military log, I suppose."

He turned over the letters, searching the inside of the book's cover for the name of its owner.

"Yes, just as I thought, this is Lieutenant McGiver's log. But, look!" Jean Paul pushed the book under Diego's nose, assuming he, too, was nearsighted.

"Well, what does it say?" Diego asked, impatiently.

"As you can plainly see, he has listed the day of the killing," said Jean Paul.

It was not at all plain to Diego and so he waited for Jean Paul to enlighten him.

"See? Here are three columns and they're neatly filled with dates, places, and... Well, I don't know what the third column actually means, but ..."

Two Bears and Miguel joined Diego and Jean Paul by the flickering candle. Together, they tried to interpret the log's purpose. Jean Paul read aloud.

"The first date is June twenty-sixth, the place ... Blue Mesa.   In the right hand column it says ...15 children - Sanchez."

There were several gasps as, one by one, the children understood.

"What is written next?" Carlotta spoke for all of them.

Jean Paul's eyes squinted and his thin face pinched even more than usual.

"July second, Valenzuela hacienda, silver shipment - Sanchez? What do you suppose it means?"

"We've ... I mean, I've got to go to the hacienda at once!" Diego cried. "The second of July is tomorrow! McGiver and Tito Sanchez must be planning a hold-up. I must warn Señor Valenzuela!"

"We'll go with you, of course," said Pilar.

The boys turned to face the child who seldom contributed to the conversation.

"I don't think that would be such a good idea ..." Diego began.

"Really, Pilar! You're just a little girl and ..." Miguel tried to intercede.

"You're not going anywhere without us, Diego!" Carlotta said emphatically.

"Pilar is my age, so she is plenty old enough," she added.

"Dios mio!" Diego muttered, shrugging his shoulders. Four years was not enough difference in their ages, he thought.

Following the massacre, the children of the mission had intuitively sought each other's comfort. They weren't anxious to abandon these new feelings of security.   Each child was beginning to recognize the strength derived from their numbers; each unwilling to be left behind, alone.

***

Half-hearted attempts by the boys to exclude the girls didn't seem to be succeeding. These were old childish games and seemed, increasingly, to have little place in the lives of children forced into an adult world. The group now deferred to Diego's leadership, because he was the only one who had worked at the Valenzuela hacienda.

In order to reach their destination it was impossible to avoid going through town. Though San Ramon was mostly sleeping at this hour, they couldn't be too cautious. Diego suggested they split into smaller groups and follow each other at a reasonable distance. San Ramon had one main street with several random structures built on outlying land. Diego led the children behind the livery stable on the edge of town. He looked suspiciously at the open stretch of land, bathed in moonlight, which lay between them and the next building.

"I'll take Carlotta and Jean Paul with me," Diego said. "When I give the signal, Two Bears, you follow with Pilar and Chuey. Miguel, you watch for Two Bears' signal and bring Virginia and Chano."

Diego's group dashed across the lot and disappeared into the shadow of the assayer's office. From across the street, a figure descended the stairway leading from the witches' rooms above the cantina. Below, several drunken vaqueros noisily exited the cantina's swinging doors, their loud singing floating on the night air.

Two Bears was about to run when he saw Diego's hand emerge from the shadows, flagging a warning to stay under cover. He pressed his body against the barn, and whispered to the others behind him to wait.

With a great deal of commotion the cowboys managed to mount their horses and ride out of town. Again, the street was quiet, and the children continued toward their destination. Once on the outskirts of San Ramon, the groups reunited and began walking down the moonlit road to the Valenzuela hacienda.

As they approached the ranch, Diego stopped.

"Wait," he said. "Before we get any closer, let me go ahead and talk to the dogs. They know me and I can quiet them before they wake up everyone. Two Bears, make sure the girls stop that giggling, or we will be caught for sure!"

The girls' inappropriate behavior had puzzled the boys as they led the way down the road.

Two Bears nodded and turned to the girls.

"Shush. What's so funny, anyway?" he asked.

Pilar put her hands over her mouth to keep from laughing out loud, the motion only driving Carlotta into another round of hysterical laughter.

"Two Bears, you leaned against the side of the stable in town and your seat is all covered with paint!" she said.

Two Bears looked behind him and discovered his white muslin pants were, indeed, red. Before he could respond, Diego returned.

"I quieted the dogs and woke Joaquin with a few pebbles thrown at his window. He's coming down now."

***

"What's going on here?" asked Joaquin, still tucking his night shirt into his pants.

Joaquin addressed Diego, but was alarmed to see all of these children at the hacienda in the middle of the night.

Diego spoke quickly, introducing the others simply as los niños from the mission.

"We really don't have time to explain everything, Joaquin, but you must trust me. We have come to warn you and your father that someone is planning to steal the shipment of silver."

"How do you know about the silver?" Joaquin was shaken, but immediately added, "My father is at Fort Granger, Diego. What is this all about?"

Joaquin knew they shouldn't be standing in the open like this and suggested they go behind the barn.

The children gave a wide berth to the corrals and the entrance to the barn. They could see two men playing cards by lantern light, each with a bottle in his hand. The men, intent on their game, were oblivious to their surroundings and gave no indication that they heard the dogs or any of the children.

With relief, the children sat down on a pile of rocks next to the old dry well. Diego tried to explain.

"You remember what I told you ... about the massacre on Blue Mesa, and the plan my sister and I had to go up there and look for clues?"

Carlotta had slipped in quietly to sit by her big brother and she now peered into Joaquin's face.

"Yes, I remember," said Joaquin. "And did you find any?"

"We found saddlebags!" Carlotta interjected excitedly. "Tell him what Jean Paul found in the log."

"Joaquin, Sanchez is planning to rob your silver shipment with the help of Lieutenant McGiver's men. It is all written in the log ... along with the payment made for the children delivered on the mesa."

There was no purpose in keeping his father's plan a secret any longer. Joaquin told the children about the wagon, loaded and waiting in the barn, and the reason for his father's visit to the fort.

"My father and the military escort should return tomorrow, mid-morning. This is the very thing my father was trying to prevent ... and you're saying that it is the soldiers who will steal the silver?" Joaquin asked, appalled.

Joaquin had no reason to suspect an adult of such treason. This was preposterous. But his good friend Diego was standing before him, and he trusted his answer to be truthful.

"Yes," Diego said with certainty.

"We can't fight them, Diego," Miguel protested. "We don't have any guns!"

"There is no way we could win in a war with the soldiers and the Comancheros!" said Two Bears.

"Then we must find a way to outsmart them. There's no other way," Joaquin was convinced.

One by one, the children offered their comments, which seemed futile against such odds. Chano and Chuey were silent until every idea was thought exhausted.

"When we were young," said Chano, "our warriors were outnumbered many times, yet they always found a way. Sometimes, if you are brave and daring, you will accomplish many things that only seem impossible."

"Yes, there are stories in our tribe that speak of clever ways to win against an enemy," added Chuey. "We may be only children ... but Indian children are taught the ways of the braves. White men would never suspect us, would they?" Chuey directed his question to Diego.

"You may be on to something ..." said Diego.

"We are not seen as a threat; that is our strength." Joaquin repeated slowly, letting the meaning sink in.

"Like ... when Maria knows that we sometimes take extra food, and she tells the friars that the mice are eating it," Pilar said.

Joaquin smiled at this little señorita. She was very quick, he thought.

"In our tepee, we were taught when something is not as it seems, that the coyote, the master trickster, has done it." Chano smiled.

Chuey laughed as he remembered the happier times of their childhood. On many occasions the twin boys had blamed their dual mischief on the coyote.

"That's it!" said Diego, "What if we let them steal the silver ... only we steal it first ... and blame it on someone else!" Diego emphatically answered his own question.

The twins were smiling. "It looks like the coyote strikes again!" Chano said.

"I don't understand," Jean Paul said. He was thoroughly confused. Everyone seemed to understand, but him.

"Look at the bigger picture, Jean Paul," said Diego. "Wonder if we ... say, unloaded the silver and put something in its place ... like rocks! We would avoid a fight ... save the silver, and most importantly, no one would need know we had done it."

Yes, this did make sense, conceded Jean Paul, and wondered why he hadn't thought of it.

Joaquin suggested how to implement the plan. He told the others about the two men guarding the barn and the wagon. They were notorious for their ability to quickly reach an inebriated state, from which even Joaquin's father couldn't wake them.

"And the rocks. Well, what about the rocks we're sitting on?" he asked.

"First, we must hide the silver!" Diego reminded him.

Virginia was sitting between Joaquin's two dogs, quietly stroking their heads. The dogs were completely mesmerized by her gentle manner, and were startled when she suddenly rose from the pile of rocks. All eyes were on Virginia as she walked over to the well and pointed into its dark hole.

"Yes! That's a good place, Virginia!" said Carlotta, delighted with her obvious solution.

"Well, let's get busy," Pilar insisted.

***

"Sometimes I think Pilar should have been named Andale Pronto!" Miguel said, his eyes rolling in exasperation.

Joaquin made his way to the front of the barn to see if the guards had fallen asleep as he hoped. Both men were seated, their backs slack against the side of the barn. They were contentedly snoring, but still managed a fair grip on their bottles. Joaquin cautiously picked up the lantern and entered the barn, closing the big wooden doors behind him.

Several mares, whose time to foal was close at hand, whinnied a greeting as he entered. Joaquin spoke softly, calmly assuring the horses. There was a back door to the barn, very seldom used, but an important avenue for escape in case of fire. This was Joaquin's destination.

He unlatched the door and quietly ushered in the others. The wagon was in the center aisle, ready to be hitched to a team of horses. The children were soon climbing all over the wagon.

"There is no silver here!" whispered Two Bears.

"Oh, yes, there is," said Joaquin. "Check under the floorboards ... there's a false bottom."

Diego held the lantern and it shone on the exposed cargo, a soft glow more like lead than silver. The children went to work, forming a line from the barn, out the door, to the old well and circling back again. The brigade soon unloaded the bars of silver, lowering them with a bucket into the well, and then replaced them with the rocks.

At last, Two Bears climbed down from the wagon, satisfied with his repair of the concealed box. It was very late and the children were growing sleepy. They had a long walk ahead of them, but Joaquin pointed out there was still a problem.

"My father will be very upset, because he won't know where is the silver. But, if I tell him what we've done, he'll be even more upset ... with all of us!"

They hadn't considered this. There had to be a way.

"I've got an idea," said Chuey. "Remember our old friend, Laughing Coyote, Chano?"

"Right! Maybe, it was he who struck again," said Chano.

The twins obviously had a plan, as they sent Joaquin on a quest for a scrap of paper on which to write. Joaquin rifled through the pockets of an old jacket hanging on a nail, but found nothing. Suddenly, Jean Paul remembered.

"Here!" he said, producing the log book and a pencil. He carefully tore out a blank page and handed it and the pencil to Chuey.

Chuey bent over the piece of paper, his mouth firmly fixed in concentration. The others encouraged him to hurry before the guards awakened. After what seemed an incredibly long time, Chuey grinned and proudly handed Joaquin his note. It read,

No matter what you see, the silver has not left.
It's in the old dry well, instead of lost to theft.
Lafing Coyote

"You should put the note in a place where your father will find it after the soldiers leave with the 'silver', Chuey said.

"I know just the place!" said Joaquin. "This will get us off the hook, but … it would sure be great if your "trickster coyote" would say something to the crooks."

Chuey thought a minute and then asked Jean Paul for another piece of paper. He scribbled fiercely across the page, crossing out a word here and there. Finally he presented his second poem.

Thank you for the silver. It's wonderful to touch.
I hope you'll like the rocks, every bit as much.
Lafing Coyote

Joaquin laughed out loud. There was instant silence, as the children anticipated a dreaded response from the guards. Their drunken snores continued, however, and Joaquin said he thought the note was grand. He handed it to Diego, who read it aloud.

"We'll slip it in under the boards covering the bottom of the wagon. The thieves should enjoy a letter from one of their own!"

***

CHAPTER 9

THE COMANCHEROS

THE COMANCHEROS

Señor Valenzuela watched the men eat, fascinated. The soldiers were ravenous when they arrived, and were eagerly mopping up their plates of juevos rancheros with steaming tortillas. It was the reputation of the hacienda that no one left without the benefit of the Valenzuelas' hospitality. This would be a long trip for the soldiers, who were to return to Santa Fe with the Valenzuelas' wagon.

Lieutenant McGiver pushed his chair away from the table and wiped his face with the linen napkin.

"You have been most gracious, Don Luis," said McGiver. "I believe we had better be on our way. There has been talk, after all, of strange desperados in the area."

Joaquin looked up from his plate, curious that this soldier would dare to imply a robbery might take place, when he fully intended to mastermind one.

"You're not hungry, son?" Don Luis asked.

"Oh, no, Father." Joaquin had been fidgeting with his fork, and before his father's unexpected scrutiny, he dropped it noisily to the plate.

"Well, then ..." Don Luis smiled, "if you and your men have recovered satisfactorily, Lieutenant, let's see about hooking up the team."

Joaquin walked uneasily beside his father and the soldiers to the barn. He had never deceived his father and felt extremely uncomfortable in this role, which yesterday's events had dictated. Conflicting loyalties were new to the twelve-year-old boy. He could only hope his father would find the note in his study as soon as McGiver and his men left.

Don Luis spent time in his study every afternoon. The myriad details and paperwork having to do with the Valenzuela holdings almost always required long hours. Joaquin would frequently look up to the house and see his father working at his desk. Everyone who lived at the hacienda knew of this daily pattern. Physical errands and work were accomplished in the morning. Records, bookkeeping, and letters were taken care of in the afternoon, while everyone else seemed to be enjoying a siesta.

Joaquin had read Chuey's note one last time before placing it conspicuously on his father's desk. He tried to imagine Don Luis' reaction. Immediate alarm, he supposed. After all, on one hand his father would read this and know that his silver was safe, but then he would, also, know that it had been stolen. His father would feel vulnerable. This didn't make Joaquin feel any too secure, either. He was obliged to see that everything went as planned, because of his loyalty to Diego and los niños.

He followed his father and the soldiers into the barn. Amazingly, the wagon stood in the dusty sunlight, un-tampered and lifeless, just as the children had left it.

Don Luis and the men worked together, hooking up the four horses Pedro brought from the paddock.

"I'll pick up the wagon and team in a day or two, when I return to Santa Fe for supplies," said Don Luis.

"Captain Sedlow has received my invitation, which is meant for you and the other officers, as well," he added cheerily. "On the twenty-ninth of this month the Valenzuela ballroom will ring once again with music. I hope you and your men will join us."

Luis lifted his hand from the box seat to give the driver the reins, and noticed a trace of the sticky red paint, which had been used to stain the wood, now on his hand. He said nothing.

"I would be delighted!" said McGiver, obviously impressed with his new status in the eyes of the wealthy haciendado.

***

The men reluctantly rode away from the Valenzuela hacienda. The beautiful hacienda, and the sampling of Spanish cuisine, served so graciously, was a needless encouragement for James McGiver to improve his lot. Army life would never offer it ... directly, but in a strange way it was the key. The prestige of authority, legitimized by the recent American involvement in the Territory's affairs, was opening the gates of neighboring haciendas in welcome. He could see his future unfolding and congratulated himself. Don Luis' invitation was just the beginning. He needed these kinds of social introductions; they were necessary to an officer's career.

Once the silver was in Sanchez' hands, McGiver's own debt, payment for the Mesa affair and his mounting gambling debts, would be paid, as well. The thought of his own stupidity made his face burn. He knew better than to think there was such a thing as an honest poker game with the Comancheros. Where had his head been? It was one thing to lose a game among the men at the fort, when their own pay limited the bets, but quite another to gamble against these notorious thieves of the Plains.

McGiver would begin again with the proper leverage his authority guaranteed. Free from personal debt, he would devote his attention to keeping his men in line. The three that rode with him today were men he could trust to follow orders, unquestioningly. It was imperative if they were to implement the raids on the list.

For a moment he thought of his log and felt his heart palpitate in fear of his own exposure, but Alcazar had assured him he would sweep the mesa in the light of day for any evidence. Though he didn't trust the friar, still Alcazar's concern was as much for his own implication in the massacre, as it was for the lieutenant's. Circumstance had dealt him strange bed-fellows, McGiver thought. He, of course, was privileged to the maneuvers of troops and protected cargo, because of his mapping expeditions. Tito Sanchez, and the Comancheros' role as the feigned ambushing Apaches, was an excellent suggestion from Alcazar.

But the friar was cause for speculation. What were this man's reasons for involvement in such a risky venture? Now that McGiver knew Alcazar better, he had no illusions about the man's love for the Church. There was something in this for Alcazar, but it was not quite as obvious as he had first thought. Money, yes, power, certainly, but there was an attitude of almost natural superiority, as if Alcazar had been born to it. Ah, he would never understand this black-robed benefactor of children, who could preside so coolly at their funeral on Blue Mesa. Did it matter? The lieutenant guessed not.

McGiver cracked the whip in the air over the lead horse's head. The team lunged forward, obediently extending themselves toward their destination.

***

The band of men shuffled restlessly in their saddles. Tito scanned the plains for any sign of movement, as he had all morning. There was no relief from the insufferable sun, and he felt his perspiring head squander precious moisture beneath his soiled hat. Snatching away the sombrero, Tito wiped his brow and the burning salt from his eyes with a dirty bandana.

The Comancheros' leader was an aggravated man and the sounds of jingling spurs and squeaking leather were annoying him even further. They were reminders of wasted time and the most recent trade gone sour. Tito eased himself upright in the stirrups and squinted under the glare of the sun. On the horizon a cloud of dust appeared, its progress toward them agonizingly slow. It had to be McGiver.

Tito recognized the young lieutenant riding escort with three men, but his eyes fixed on the heavily constructed wagon that inched along the trail. It was almost as welcome as the silver, he thought. In his more legitimate dealings, a good wagon was an asset and certainly superior to the broken-down ox carts, or carretas, he had abandoned along the way. He decided he would take the wagon and its four-horse team, even though it hadn't been part of the deal.

McGiver owed him, after all, for the blunder on Blue Mesa. Tito gritted his teeth, seething with the memory. If this transaction went no better by the end of summer he might have to return to legitimate trade. These dealings between McGiver and himself could make them both wealthy men, even though the brash young lieutenant was proving to be as foolish as he was greedy. Ah, but he had to admit, he would not have known about the silver from Chihuahua otherwise and it was certainly an easier asset to handle than sending children there as slaves.

The wagon entered the long gorge and Tito Sanchez decided it was time. He slapped his pinto, welcoming the freedom of movement, and signaling to his men, they made their descent to the canyon floor.

There was little said, the men exchanging only curt greetings. One of Tito's men drew up on the harness of the team, and Lt. McGiver swung from his horse to the wagon seat to help unload the cargo.

"Where is your carreta, Tito?" McGiver asked, mockingly. "Certainly you and your men aren't going to carry the crates back to your hideout!"

The trader moved slightly in his saddle.

"No. We're taking the wagon, soldier." Tito's jaw tilted forward, a subtle challenge to the lieutenant.

Quickly, Tito's men each pulled an arrow from their quivers, and drawing back on their bows, hurled shots at the astonished soldiers. The lieutenant's men reeled from their saddles and were flung sprawling to the ground.

McGiver went for his gun, but Tito had already drawn his.

"There's no need for that," Tito said, his voice as steady as steel. "I just saved you a walk back, McGiver."

There was no mistaking Tito's intention. James McGiver was looking down the barrel of his gun. It was only the comanchero's whim whether McGiver lived or died, and apparently it was going in his favor, so far.

The Lieutenant slowly took his hand from his holster.

"The Apaches did this," said Tito. "Shouldn't be any questions this way. They took your wagon and horses and killed your men."

McGiver looked down. There wasn't a movement from one of the soldiers. He looked up again at the ragged band on horseback, half-breeds, Comanches mostly. It was believable, he thought. He had just seen what Indians could do, but he knew better than to let himself think about this horror now.

"I'll settle with you after my men open the crates," said Sanchez. "You go now, you and your horse. Ride back to the Valenzuela hacienda and tell the jefé about this terrible ambush by Apaches, eh?"

The Comanchero thrust his fist in the air and yelled what seemed unmistakably to McGiver as a war cry.

***

The tension broke and the men rode whooping and hollering back to camp with the Valenzuela wagon, their smoldering discontent left behind in the dust with the bodies of the soldiers. All of the hours of anxious waiting had paid off, and each man renewed his allegiance to Sanchez, their leader.

Tito Sanchez' band of Comancheros were a mix of misfit traders and outlaws and seen as such by the New Mexico territorial government. Tito's own reputation had prevented the traders from being licensed, but not one man now considered this to be worthy of losing his independence. The renegades made their own rules; Tito had shown them how. They headed back, victorious, to the stronghold where they would savor the profits of the day.

Men, women, and several ragged children boisterously greeted the returning Comancheros as they entered the valley. Premature celebration was already taking place. Liquor was flowing freely as bottles were passed among those who lined the way.

Here, nestled protectively between two mountains, a shanty town of lean-tos housed the comancheros. Tito, who rarely smiled, rode triumphantly up to his shack, grinning from ear to ear. He took a swig from the bottle someone had handed him and spat explosively in disgust.

"Break out the new shipment of whiskey!" ordered Sanchez. "I'll be damned if I'm going to drink this rotgut!"

He slid off his horse into the waiting arms of two Indian women. The sisters, dressed more like women of the cantina than of their native pueblo, tugged playfully at Tito's clothes. The two were willingly caught up in the Comanchero's wild merriment. They grandly ushered their leader onto the rickety porch, past the unhinged door, and into the room.

"Bring the crates onto the porch, pronto!" Tito barked at his men.

A new bottle in hand, Sanchez clapped the shoulders of his compadres as they unloaded the crates from the wagon onto the groaning floor boards.

"We did well today, eh Antonio?" he asked.

A lengthy exchange of congratulations ensued, delaying further interest in the unopened cargo. More liquor was brought in, whiskey whose destination had been one of the local haciendas. The liquor was passed around and the celebration grew louder.

Several men brought musical instruments - guitars and a fiddle - which they began to play. The small one-room dwelling grew hot and sticky with the large number of revelers who joined the fiesta. The women danced with the men, spinning dizzily with the mariachi music, and the floor resounded under the weight of their thumping boots.

The sun had set when Tito escaped to the porch for a breath of cool air. He was roaring drunk and found it difficult to focus on any one person, but the sight of the wooden boxes was all that he needed to see. This would be just the beginning of other successful ventures, he assured himself.

Tito eyed the crates magnanimously, and called to his women, thinking to please them with the opportunity of opening the treasure. There was a noisy commotion as the two women, giddy with alcohol, attempted to pry up the nails. Tito finally brushed aside their efforts and impatiently tore open the wooden boxes himself.

The crate was full of riverbed rocks. Tito began the task of removing the rocks, certain that he would find real wealth just underneath them. One of the rocks felt tacky and he was idly curious as to how red paint could have been introduced in this shipment. Tito quickly emptied the crate. There was nothing below, not even a false bottom to the box. Nothing.

It took several moments for the truth to set in, time in which Tito sat back heavily on the porch, staring into the empty crate. A dirty scrap of paper lay at the bottom and Tito picked it up and read:

Thank you for the silver. It's wonderful to touch.
I hope you'll like the rocks, every bit as much.
Lafing Coyote

Finally, the terrible reality penetrated Tito's alcoholic stupor, and he rose from the floor like a raging bull.

He had been taken. Tito Sanchez, the most clever of traders, the leader of the most successful band of Comancheros ... licensed, or not, had been taken! And it appeared the thief was an Indian. Who else would have the name Coyote?

The two young women stood obediently by the crate, unable to grasp Tito's loss. They only knew the reason for the celebration was the plata that Tito had brought into camp. Everyone was talking about it ... this "silver." The only plata they had ever seen was in the chalices they had stolen from the kiva and brought, so long ago, to the Comancheros.

"Are you looking for more shiny vessels, Tito?" the eldest sister asked, shyly.

"We know where there are more!" the younger sister said, excitedly.

"Fools!" Tito cried. "No ... you think I'm a fool, right?"

His arm lunged out, back-handing the younger girl across the face, sending her careening against the wobbly railing.

"Who is this Lafing Coyote?" he demanded.

The young woman hit the railing, somersaulting over the side, her colorful petticoats flying. A deep moan came from her direction, but no answer.

Tito grabbed the older sister's arm, yanking it behind and up between her shoulder blades. She screamed in pain as her feet left the floor.

"Who is Lafing Coyote?" Tito hissed viciously.

"I ... stop!" she said through burning tears. "I don't know any ... Lafing Coyote!"

The Comanchero released his fierce grip and the woman sagged to the floor.

"Get out!" he boomed. "I don't need any Apache traitors around here!" he yelled.

"I am not Apache!" the woman cried. "I am from the pueblo," she pleaded.

"So you say! All I know is you are both witches! You've brought bad medicine to my men. We don't need you. We don't want you!" Tito's heavy boot sent her sprawling across the wooden porch.

The woman scrambled to her feet, staggered down the stairs, and limped painfully to her sister's side.

***

The men of the camp gave Tito a wide berth as they made their way home. No one was willing to test the half-breed's patience when he had been drinking.

Tito sat on the porch staring into the black night long after the moon turned the hills to silver. The only silver he'd seen today, he thought. With the moon's light came the calls of the coyotes. The manic yips and howls of the pack carried across the valley, and Tito was reminded of the legends taught about the coyote.

His Comanche mother had repeated stories told by her mother about the trickster coyote and how he made death inevitable for humanity by throwing a stone into the water and declaring that, if it sinks, living beings shall experience physical death. She told him the coyote introduced all of the wicked things man has done, and her concern was that her son seemed inclined to follow the coyote's trail. It had to be the Powaqas' spell that made the coyote mock him now with his riotous laughter.

***

"Just a doggone minute," called out the doctor. "I'm coming!"

He had wakened to the pounding on the door downstairs. Certainly someone was in need of his services, he thought, as he hurriedly pulled up his suspenders. Dr. Gentry mentally checked off all of the townspeople who might need him at this hour and found he couldn't think of one. There wasn't a baby due for two months and no one that he knew was suffering from consumption.

The doctor opened the door, fully prepared to be called out for a gunshot wound, and was surprised to see the Indian sisters who lived and worked above the cantina telling the fortunes of visiting vaqueros.

Even in the early-morning light, he could see they were badly beaten. The doctor let them in and motioned them under the light where he could see the extent of their injuries.

Ugly purple and blue bruises marked their faces, neck, and upper arms. The first young woman held her arm close to her body in a way the doctor had long associated with a break. Her sister was almost doubled over in pain, pressing her rib cage with both hands so that she could bear to breathe.

"Who did this to you?" the doctor asked.

His question went unanswered, and determining not to press the issue just yet, he attended to their wounds. The doctor had seen his share of suffering during his career, but the reprehensible evidence of physical violence to women and children was always the hardest.

The women were known to spend much of their time out at the Comanchero camp, and that was explanation enough, thought Dr. Gentry. Tito Sanchez' reputation was as foul as his hygiene. There were others he had hurt, mostly men who were probably deserving, but Gentry remembered one child brought to him in the middle of the night. The young boy was badly beaten and couldn't speak. His mother, who came with him, was too frightened to say who had done this terrible deed. At the time it made little difference, because the child died during the night. The doctor vowed it would not happen again.

The door to the office opened and a Pueblo woman entered. She carried a large basket and the doctor could see that she had brought the herbs he requested.

"Hello Owl Woman," the doctor greeted, warmly. "You may set the basket down over there. I'll be with you as soon as I'm through here."

Owl Woman hesitated a moment as she recognized her sisters. Dr. Gentry watched as his patients, who were occupied with their own pain, looked up startled. She held their gaze and nodded evenly.

Dr. Gentry knew of the sisters' banishment from the tribe, as everyone in town had learned over time. Also, he knew of Owl Woman's good reputation as a healer, and her acceptance back into the pueblo. Her knowledge of herbs was invaluable, and the doctor's shortage of medical supplies had encouraged him to seek her. He was just beginning to learn of their many uses, but restrained his enthusiasm in the presence of his usual patients, who were inclined to expect more.

"Would you have a suggestion to help knit this broken arm?" he asked.

Owl Woman smiled gently, and picked some slender green leaves from her basket. Dr. Gentry recognized the plant as comfrey and listened as she told him how to make a poultice for the broken bone. He thanked her and decided to press his luck.

"Owl Woman...one more question. Would you ask your sisters who beat them?"

The pueblo woman looked steadily at the doctor, attempting to comprehend his motive. She then turned to her sisters who retreated, almost withering under her scrutiny. In rapid-fire manner, Owl Woman asked the question in their native language.

For the first time Dr. Gentry recognized fear in the women's faces, fear that was stronger than their fear for the one who beat them. They appeared to be cornered animals.

The youngest looked at Owl Woman and blurted, "Laughing Coyote!"

"You mean Tito Sanchez," corrected the doctor.

"No!" the eldest sister protested nervously. "Laughing Coyote ... he is the one who beat us."

There didn't seem to be much point in pursuing the matter. The doctor finished dressing their various wounds and even used the poultice Owl Woman made, before fashioning a sling for the woman's arm.

The doctor hadn't expected any payment for his services. This was one of those visits, like many as of late, which honored his oath but not his pocket. Issuing final instructions, he saw the women out the door. Owl Woman, also, prepared to leave, but the doctor asked her to wait so that he might pay her for the herbs.

"You do not owe me," she said. "You have given my sisters good medicine. Thank you."

Owl Woman slipped out the door before the doctor could protest.

The sisters from the Comanchero camp exited the doctor's office on to the boardwalk and saw Friar Alcazar. They hurried off, eager to be out of the street and away from the stares of passersby.

Owl Woman was left standing alone, and quietly watched the priest of the White Man's religion. She concentrated hard, trying to understand the man who walked toward her.

***

CHAPTER 10

ALCAZAR

ALCAZAR

The rider and his horse tore through the open gates to the hacienda, exploding puffs of dirt dotting the trail behind him. Luis Valenzuela recognized James McGiver and marveled at these unfolding events, as predicted by "Lafing Coyote."

Luis left his study and descended from the veranda that fronted the house. He was mildly surprised to find Joaquin sitting idly on the steps, and was about to ask his son if there was something he wished to discuss when the lieutenant rode up, hell-bent-for-leather.

Lt. McGiver's neat, organized, earlier appearance was transformed into that of a disheveled, sweaty rider. McGiver dismounted, his excited words lost in the sounds of his horse's braying.

Luis waited for them both to settle down.

"We were attacked!" he yelled, choking on the dust. "Apache ambush! They've killed my men and taken the wagon!" McGiver added.

Would Don Luis have seen this confession any differently had he not read the note? Probably, he admitted to himself. McGiver was a good actor; he had to give him that. Or, things had not gone exactly as he planned. It then occurred to Luis, if this were the case, the soldiers who accompanied McGiver might very well be dead.

He listened as Lt. McGiver recounted how they were surprised while passing through the gorge. His men died instantly under the full attack of the filthy Apaches' arrows, he said. As evidence, he handed Luis the feathered end of a broken arrow.

Luis turned and looked at his son's face, which was drained to an ashen color. Joaquin's eyes were on the lathered horse and the arrow. Luis decided his son was equally amazed. There wasn't an immediate reason or advantage in confronting McGiver, Luis thought. It would be much more interesting to give this man lead and observe where the falsehood would take him.

***

This military contract was only the beginning, Alcazar reminded himself. His own patience was finally being rewarded. The annual monies Alcazar personally received from Spain, for the care of the Medina children, had enabled him to invest in cattle herds. These herds, raised on the mission's outlying ranches, would now feed the soldiers at Fort Union.

Certainly the citizens of the Santa Fe and Taos areas would gain needed protection from hostile Indians with the building of Fort Union, but it was Alcazar's foresight and influence that enabled him to profit financially.

Alcazar's meeting at Fort Granger to sign this lucrative contract, and the discussion that followed regarding the military's handling of local Indian matters, were on his mind as he left the livery stable. He looked down the long boardwalk and saw Owl Woman and her two sisters in front of Dr. Gentry's office. Owl Woman's sisters hurried off, their movements indicating they suffered pain.

The woman the Indians referred to as a Tuhikya stood alone. The significance of having seen the three sisters together was initially a shock, but Alcazar would not let the opportunity to learn the reason pass him. He decided to question her. They greeted each other tentatively, as old adversaries finding themselves on neutral ground.

"Good morning, Owl Woman. I see your sisters have required the attention of the good doctor." Alcazar explored carefully. "You have your health, I pray?"

"Yes. Thank you." Owl Woman answered.

Seeing that this was all she would offer, Alcazar asked, "What brings you to town this morning?"

"I have brought herbs to your medicine man," answered Owl Woman.

"You mean doctor," he corrected, agitated with her deliberate reference to her own status within the pueblo.

Owl Woman made no effort to contradict him and asked, "I have a wish to see Sak-mo-i-si's son, Two Bears, and the other children, Friar. May I walk back to the mission with you?"

"The children have their studies, woman," Alcazar answered abruptly, goaded by her impertinence.

"Furthermore, I think it best you distance yourself from Two Bears until he returns at harvest time. If he is to receive an education, as I promised his father, your ways will only confuse him."

Owl Woman remained silent. She was trying to understand this reference to confusion, an attitude she had never felt before her pueblo's dealings with the men of the mission. Purposes were always projected honestly by the tribes with which her people had dealings. Even the raids between tribes were foreseen as the unfortunate consequence of drought and famine. There was no reason to disguise their necessity.

She knew her own expulsion from the pueblo was determined by the evidence of theft, and she'd accepted this as her fate until an opportunity arose to prove otherwise. It had never occurred to Owl Woman that the truth might not be considered because it was confusing, just as she would never have thought to use truth as a ploy against an enemy. Confusion seemed to be a White Man's tactic, the deliberate attempt to disguise purpose.

Alcazar said good day and, leaving the perplexed woman standing on the boardwalk, entered the doctor's office. It was appropriate that he ask after the poor Indian women who were seen leaving earlier. Dr. Gentry obliged with a detailed account of broken bones, abrasions, and bruises.

"Who would do this to them?" Alcazar asked. "One of their upset vaqueros, I would guess," he added.

Alcazar thought the sisters' practice of selling potions had not brought the expected romance for which a visiting client had paid. Perhaps it was the wealthy haciendados, each vying for the hand of the same señorita, who instead bought trouble.

Dr. Gentry was busily dividing the dried plants, placing the leaves and faded flowers in apothecary jars. He stopped at the mention of vaqueros and said, "Actually, my first thought was Tito Sanchez, but the women wouldn't tell me anything. You know how stubborn and quiet these Indians can be! If Owl Woman hadn't happened by with these herbs, I wouldn't know yet.

"For some reason the girls seem to have a great deal of respect for her, maybe even a little fear ..."

Dr. Gentry was recalling their compliant behavior, and his rheumy blue eyes became distant as he lost track of the conversation.

"But you know now," Alcazar reminded him.

"Yes," Gentry laughed, his eyes settling back on the friar "... if you can believe there is a character named Laughing Coyote!"

***

He sat at his desk staring into the dark, oblivious to the setting sun and the unlit oil lamp. The day's events brought Friar Alcazar many things to ponder. The errands that eventually led him to the general store proved the story of Laughing Coyote had preceded him throughout the small town. Two women, picking over the dusty bolts of cloth in the dark corner of the mercantile, were gossiping.

The Indian sisters were seen stealing up the stairs to their rooms above the cantina. They were obviously battered and anxious to be out of public view, said the assayer's wife, who had entered the street particularly early this morning looking for her husband's small dog. The other woman knew for a fact that the culprit was a character called Laughing Coyote, because she overheard Dr. Gentry discussing his terrible deeds when she passed by the blacksmith's.

The friar tipped his hat graciously when the women approached the counter to pay for their purchases. He was, indeed, in their debt.

Rumor was a delicate asset, Alcazar thought. When fastened carefully to remnants of truth and intricately woven, the fabric could be made quite sturdy. In little time it would be difficult, if not impossible, to discern truth from lies. Here were newly spun threads, waiting for Alcazar to introduce to the Indian problem.

Alcazar had little doubt that it was Tito Sanchez who beat the women from the pueblo. When drunk his raging temper was known by the ranchers and townspeople. The women would fear his retribution if they named him as their assailant, and therefore it was plausible they would invent the character Laughing Coyote as a diversion.

Laughing Coyote was a most providential choice, Alcazar thought. He knew how the Indians regarded the coyote and his introduction of wickedness into the world. He and Father Serna had corrected the Indian children's belief in the coyote as the source of their own evil. It was entirely compatible with what the friar knew of the different tribes' beliefs that a mocking coyote take the blame for the girls' beatings. A man bearing this name would have to be Indian, Alcazar realized, and an Indian villain would only help further his own purpose.

On Alcazar's desk, somewhere in the blackness that filled the room, lay the letter of invitation to Señor Luis Valenzuela's ball. He thought about the others who would be invited to this important social affair, men who would be crucial to the furtherance of his objectives. Yes, he would certainly attend.

Friar Alcazar reached in the dark for the lamp. Striking the match, he set it to the wick and watched with pleasure as the small flame climbed the woven threads.

***

Captain Sedlow stormed out of the barracks and barked out his orders to the detachment, his curling mustache systematically lifting under the sharp ejections of his breath. He ordered the nineteen men and three scouts riding under the command of Sergeant Davis to depart immediately, round up the renegade Apaches, and retrieve the silver.

"You're certain you won't require my men, Captain?" asked Lt. McGiver.

"No!" Sedlow answered brusquely.

Sedlow was barely able to contain his temper as he reflected on this most recent threat to trade, the attacks on the tributaries to the Santa Fe Trail. Three of Lt. McGiver's men had been killed, riding escort with the Valenzuela shipment. How had this lieutenant managed to succumb to such a predictable ambush? As commanding officer, the captain felt fearful his own reputation would slip in the eyes of the territory's green new governor.

Friar Alcazar had made a good case for a fort at San Ramon and Captain Sedlow had to agree. Troops had to be dispensed quickly, if they were to be effective. Swift retribution was the only way to deal with the warring Jicarilla Apache.

He would not be able to wait any longer for Washington's reply. His appeal to the new governor and Indian agent, John Maxwell, had been made when Lt. McGiver returned with Friar Alcazar from Blue Mesa. The Jicarilla massacre of sixteen orphans was reason to request military authority in this area. Permission to squelch these Indian uprisings would surely be granted, but the lengthy process was an abhorrence. Captain Sedlow thought the cost of delay was already too high.

Sergeant Davis' eyes met those of James McGiver as he crossed the parade ground. He could still feel McGiver's smoldering resentment as he saddled his horse, but tossed off the lieutenant's inference that he thought himself more suitable to lead the campaign. Davis bore the confidence of an experienced Indian hunter; besides, he knew that McGiver had bungled his more recent assignments.

There was the added matter of trusting the lieutenant. Davis knew of McGiver's penchant for gambling and suspected this could lead the ambitious to misplaced loyalties and perhaps even desertion. Not the sort of man on which Davis would want to depend during an Indian campaign.

The march from Fort Granger began at first light. The troopers formed an eerie, ghostly procession that faded intermittently in the early morning haze and dust that followed the commanding officer.

Sgt. Davis had convinced Capt. Sedlow of the value in employing the skilled Mescalero Apaches as scouts. The three Indians had proven their worth as trackers and were now scouring the rough country for any sign of the Llanero band of the Jicarilla.

The unrest within the tribe of the Llanero Jicarilla, or "plains people," was mounting with the suspension of all licenses to trade with their tribe. Since being forced away from the settlements, the Indians were becoming bold with hunger, frequently attacking the wagon trains in the Santa Fe and Taos areas. The new Fort Union would soon provide for control of the Jicarilla, but in the meanwhile it was the army's task to stop the raids and warfare. This was becoming increasingly difficult now that the Jicarilla were often joining with the equally unhappy tribes of Navaho and Ute.

In a northwesterly direction, Sgt. Davis rode with his men. He had considered the possibility of the Indian band remaining in the area of the Comancheros, and discounted it. Davis knew a wagonload of silver would not feed their bellies. He asked himself, when the Indians discovered their ambush on McGiver's men hadn't netted any supplies, where would they go? He thought it a good bet the Jicarilla would retreat to an area less populated by army personnel, a place where they could plan their next raid on unsuspecting ranches or even the quiet town of San Ramon.

Davis' intent was to circle a wide area, drop down from the north, and hopefully attack with surprise. The scouts were invaluable in combing the hills, reading the signs of the band's movements, and by mid-afternoon had reported finding a campsite of the Llanero.

The scouts led the sergeant and his men through the dense scrub pine and up a small hill. The unsuspecting Indians were encamped in tepees in a hollow down the other side. This was a small band, only recently settled according to tracks still visible from the recent rain, which led to their camp. Sgt. Davis felt certain he had found the warriors who had ambushed and killed the Valenzuela escort.

Rather than risk their own exposure, and with only a couple of hours of daylight left, Sgt. Davis ordered his men to charge. The soldiers descended the hill, guns firing. Faces of astonishment lifted as the people realized they were under attack by the advancing troops. Men and women fell silently underneath the first volley of fire. Then, comprehending, the Indians' screams echoed between the walls of the boxed canyon as old and young men and women ran for cover. Several children darted from their tents, hoping to scramble for a place to hide in the scrub pine.

A few braves managed to unleash their arrows, and Davis felt a singing missile fly by his ear as it barely missed its mark. One of his men was not so fortunate and was hurled from his falling horse as the injured steed plowed through a tent, legs flailing. In the chaos, the fleeing children repeatedly fell as they turned to look back on the fate of their people.

Davis and his men made a thorough search for the missing silver, but it was evident the Jicarilla Apache had nothing, not even food.

In the end, Davis thought his company had suffered little. Five men were wounded, only one taking an arrow in his leg.

Eighteen Llaneros were dead or dying, and his soldiers had captured three small children.

It was the children who were the problem. The sergeant hadn't allowed the slaughter of the younger children, not having the stomach for such a deed, but now he had to make a decision for their care. His remorse did not extend to the others, and he felt satisfied that he had dealt with the Indian problem that had overcome Lt. McGiver and his men.

Davis decided to set up camp on the outskirts of San Ramon, where the man who had taken an arrow in his leg could receive the town doctor's attention. There was no military surgeon riding with Davis' unit and he understood the necessity for the arrow wound to receive quick attention. The sinew that held the arrowhead to the shaft would soon begin to soften, making its retrieval all but impossible.

The mission was the logical place to leave the children. Sergeant Davis would personally see that they were delivered to Friar Alcazar after the soldiers had tended to the casualties. Following the Rio Grande in a southwesterly direction the troopers reached San Ramon before nightfall.

Davis and Private Girard, the only man with medical training, drove the wagon with the wounded soldier into town. They had left the teamsters and remaining troops to prepare camp, treat the remaining wounded, and set the horses and mules to graze.

The injured man was in agony. Davis gritted his teeth as he heard the man moan with each bounce of the wagon. They rode up the main street of San Ramon at dusk, drawing the attention of the few folk who were in town at this hour. A couple of ranchers on horseback followed beside the wagon and questioned Davis about the attack. "What tribe were you warring with, Sergeant?" asked the oldest man, as he leaned over the wagon to take a closer look at the arrow lodged in the thigh of the writhing soldier.

The concern by the settlers who lived on the outskirts of town was reasonable, thought the sergeant. Just the very presence of the military had to be reassuring this far from Santa Fe.

"The Jicarilla Apache," Sergeant Davis answered. "I guess you've heard about the raid on the Valenzuela wagon?"

"Yea. That would be Laughing Coyote, wouldn't it?" The eager face of the younger man passed from view as Davis saw the old doctor step into the street.

"Come on men, give me a hand here," instructed Dr. Gentry, as he assessed the situation. "No diddling now, we've got a man in a helluva lot of pain!"

The room had turned dim with the setting sun and the old rancher lit the lamp by the doctor's examination table. They eased the patient off the litter and onto the table, but in spite of their best attempts at gentleness the soldier howled in pain.

Gentry looked the man over carefully. "It's remarkable. This the only arrow, huh?" The doctor had attended his share of arrow-wound victims in his time and thought his patient's single wound unusual. In a skirmish, the Indians were known to rapidly discharge their arrows, and if one arrow found its mark, too often others would, also.

"Lucky fellow," the doctor mumbled to his doubtful patient.

The placement of the arrow eliminated the possibility that it was lodged in bone and had prompted the doctor's remark. His real concern was the length of the protruding shaft. A good two feet was visible, indicating a shallow wound, one he would not want to chance forcing the arrow all the way through the leg for fear of destroying more tissue.

One way or another the doctor intended to remove the arrow, and so set about preparing his patient the only way he could, by getting him drunk. As the men encouraged whiskey down the soldier's throat, Dr. Gentry laid out his medical supplies, including the duck-bill forceps that he intended to use to retrieve the arrow. He considered the private's chances for survival. If he survived the shock of surgery, he ran the risk of a severed artery or blood poisoning.

When Dr. Gentry felt the soldier's senses were dimmed enough from the imbibed alcohol, he tentatively rocked the shaft of the arrow back and forth in the wound. There was little resistance, other than the patient's vocal protest. Deciding not to delay the inevitable, the doctor pulled steadily back, removing the arrow in one motion.

The soldier's scream ended in pitiful moans. As they finally subsided, the men in the room began to breathe regularly once again.

Gentry held up the arrow with its arrowhead still intact and said, "This isn't a warrior's arrow."

The men gathered around to inspect the arrow.

"See," said the doctor, "I'd never be able to pull out a barbed arrow. Besides, they're attached at a horizontal plane to the shaft, so that when released from the string at the other end of the shaft's vertical notch, they often find their deadly mark in a man's rib cage. Nope, this is a hunting arrow, intended for an animal's vertical ribs."

"Well, no matter," said the sergeant. My man's gonna make it, huh?"

Sergeant Davis agreed with the doctor that it would be best to leave the patient under his supervision for the night. He would return in the morning with the litter, before the troops returned to Santa Fe.

***

A commotion was coming from the adjoining room, and Carlotta raised up on one elbow in order to hear better.

"What's going on?" whispered Pilar.

"I think they're bringing in more children. Do you hear Maria?"

The girls listened intently and could faintly detect Maria's soothing voice. They recognized the soft, reassuring words they had heard her use so often to comfort Felicia.

Soon the room became quiet, and except for an occasional small voice whimpering in the night, everything returned to normal.

***

The noisy birds were the only indication it was morning, and Carlotta woke with a start. She could hear the boys talking among themselves in the dark, and she rose quickly from her bed, as if sleep had been a stalking thief that she had just escaped. This same sense of urgency led her to dress quickly, smooth out the bedding on her cot, and join her brother.

Jean Paul, with the army log grasped firmly under one arm and a lit candle in his free hand, joined Miguel and Two Bears on Diego's bed. Though their voices were low, Carlotta saw they had obviously been arguing a point and were expecting McGiver's log to settle the debate.

Familiarly, the French boy opened the book and pointed to an entry.

"See, the date is August third, but there is nothing indicating place," said Jean Paul. His usual neatly combed hair was in disarray, and Carlotta guessed he had not slept well.

Jean Paul continued, "Then the words 'Ordnance Department' and again, 'Sanchez'. We're missing an important piece of information, don't you agree?"

Diego studied the book. "What are these marks?" he asked.

He pointed to another column that had a date and a check mark, written in pencil, which he hadn't remembered seeing.

"Oh, that's my writing. I was just keeping track of our missions."

Carlotta moved in close to her brother and peered over his shoulder at the open log. Jean Paul's marks emphasized their accomplishment in a way she had not considered. The boy's bookkeeping skills in adding this column of new entries registered a finality to the balance sheet. Wasn't this a payment column of another kind? Carlotta wondered, was this justice?

"Well, what can we do about it?" asked Miguel. "We can't stop everything McGiver, Tito Sanchez, or Friar Alcazar does!"

"Maybe not, but we're in a better position than most, because we know what they have done and they don't know that we know," said Two Bears.

"So ... we keep our eyes and ears open!" Diego said, completing the thought.

"What's an Ordnance Department?" Carlotta asked.

"I don't know," Diego answered, hopelessly.

Carlotta left the boys as the first rays of sunlight were coming through the high window. It seemed futile worrying about things in the future. Especially because she knew there were now more children in the mission, possibly more children in danger.

Pilar and Virginia were just rising when she returned to the girls' side of the room. The three agreed to visit Maria and the small children they had heard during the night.

Maria had her hands full. She was standing at the fire stove, a struggling Indian child in her arms, while she attempted to stir a pot of beans. Two other babies were on the floor, frightened and crying. With great relief, Maria handed the older toddler to Virginia, and instructed Carlotta and Pilar to help with the little ones.

Carlotta took a warm tortilla from the stack on the stove, tore it in half, and sat on the floor with Pilar and the babies. She could feel the children's fear, and gingerly held out a small piece of tortilla as a peace offering. A little brown hand, far less plump than any child's should be, reached out to accept the food. The girls comforted the hungry babies as best they could, tempting them with beans and tortillas, hoping to gain their trust.

Carlotta thought of the Indian children's loneliness, remembering her own feelings of abandonment in the mouth of the cave. How could she help them, as Owl Woman and the people of the pueblo had helped her? And then she remembered her Kachina doll hidden behind the adobe wall. When the children had their fill, Carlotta suddenly got to her feet and excused herself, telling Maria she would only be gone a minute.

All consideration for risk left Carlotta's mind, as she hurried around the corner to her secret place. The doll was just as she had left it, wrapped tightly in Diego's shirt. She clutched the bundle to her chest and ran back into the cocina unobserved.

Sitting on the floor, Carlotta unwrapped and presented her treasure with complete confidence. As she expected, the children were fascinated, and curiously touched the little figure of feathers and a painted body. Maria, Pilar, and Virginia, who had stood watching, came closer.

Virginia gasped in surprise. Pilar and Carlotta were startled to hear a real sound come from their mute friend and watched as Virginia struggled with her desire to speak. But nothing further came from her mouth. Virginia was as astonished as the little ones to see Carlotta's miraculous possession, and Carlotta willingly held the doll out for her to examine.

"Hactcin," said the oldest of the Indian children and then retreated shyly behind Maria's skirts.

Virginia slowly shook her head and again tried to force a word from her throat.

"G ... Gan," she finally managed.

Carlotta looked from one to the other and recognized a communication had taken place.

"Gan?" Carlotta asked, tentatively.

Virginia's blonde head bobbed up and down in affirmation.

"Hactcin?" Carlotta asked the Indian child.

The Indian child smiled sweetly, in much the same way as the children of the pueblo, Carlotta thought.

"Kachina!" Carlotta said triumphantly.

***

CHAPTER 11

EL NORTE

EL NORTE

Carlotta was astonished. She had never seen so many horses in one place. Beautiful horses, their glossy coats sparkling in the sun, nervously pressed forward as they funneled through the narrow gateway to the empty corral. To get a better look Carlotta climbed on the wood railing, with Diego and Joaquin on either side. She didn't want to miss observing the hacienda's guest make his final decisions for purchase from the moving tide of horse flesh.

Vaqueros were cutting the herd, responding to the hand signals of the Californian. Adroit in their movements, they separated the animals who would become part of the drive to their new home. Señor Valenzuela and the Californian exchanged observations, indicating first one and then another choice. Luis Valenzuela pointed to a sorrel.

"I've been watching that little mustang. Pedro, my foreman, broke him, and I think he'll work out well for you. He's a natural cutter."

The children looked over the herd to the sturdy little range mongrel running along the fence. He, like the others in this corral, was smaller than the herd they had just visited.

"They don't look like much," Joaquin explained to Diego, "but they're tough little horses, related to the Spanish breed, and the men who work with our cattle say they have the "cow sense" that's needed."

"The military doesn't like them much, at least not for their long campaigns. They need a heavier horse that will carry their men and equipment for longer periods," he added.

Joaquin's remarks held just a hint of disdain. He was obviously quite proud of his horse, which differed in look from the horses they watched, Carlotta thought.

Valenzuela's son had walked with his friends down to the corrals, where his father's holdings included horses specifically bred for the demands of the new frontier. Carlotta never dreamed that horses would have such diverse characteristics. Apparently, they were bred to serve different masters. As Joaquin had said, some would be ridden by the working cowmen, the vaqueros of large cattle ranches, others were the beasts of burden the military required, and yet others, like El Norte, more closely resembled the regal, proud descendants of Arabian stock.

From the moment Carlotta stepped foot on the hacienda's land she was caught up with the magic of the horses about which Diego had long talked. Again, she felt the good fortune that had occurred in being allowed to come with her brother for two weeks. At the same time she felt some anxiety for the children left behind at the mission.

Friar Alcazar had called Carlotta and her brother into his rectory only yesterday. They had appeared before him quietly submissive, fearful that someone had linked them to the "theft" of the Valenzuela's silver. Diego held his sister's sweaty palm contemplating their punishment as they stood on weak and trembling legs before Alcazar's desk.

In the friar's hands was a letter that Carlotta imagined to be the one Chuey wrote. Her eyes were riveted on the piece of paper as she tried to guess which poem was in his possession. In fierce concentration, Carlotta was barely aware of the friar's voice, and visibly jumped when she heard the name of the poem's intended recipient.

"Señor Luis Valenzuela is planning a dinner and ball, and has written requesting the services of the mission's older, more capable children," Alcazar eyed the two pale faces before him.

"What is the matter, child? Are you ill?" the Friar asked Carlotta.

"No, Father ... I feel fine." Carlotta swallowed hard.

Had Luis Valenzuela linked the children to the theft? Was he planning some terrible retribution? Carlotta's imagination ran wild with these possibilities.

"I have decided that because Diego has frequently been asked to work in the barns, it would be appropriate that the two of you stay there to prepare for the ball.

"Carlotta, you've helped Maria in the cocina. I'm sure you can be useful in the hacienda's kitchens. Am I right?"

"Oh ... oh, yes, sir. I mean, Father."

Carlotta was having difficulty addressing the friar as he had requested. The word "Father" caught in her throat, just as the falseness of his benevolence had caught and suspended her in his web of deceit.

"Do you suppose, Father, that the others could come, also?" Diego asked, guardedly.

"Out of the question," Alcazar answered. "There is other work to be done, here and outside of the mission. Diego, I want you to pay particular attention to your lessons in horsemanship. Later, it will be your responsibility to train the Indian children as vaqueros for my ... the mission's cattle herd."

Diego's eyes lifted, betraying his interest. This was the first time either he or his sister had heard about a cattle herd belonging to the mission. He was, also, mildly shocked to learn that Friar Alcazar knew something of his hours spent riding rather than attending to the menial duties in the barns. But the prevailing thought was the miracle, his calling ... his being asked to do what he loved more than anything in the world ... to ride a horse. Diego labored to keep his gaze steady and his heart, which threatened to burst with joy, beating unnoticeably. Mercifully, the friar continued.

"Of course, the day of the ball, I will send over the others to help with the preparations and the serving of the food.

"Now tell me, do you think that I can trust the two of you to honor this privilege?"

Diego and Carlotta nodded, eager to withdraw from the friar's scrutiny. Once on the other side of the rectory's door it was impossible to contain their pleasure. This would be the children's first overnight stay away from the mission. Carlotta's excitement was equal to her brother's. She had lived Diego's dreams of El Norte vicariously, listening to him recount each day spent at the ranch, and would now have her first opportunity to see this marvelous horse.

They hurriedly packed their few belongings amidst the curious stares of their friends.

"It is very good fortune," said Two Bears with a smile.

"Do you really think so?" Carlotta asked, doubtfully. She was thinking of those they would leave behind.

"Please be careful! Alcazar is dangerous," she added.

"This is true, but we know that now," said Two Bears. "It will not be the same as on Blue Mesa. We are smarter now."

With that affirmation, Jean Paul's wrinkled brow relaxed. "You know," he said, "you might be able to learn more about the next holdup!"

Virginia was sitting on Carlotta's cot, her head resting on her folded arms. Carlotta saw one lone tear make its way down Virginia's cheek and fall, unobserved by the others.

The girl had not spoken since she struggled to say her strange word for Kachina, but Carlotta was confident other words would follow. The clue was in Virginia's blue eyes, which seemed, more and more, not only to observe her surroundings, but express a desire to comment on them.

"We'll be together again soon, Virginia!" Carlotta tried to assure her friend. "Then you and Pilar and I will be fine ladies at the Valenzuela ball!"

Pilar giggled, delighted with the thought. Virginia raised her head, searching Carlotta's face for an explanation.

Sister and brother left the mission with the promise to their friends that they would all meet again on the eve of the ball. In return, Carlotta extracted a vow from the older children that they would care for and comfort the Indian babies in her absence.

And so the Medina children arrived at the Spanish hacienda, Diego barely reintroduced to a heritage deprived him at the age of six, securely clasping the hand of his little sister, who had only visited the hacienda at night and had no hint of such grandeur or even the suspicion of its existence.

Joaquin and Don Luis greeted them at the gate, and Diego took care to formally introduce his sister. He was relieved to see Señor Valenzuela was convinced of the children's first meeting, and mildly surprised when the don suggested they take Carlotta on an unhurried tour about the ranch.

The child was delighted. Flowering vines drooped with cascades of perfumed blossoms from the roof's red clay tiles, an overwhelming enticement for Carlotta to climb the stairs of the long cool veranda and explore the rooms beyond. Diego reached out to check Carlotta's unmannerly venture, but Señor Valenzuela stopped him, giving his approval.

"Let your sister be, Diego. There is nothing she can harm and there is certainly nothing here that would harm her."

Two large French doors stood open and inviting. Carlotta entered slowly, not in fear but lest she, in her hurry, miss some small wonder. The room was large, the length of the veranda itself, and its presence was dominated by the long, square, carved vigas that supported the roof. Rays of light flowed through the doorway and the open windows recessed in deep adobe block, falling softly on the ornate rugs and turning lacquered and golden as they touched the room's few pieces of heavy wooden furniture. Carlotta approached the massive hand-carved table in the middle of the room and touched its Spanish lace cloth, watching it flow and dance before her eyes like delicate snow flakes flying through the air. She looked up at the great crystal chandelier that had liberated the sun, rerouting shards of splintered light across the room. The vision was magnificent and it took her to another place, a white horse running on a field of snow. A memory, a dream she was helpless to fully recall.

Don Luis watched her turn to her brother, her face exposed and vulnerable, and felt something of the child reach into the unknown. It was a fleeting moment, quickly replaced with a wistful smile.

Joaquin and Diego were not to be put off any longer. They had waited patiently, but were now eager to show Carlotta the horse, El Norte. The group retreated from the coolness of the villa into July's bright sunlight. Carlotta happily skipped ahead, frequently stooping to examine a flower or pet the head of one of the ranch's numerous dogs.

In a paddock off the barn stood a sleek black horse, such as Carlotta had never seen. El Norte's body appeared shorter than most and his sculpted head small for his body, but there was nothing out of proportion in the way he was put together. He stood alert and graceful, and as they approached the corral his slender, arched neck dipped and rose to reveal a wide forehead and bright, intelligent eyes. The young stallion whinnied at the sight of company, his mane swirled and an unruly forelock fell over one eye.

The boys quickly shimmied the rail to stand at either side of the majestic horse. They stood, stroking a hide that rippled like blue and black satin, while Carlotta gazed into El Norte's one liquid dark eye not inhibited by the wayward forelock. It was an invitation and she felt him beckon her to mount.

"Do you think I can?" Carlotta asked.

"What? Ride him?" Diego asked, incredulously.

Joaquin looked at his friend's sister as if it were for the first time.

"Have you ever been on a horse?" He was certain she hadn't, but her familiarity with El Norte puzzled him.

"Yes ... sort of," Carlotta dropped her head, answering softly.

"Carlotta!" Diego chastised her. Where did she ever get some of her notions, he wondered.

Don Luis, also, stared at the child, but intrigued by her sincerity, made the suggestion they only allow her to mount for a few moments.

"Diego, why don't you fetch the bridle and a blanket from the barn?"

The boys eyed each other warily. Diego and Joaquin knew the gear Luis was suggesting. A cruel Spanish bit, which caused the horse pain with any but the gentlest touch. A bit that Diego had managed to convince Joaquin was unnecessary, after a morning session in which he controlled El Norte's movements with just a bozal and flicks of the reins to his neck.

Diego walked to the barn, undecided and troubled. It wasn't until he arrived before the wall of dusty tack supported on rusty nails and hinges that he made his decision. Both headstalls would bring the responsive horse to his rider's submission, but only the bozal was painless. Diego reached for the headstall with its heavy rawhide noseband.

He wasn't at all sure how Don Luis would react, but he was absolutely certain he couldn't bring himself to inflict torture on the beautiful black. His rapport with the stallion had grown, and could no longer be denied. Joaquin's own recognition of their relationship had initially caught him off guard, but no longer. He loved this horse, El Norte. Perhaps, he thought, even as much as his love for his sister. He would live with the guilt of that fact before he would admit it.

Confidently, Diego returned and slipped the bozal over El Norte's muzzle; the knot, its only means of control, nestling beneath the horse's jaw. He wouldn't allow himself to look in Luis Valenzuela's direction, but brusquely took the reins up and over the horse's head, as if his quick and assured movements would suffice and replace, in Don Luis' expectations, the cruel Spanish bit.

Miraculously, it was to be. Joaquin stood silently beside his friend, his eyes wide but staring down at the dirt. He was not about to betray his friend, but wondered if Diego had lost his mind. Diego hefted the blanket onto the horse's back and called Carlotta to come over.

Luis watched as Diego gave his sister a boost and the child found her place upon the stallion. He overlooked nothing, but had the advantage of being a witness that earlier morning when Diego proved his worth.   It was on the basis of this observation he had suggested to Friar Alcazar that he consider Diego's talents. Luis heard about Alcazar's investment in cattle, and though he considered the friar's motives of a greedy nature, thought it a good opportunity to train Diego for gainful employment.

The future of the Medina children, mission orphans, held little promise Luis guessed, and if there was some way he could help prepare Diego to fend for his sister and himself he felt obliged to offer his guidance.

Carlotta beamed. She, the only one who was not aware of the spirited stallion's unusual trust and acceptance, sat easily on El Norte's back and calmly stroked his mane.

Diego and then Joaquin led El Norte around the corral, the horse submissive and relaxed. In spite of himself, Luis felt his shoulders lose their tension as he recognized his own anxiety had been for the child. He watched the little dark-haired girl, whose faded dress was most likely her very best, as she melded happily with her mount, bare feet dangling innocently against his flanks. The sight touched him in a way that he found disconcerting.

He feared for these children and his own son, who were involved in something beyond their abilities. Luis had no hard evidence, just a childish note and a stolen shipment of silver, which had never left the hacienda. But when he had gently asked his son, Joaquin adamantly denied any knowledge. His son was not one to lie, but he held a fierce, stubborn loyalty to his friend Diego, and Luis knew enough not to press the issue.

Luis began to understand that if he were to learn more he would have to bide his time and allow Joaquin to find his own way. It was all part of his son's becoming a man.

***

From Carlotta's first opportunity to mount El Norte, it became a competition between brother and sister for permission to ride Joaquin's black stallion. Diego acquiesced, reluctantly at first, but as he met Don Luis' challenge to work with the green prairie horses, breaking the spirited little mustangs to saddle, he became more generous with the horse of his dreams. Pedro, the ranch foreman, oversaw Diego's training, matching each of his accomplishments with the next level of difficulty, and though the boy fell into bed each night exhausted and sore, he was spared any serious injuries.

That first evening Carlotta and Diego learned they were expected to share their meals with Joaquin and his father. Unprepared for their employer's generosity, they shyly slipped into the high-backed chairs, uncertain as to their expected manners.

With hands folded in her lap, Carlotta stared across the table. The table, though a lesser size than the massive piece of furniture in the room off the veranda, was exquisitely appointed with a white cloth covering and a bowl of roses of vibrant color set in its center.

Don Luis observed the nervous children and set about to make them feel at ease. An Indian woman entered the room bearing dishes with heavenly smells. She was dressed in the clothing of her people and still seemed quite at ease serving Spanish society. When she placed the platter of wild fowl down before Luis, he introduced her to the children as Cuenta, his cook and housekeeper.

The Indian woman gave an easy smile, and Carlotta recognized in her lined, brown face a long association with laughter. Cuenta was Apache, Don Luis said, and had lived with the Valenzuelas for many years.

After dinner Don Luis retreated to his library and study. A room, Joaquin said, where his father spent hours reading from a great collection of books. Much of Joaquin's own education was explored through the travels and research of the books' authors, he added.

Carlotta stared at the heavy carved doors that led to this secret world. She thought of her single introduction to a world of learning, the book Friar Serna had loaned her. What would it be like to have access to so many books? To want to know or understand something, and then just because of this desire find the means to the answer, behind closed doors? The idea was as remote as heaven.

"Come on, Carlotta!" Joaquin said, interrupting her thoughts. "Let's go sit on the veranda and watch the stars. I will show you my favorite constellations."

It was so tempting, but Carlotta suddenly realized why she was here. She had not offered to help Cuenta in the cocina, and she felt confusion, and just a small amount of guilt, that her day had been so wonderful. It had not been Friar Alcazar's intention that she be treated like a guest.

"I think I should go to the cocina, Joaquin," she said sadly.

Joaquin looked at her uncomprehendingly. "Oh, no, no. You don't have to work. My father wants you and Diego to be my company. He thinks I spend too much time by myself ... or with the wolves!" Joaquin laughed heartily.

"Yes, but he told me I will be needed to break the mustangs," Diego sternly reminded Joaquin.

"Of course, Carlotta can, too, if she wants to," said Joaquin.

Carlotta's dark eyes flashed, but Joaquin was grinning, and she saw he was only teasing.

There wasn't anything about which Carlotta would complain, and so she didn't reveal the thoughts that had been in her mind. Joaquin could not understand what this day had meant to her. The grandeur of the hacienda's rooms, the flowers and their smells, her first time on a horse, these events and more had made this day so very special. Nothing could upset her now, and so Carlotta joined the boys on the veranda and listened as Joaquin pointed out his constellations, and thereby gave new names to her friends who'd died on Blue Mesa.

The night grew moist with dew, and a closeness rose from the earth and encircled the children who grew sleepy in its fragrant embrace. Their shared excitement, at last exhausted, gave way to quiet contentment, and Cuenta appeared in the doorway to show them to their rooms.

Carlotta was alarmed to learn she would be sleeping alone. Not just on a bed alone, but in a room all by herself. She wanted to protest, but this was not the way to show her gratitude. She realized that something more was expected of her after all. Perhaps this was growing up.

Cuenta dipped the candle she carried to light the one placed on the small table, and the room where Carlotta was to sleep took on a yellow glow. A lovely dark wood poster bed with flowing canopy graced the room, and Carlotta watched as Cuenta turned back the comforter to reveal snow-white linen. The housekeeper pointed to the wash stand with its bowl and pitcher filled with water.

"You wash," she said simply, and then handed her a muslin gown.

The child's eyes were large, and Cuenta smiled in understanding.

"It is a good thing for you to sleep here. Señor Valenzuela is a kind man, and no harm will come to you in his hacienda."

Their first day swam through Carlotta's head. She lay with the comforter pulled up beneath her chin and examined the painting on the wall across the room. Her body was still chilled from the quick scrubbing at the wash stand, and it emphasized the luxurious textures that now enveloped her. She reached out and absently stroked the laced-edged covering of the pillow on which she lay.

The painting was of a diminutive woman, elegantly dressed in Spanish riding attire. She was holding the reins to a horse who looked similar to El Norte. The expression on her uplifted face was proud, but something in her warm eyes betrayed a friendliness; a gentleness. Carlotta felt comforted with her presence now that Cuenta had closed the door. She found it was too difficult to keep her thickly lashed eyelids open any longer, and reached to the table beside the bed to blow out the candle as the housekeeper had instructed.

***

The days ahead were warm and sunny. Days in which Carlotta smiled and laughed as she never had. She explored and played, freely expressing her delight with all things living. And once in awhile the child would stop in the middle of her play and reflect on the other children. The pueblo children, who were loved and accepted by their people; children who were allowed to run splashing in the creek, were yet attentive to their people's teachings of modesty and dignity.

Don Luis noticed how, in the midst of the children's happiest times, Carlotta would turn quiet and distant, her thoughts somewhere else. He wondered if she was remembering her life within the mission walls, a life of servitude and constant repentance. He thought it a suffocating, dreary existence for any child.

Carlotta weighed her own worth in light of her free time to roam the hacienda and permission to enjoy its many pleasures. Frequently, she would show up in the cocina and quietly assist Cuenta by cutting up the vegetables or stirring a boiling pot. Carlotta followed the housekeeper, as she made her rounds dusting and cleaning the many rooms, and it wasn't long before she had learned to predict Cuenta's routine and hurriedly cleaned the last rooms on her schedule. Smiling proudly, the child would greet Cuenta as she came into the library and explain that she could leave now because her work was almost done.

On one such afternoon, Luis entered the library, the heavy carpet muffling his footsteps. The girl, apparently unaware, was sitting cross-legged before a wall of books with a large volume in her lap. Her attention was so preoccupied she did not hear Luis approach.

"Which book has you so captivated, Carlotta?" Luis asked.

"Oh!" The book slammed shut and Carlotta quickly rose to her feet.

"Pardona me, Señor. I was just dusting and ... they're so beautiful and ..."

"You mustn't apologize, child. Never apologize for wanting to learn," said Luis. "That is what you were doing, isn't it? Reading, learning?"

Luis gently took the book from her hands.

"Yes," he said. "A fine choice! A book about Thomas Jefferson, a man who understood that liberty requires vigilance."

"He is an American, is he not, sir?" Carlotta's fear of being caught in the Valenzuelas' library was momentarily forgotten with her interest in the book.

"Yes, he was, child. He was a man who was able to explain convincingly to others the splendid ideas of freedom and equality, a man whose ideas found their origin in this America of the north."

Luis watched as Carlotta mulled over his words and her apparent struggle with a thought.

She looked directly into his face and said, "I believe I understand about freedom, because that is how I feel since I came here," she smiled wanly. "But what does the word equality mean?"

Luis was dumbstruck. He had watched this child, had observed her intelligence, but she was asking a question that required her to reach beyond her years for understanding.

"Equality means the same opportunity for freedom for all," Luis answered.

Again, the child's countenance reflected her struggle to comprehend.

"Perhaps I can explain by telling you a little story," Luis said.

"Years ago, when in my youth and ignorance, I thought some people were different, more entitled than others, I took into the hacienda ... No, no, I bought an Indian slave from a Comanchero. It was the way that I was raised, to believe that some shall govern and others serve. I had never considered that it might be against a person's will ... that the person had no choice."

Carlotta's eyes held Luis's, riveted on what he was saying.

"The woman I bought was one of several Apaches I was taking back for myself and other haciendados. The Comanchero, whose spirited horse team momentarily required his full attention, told them to follow me to my wagon where I counted out his payment in silver. When I had finished, I sent the woman back to hand the silver to the Comanchero with a final instruction: 'Cuenta el dinero'. She obediently took the silver to the man who had sold her and quickly returned. I asked her, 'Le dijiste, cuenta el dinero?' Asking whether she had requested the Comanchero to count the money.

"It was only then that I realized she spoke such little Spanish, as she answered, "No cuenta!" At the time I thought it amusing, and on the long ride back with my newly purchased slaves in the back of the wagon, I decided to call her Cuenta.

"We had been traveling for some time when suddenly I saw the real meaning of her words, 'No cuenta', or 'no count.' This woman had expressed the reality of her situation, perhaps unwittingly but true nonetheless. She did not count. Her wishes, her choices, her life simply did not count.

"It was a tremendous lesson for me. Some men, actually many men, believe they are entitled to freedom and they will fight and often die for this right. And yet they do not consider others to have this same right, because they do not regard them as equal. They will say they value human life, but what they really mean is only their own life holds value.

"I saw I could not have it both ways, and though I could not undo the transactions for my friends, the other ranchers, I was determined it would be different in my household. I told Cuenta that she was free to return to her people. She didn't believe me at first and stayed on. I supposed she didn't dare. But she never left, and I found out later that she fully understood ... and chose to stay."

For a long while after Carlotta left, Luis sat staring at the closed library doors and asked himself who had benefited most, the student or the teacher? Luis smiled to himself. Who was the teacher? He wondered.

***

CHAPTER 12

THE BALL

THE BALL

"You no move, please," Cuenta begged for the fifth time.

"I am trying, Cuenta!" Carlotta said, earnestly. "But please hurry!" Cuenta was doing her best under the difficult circumstances imposed on her. The child standing on the stool would not hold still much longer, but how was she to finish shortening the hem of the gown in time?

Through the open window of the upstairs balcony, the woman and child could hear the approaching carriages and buggies rolling on the gravel path. It was way too late for both of them to be involved with such alterations. Cuenta was needed in the kitchen, and Carlotta must return to the children in the dining room where they were to wait for further instructions. The puertero would, at any moment, be ushering guests into the ballroom.

Carlotta's excitement was mounting. To think, in only several minutes she would descend the stairs dressed as a lady! She had never dared to dream of the image reflected in the mirror across the room.

The dress had been the reason for their delay. Don Luis had called the children before him for a last-minute inspection. They appeared, scrubbed and shining, the girls presentable in clean muslin gowns, and the boys in muslin shirts and pants. But after they returned to the kitchen, Luis called Cuenta, and a hurried order was given.

Luis had decided that one of Señora Valenzuela's gowns, laid tenderly in a trunk so long ago, would better serve her wishes if put to use, rather than succumb to mice. The dress Don Luis chose was made of creamy silk, which harbored soft hints of pink and yellow, accented with similarly colored ribbons. Now that Cuenta had severely tucked in the bodice, it fit smoothly over Carlotta's childish figure.

The child gawked at her reflection. Her hair had been combed back and upward, tamed into submission with two tortoise-shell combs. The rag curls about which Carlotta had protested when Cuenta put them in place that morning, were now removed, allowing her hair to fall on her shoulders in individual long dark curls. Was she the same little girl who only two weeks before had come to the hacienda? Carlotta did not think so. She remembered the reflection that mocked her, shortly after her arrival, as she was helping Cuenta dust and polish the furniture in readiness for the ball. They had worked upstairs preparing rooms for those guests who would be lodging for the night, when a horse-drawn wagon brought a delivery for Don Luis.

The commotion downstairs was unusual, emphasizing the rare occasion when the Valenzuelas received a package from France. Luis bounded up the stairs, skipping steps with his long stride. He was looking for Cuenta to help him appraise the contents of the package. The gown, a gift from Governor Maxwell for his niece, Rebecca, had arrived in time for the ball!

Luis found Cuenta and Carlotta airing the blankets on a balcony in one of the bedrooms. He excitedly shoved the package into Cuenta's arms and impatiently asked her to open it. Many an instruction could be misinterpreted in this long-distance communication from America to France.

"Will Rebecca be disappointed? Tell me honestly, Cuenta."

Luis had agreed to make the arrangements, but as the time grew nearer, he wasn't certain this had been a wise decision. Rebecca was quite excited at the prospect of a Paris gown, her expectations growing with each passing day.

Cuenta tore away the last of the tissue, exposing a glimpse of rich black lace. Carefully, she lifted the dress from the box and let fall the folds of shimmering taffeta. She then dropped the gown over the dress form standing in the corner and stood back so that the three could appreciate its beauty.

The gown was breathtaking, a marvel of black taffeta and graduated tiers of black lace, beginning with the most intricate narrow trim on the bodice, to the yards of deep lace that scalloped its sweeping skirt. Each row was studded with dropped pearls. In the light from the balcony doorway the pearls reflected the dress's black shadows and their own inherent luminosity. The affect was reminiscent of dew on a moonlit forest floor.

The Apache housekeeper, though accustomed to the finery worn at the hacienda on other occasions, was duly impressed with this latest fashion from France. Cuenta stroked the taffeta fabric that played deceptively in the sunlight and smiled her approval.

Luis was pleased, and looked to the child, seeking her opinion. Carlotta had turned away from the unveiling to face the dress-length mirror in the opposite corner of the room. All memory of the gown had left her face and in its place was the acceptance of her own drab reflection.

Carlotta's hand touched her throat and moved slowly, involuntarily over her own dress of coarse muslin, as if reading the reality in the mirror. Her hand followed her body, smoothing the waistline and the skirt below it, faithfully adhering to the image. Resigned to the truth, Carlotta dropped her hand to her side.

With this gesture, Luis felt the child's futility, and his heart ached to find her so accepting. If this had been his child ... if his dear wife had given birth to the daughter they had hoped for, as a sister for Joaquin ... could they have wanted more than the unspoiled little girl before his eyes? A child who, he had learned, embraced life with such enthusiasm and still had the ability to face the truth.

Luis turned to Cuenta, not quite willing to leave these thoughts.

"Yes, I believe the gown will meet with the approval of both Governor Maxwell and his niece" Luis said and hurriedly left the room.

A soft rapping on the door brought Carlotta's attention back to the big brown eyes staring at her from the mirror. This startled her. Behind the beautiful creamy pink vision, she still looked the same. In the past two weeks she had seen so many new and wonderful things, things of which she had never dreamed. She knew so much more today than she had known yesterday. All the things that she had seen and done had changed her. Surely, she would look different. People could see the difference in her, couldn't they?

Cuenta opened the door to find Pedro, the foreman, standing awkwardly in the hallway. The two shared intimate words, ignoring the child before the mirror.

"Did you ask Father Alcazar about our wedding, Pedro?" Cuenta asked anxiously. "Will he reduce his fee to perform the ceremony?"

***

The last rays of the late afternoon sun spilled across the Valenzuela hacienda, casting long shadows along the wooden veranda floor. Diego stood at attention beside his friends, Chano, Chuey, and Two Bears. Luis nodded his approval.

"A fine group you have picked to help with the arrival of our guests, Diego, but are you certain these young boys are able to manage the horses?"

Luis was evaluating Chano and Chuey in particular. The Comanche twins were small for their age. Chano stepped forward hesitantly and in perfect Spanish defended their ability.

"Señor, our people, the Comanche, ride well. When we were little my brother and I were on the backs of many of our father's horses ... until the raid by the Comancheros," Chano added as an afterthought. "They stole the horses and us, but they couldn't keep us apart from each other!"

"How old are you?" Luis was more amazed at their command of Spanish.

Chano looked at Chuey, and his brother shrugged his shoulders.

"We don't know, Señor, but we have been at the mission four snows."

"Apparently, the mission has offered you a fine education," said Luis.

"Si, Señor," the twins answered in unison.

"Our guests are beginning to arrive, so I will leave you to your duties. After the ball, come to the cocina and Cuenta will give you something to eat."

***

The sun, a burning orange sphere, hung momentarily on the horizon as the first carriages pulled up to the wide stairway leading to the veranda. On either side of the hacienda's massive doors that stood ajar to embrace the western sky, lanterns flickered, cheerfully beckoning the guests inside. Santa Fe's most elite and influential citizens descended from the coaches, their fine garments wrapped in the sky's last golden glow, their steps buoyed with the rich, heady smells of jasmine and honeysuckle.

Last-minute murmurings were uttered to the boys who took the horses' reins, and tinkling laughter floated through the evening air. The swish and rustling of silk and taffeta met the soft sounds of guitar and violin, a mounting overture of genteel excitement that ushered the guests of Luis Valenzuela into the grand ballroom.

The girls fluttered about the large dining room, quickly following Cuenta's last instructions. Each piece of polished silver was placed in order, each crystal goblet wiped immaculately clean and set in its designated spot on the long carved table. Above, the chandelier, a huge multiple-tiered fixture of a thousand prisms, shone brilliantly with the flame of candles.

Carlotta remembered the table that had greeted her and her brother that first night at the hacienda, its charming warmth and beauty a memory she would cherish. The smaller room and table served the family's everyday meals. This elegant room was now rarely opened, Joaquin had said. Since his mother had died, the dining room was used only occasionally to receive his father's friends. His guests were traders and acquaintances who came from the East and Old Mexico.

Frequently Carlotta looked down at her altered dress in amazement. She was conscious of the candlelight and how it enhanced its pale cream color. It was easy to imagine another time when Luis Valenzuela's wife graced this gown and flowed busily about the dining room making last-minute preparations for her guests. Instead of haunting her, the thought was comforting.

From across the room, Pilar and Virginia beamed, the colorful ribbons Carlotta had begged of Cuenta fastened prettily in their hair. Voices were heard coming from the next room, and the girls hovered at the dining room door to watch the guests enter the ballroom.

Joaquin stood beside his father to welcome the handsome procession of ladies and gentlemen. Miguel and Jean Paul waited politely to take their wraps. Several times Joaquin recognized and warmly greeted his father's friends, drawing a comment on his own rapid growth.

The Chavez family of a neighboring hacienda were especially surprised.

"My, you've grown," Rachel Chavez patted Joaquin's cheek, teasingly. "We haven't seen you riding out our way in some time, Joaquin. Though I'm sure we wouldn't have recognized you, except for your fine Arab, of course!"

Don Luis rescued his son. Taking Rachel's arm, he turned to introduce her to a couple standing modestly beside him. Rachel was a gregarious woman, kind and warm in her own way, and Luis thought an introduction to the newest residents of San Ramon would go far in making them feel more at ease.

Friar Alcazar entered the room and reached out paternally to pat Joaquin on the head. Joaquin involuntarily shrank under the man's touch, muttering the appropriate words of welcome at the same time.

After the friar had passed, Jean Paul whispered, "Be careful. You mustn't let on," he cautioned. "We still do not have enough information about the next theft. We must find out what will be stolen and where."

Female guests in colorful, billowing gowns, fairly glided into the room, accompanied by their regal escorts, who, in a few instances, appeared rather stiff and awkward in their unfamiliar attire.

"Luis, I'm just dying to know!" exclaimed one of Santa Fe's socialites, breathlessly descending on her host with a young companion in tow. "Did you recover the silver from this Laughing Coyote person?" she asked, earnestly.

Luis was not entirely unprepared for the question, at least not about the silver being stolen. No one could know of its recovery, but certainly, by now, everyone knew of the military escort and the ambush. But, Laughing Coyote? It would be interesting to track the rumor this evening. Luis's well-founded hunch regarding the children's poem was stirring conversations already.

"Doña Isadora, so good to see you again," said Luis. Indeed, her dress of green velvet was most becoming to her eyes.

"No, I am sad to say the silver appears to be lost," Luis lied. "However, we may learn more when Captain Sedlow arrives."

Isadora Torres nodded sympathetically. Her male companion closed the imagined space between them, proclaiming his intimate relationship to Doña Isadora.

"Well, Isadora, you know that Luis Valenzuela isn't the only victim of Laughing Coyote!" the young man laughed. "I've heard that even some of your humble villagers, right here in San Ramon, have been brutalized by this rogue!"

Vaguely irritated by the interruption, the socialite off-handedly introduced the two men. Luis watched Isadora's eyes scan the room, searching for another diversion. Recognizing an acquaintance across the room, she raised her fluttering fan for attention.

Luis excused the couple, wishing them a pleasant evening, and looked up to see Rebecca and her uncle approach. He turned to give the new arrivals his full attention.

Governor Maxwell, a plumpish man, was a distinguished figure nonetheless, his fine silver hair curling just above his white satin vest. Luis thought it lent the elegant touch required to present the vivacious young woman on his arm.

Luis greeted them, but his eyes were fastened on Rebecca. He took her fragile white hand and brushed it with his lips.

"The dress has come alive, Rebecca." His smile was warm and inviting.

The memory of the black taffeta gown, so lovely that first day on the dress form, was commissural with the beautiful vision before Luis. But now the gown moved and breathed, emanating life with each rise and fall of Rebecca's breasts, and the pearls, nestled in the gown's most secret places, had become buried treasures waiting to be discovered.

Their eyes met, and Luis observed Rebecca's merriment, due to the impression she had made on him.

"Luis, your home is a beautiful example of Spanish elegance!" gushed the governor.

"I believe my uncle means we didn't really expect to find such an oasis of gracious civility on the frontier," Rebecca said, smiling sweetly.

"Rebecca, one would think from the way you talk, that I haven't spent much time on the frontier or in the territories," interrupted the governor, defensively. "After all, I had a great deal to do with helping to set up this new territory before I left Washington."

"You must remember Governor ... and Rebecca," Luis gently chided, "we have been settled here for several hundred years. It is hardly a frontier to us."

"Ah! We've both grown too fond of Washington's refinement," Maxwell admitted. "But we are coming to appreciate this beautiful land of yours, aren't we Rebecca?"

Captain Sedlow joined their group, remarking extravagantly on Rebecca's beauty. Rebecca seemed unimpressed with the captain's flowery compliments, and Luis found himself wondering about their lives in Washington. The falseness of things went beyond politics, it seemed.

Captain Sedlow addressed his host. "It appears that half of Santa Fe has turned out for the party."

"Yes, I see that most everyone has arrived," replied Luis. "Joaquin, why don't you open the doors to the dining room, and tell Cuenta and the children our guests will be seated."

Luis observed Friar Alcazar in a conversation with Dr. Gentry, and thought it an opportune time to inquire about the wedding.

"Buenos Noches, Doctor ... Father! Tell me, how are the wedding plans for Cuenta and Pedro coming?"

Admonished momentarily, Alcazar replied. "There is the matter of fees, Don Luis ..."

His voice diminished to an expectant pause, and Luis felt a distasteful hint of greed.

Luis Valenzuela's face became a rigid mask of contained anger.

"You agree, I am sure," he said, "that the request of my housekeeper and foreman for the church's blessing is my foremost concern? If it is, as you say, that they lack the silver, please see me at the end of the evening and I will take care of it."

Doctor Gentry observed his host's cold retort and squirmed uncomfortably. Unpredictably, Luis changed the subject.

"So ... let us see what Cuenta is serving, shall we?"

***

The doors opened wide and Carlotta, Pilar, and Virginia stood to the side as the guests converged in the dining room.

With familiar ease they approached the long, laden table and read the place cards that would determine the seating arrangements.

Carlotta was amazed to hear the buzzing chatter. It seemed as though everyone was talking at once. The tone was light and gentle, dotted frequently with laughter. When Carlotta was able to distinguish one particular voice over another, she heard avid tales of gossip.

Seated at the table were neighboring haciendados, who paid particular attention to the news from traders, merchants, and the freight-line owners. Any information from Old Mexico was significant, as was the subject of new taxes levied on the caravans by the Americans. There were those on their way to the California gold fields, who reported the town of Santa Fe overrun with travelers, and complained of the hotels being extremely overcrowded. One, a military officer, whose new post would be Sutter's Fort, discussed his expectations with Luis's house guest, the horse buyer from California. Interspersed, all the while, with the reports of explorations and faraway places, Carlotta overheard the name Laughing Coyote.

The children made their way from one guest to another, pouring wine and serving an appealing array of appetizers. Carlotta watched as across the table Virginia served Dr. Gentry. The kind doctor was patiently listening to a matron from Santa Fe tirelessly describing Laughing Coyote's most recent escapade.

"... the Fletcher family was devastated, of course! Just imagine driving that long distance back, to find your home burned to the ground! Well, they just knew that it was Laughing Coyote!"

A woman seated on the other side of Dr. Gentry, completely oblivious to his presence, addressed the matron.

"You see, that is exactly what we can expect when we educate these heathens. Don't you agree, Bishop?"

Carlotta had lifted the Bishop's glass and was carefully pouring the deep red liquid over its rim, when a small amount of wine splashed onto the lace cloth. The Bishop discreetly placed his napkin over the spreading stain. Smiling conspiratorially at Carlotta, he looked up at the woman across the table who was staring at him.

"And who would you be speaking of, my dear lady?" asked the Bishop.

"The Indian heathen, Laughing Coyote. Who else?"

The boys had come in to assist with serving. Tray after tray was brought in from the cocina with offerings of succulent dishes seldom seen in even the finest hotel in Santa Fe. The meal was taken leisurely, with frequent pauses between courses, and when at last the guests felt as if they couldn't eat another bite, Luis rose to toast his visitors.

"May we all prosper in the times ahead ... in spirit as well as wealth!"

Glasses tinkled as men and women rose to touch their wine glass to a neighbor's. Carlotta watched as Don Luis nodded to his son, approving Joaquin's participation in the toast. Joaquin caught Carlotta's eye and grinned sheepishly.

Don Luis made the suggestion that while the musicians tuned their instruments, perhaps the women would like to freshen themselves upstairs. The men, he said, would meet in the library for a brandy and an important announcement from the governor.

A procession of men departed for Luis's library and his fine cigars. Cuenta had told Carlotta that it was the task of Two Bears and herself to serve the men their liquor, until later when the dancing would begin in the ballroom. Carlotta ran ahead to open the library doors. Since the day Don Luis had found her in the library, it had become her favorite room.

Familiarly, Carlotta served the brandy goblets from the silver tray on the library table, handing one to the governor first, as she had been instructed.

With glass in hand, Governor Maxwell addressed the men. "I've heard your comments tonight about the risk of doing business in the area, and I want to assure you America is here as your protector. An immediate shipment from the Ordnance Department will soon arrive at Fort Granger."

The governor's serious tone captured the immediate attention of the others in the room, and Carlotta's ears perked at the reference to "ordnance department."

"We are well aware," he continued, "of the attacks by marauding Apaches and Navaho, and the danger of further inciting the more peaceful Indians to war against ranchers and settlers. The attack and massacre of innocent children on Blue

Mesa is reprehensible, and we will not rest until we find this Laughing Coyote!"

Carlotta turned to observe Friar Alcazar's expression and found that it revealed nothing.

"And I am sure you've heard about the loss of Lieutenant McGiver's men to an Apache ambush, and the theft of our host's silver shipment. This, too, will no longer be tolerated. Captain Sedlow, here, is confident the guilty band of Jicarilla Apache has been found and punished, though unfortunately Laughing Coyote escaped first ... with the silver.

"With all of this in mind, I have sent a proclamation to the governors and other principals of the pueblos."

Drawing a letter from his vest, the governor referred directly to his communiqué.

"The United States Government requests that you abstain from all friendly intercourse with the warring Navahos and Apache, and instead make war on them if they should come into the pueblo area."

The room turned silent, and Carlotta saw Two Bears wince as they heard the words that would mean certain death for so many.

"... and in addition," Maxwell continued, fixing his gaze on the concerned men before him, "I request all able-bodied citizens of the territory to enlist in a volunteer corps to pursue and attack all hostile Indians plundering the settlements."

Spontaneous applause filled the tense silence, as the men congratulated one another and the governor on the effect of their many appeals for assistance from the United States. Luis remained calm and, Carlotta thought, a little preoccupied, as if there were a more important matter on his mind.

***

The men's camaraderie spilled over to the ballroom, as each considered his own interests were afforded a measure of protection. The earlier rumors were now ignited with the attention of the Americans. The ballroom became a virtual hub of gossip and excited speculation.

Lieutenant McGiver found he was the center of a growing group who questioned him about his heroic role under the attack of Laughing Coyote and the Apaches. Several young ladies giggled appreciatively, and McGiver blushed with this surprising admiration.

Don Luis was the last to leave the library, and Carlotta took the opportunity to ask what ordnance department meant.

"Weapons, mi Corazon ... weapons." Luis looked at the child before him. Her manners, her dress so easily spoke of her adaptation to life at the hacienda. His affections had grown for the child and he knew he would miss her when she returned to the mission.

Diego approached, reluctant to interrupt their conversation.

"Come here, son. I wanted to give you your earnings, and that of your friends."

Luis reached in the pocket of his short, fitted jacket, but Diego protested.

"Por favor, Don Luis! The money ... I won't be allowed to keep it."

Diego's head dropped, and Luis insisted he explain.

"Father Alcazar orders us to turn over all of the money we earn in town or on the ranches."

"Do you mean that the money I have paid you has gone to Friar Alcazar?" asked Luis.

"Si, when I left here I walked with Virginia through town and he was waiting at the gates for us."

Diego felt a little guilty, but not enough to deprive himself of the money. It had never made any difference before. What would he buy ... a child of the mission? Now he had a dream. Some day he would buy a horse ... hopefully, one as beautiful as El Norte. It was a worthy goal, but selfish, Diego reminded himself.

As if he read his thoughts, Don Luis asked, "Do you intend on saving for a horse one day?"

Again, Diego's head dropped with shame.

"You mustn't apologize for planning your own life, Diego. When your dealings with men are honorable, you are acting as an honorable man."

Diego's head lifted as he received the children's wages.

***

The musicians were in fine form, enjoying the opportunity to play before such an appreciative audience. Their gay, light waltzes filled the room, rising to the four chandeliers that hung from the timbered ceiling. The children passed among the guests waiting by the wall. There were those who were recovering from the last dance and others who were eagerly waiting for the next. The children attended to their needs, offering to bring drinks or wraps for those who wished to escape outside to the patio for a breath of cool night air.

Carlotta asked the fragrant woman, who was brusquely fanning herself, if there was something she could bring her.

Señora Quiros looked down past her bejeweled bosom to the child before her.

"Darling, what *ever* are you doing? Isn't she adorable, Juan?" she prodded her husband. "You should leave the serving to the servants my dear! It's very sweet of you, but you'll soil that pretty dress ..."

Carlotta was eager to slip away, before Friar Alcazar turned around, but the Señora rudely interrupted Don Luis and Rebecca as they waltzed into sight. Frozen by the woman's sheer gall, Carlotta watched as Luis stopped to inquire how he might be of service.

"What are you doing, Luis, having this *darling* child work with the slaves? Is she a relative? She's absolutely precious!"

As Carlotta feared, Alcazar turned to see what the commotion was about. Luis looked at the woman incredulously and then his eyes flashed to Alcazar.

"Madam, I assure you all of the children have been paid for their services!" To the friar directly, Luis said, "I have given Diego the money the children have earned, Father. You, of course, will see that they are allowed to keep it, won't you?"

Luis bowed his departure, and taking Rebecca's arm they left the confused woman to deal with Alcazar's smoldering anger. As they continued their waltz, Luis felt a tension, almost a resistance in Rebecca's touch. She drew back from him, her mouth set in a thin determined line.

"There is a time and a place for such criticisms, Luis," Rebecca said.

Luis felt a sinking emptiness, as he looked into her scornful eyes.

"And *when*, Rebecca, is the correct time and place?" he asked.

"You must remember who you're talking to!" she answered, angrily.

"I believe I've just been reminded."

The waltz was over and they stood for a moment in the silence until the full meaning of their impasse filled its void. Luis's hands dropped hopelessly from Rebecca's shoulders and offering a scarce nod, he left her with his answer. Though no one else had noticed, Carlotta watched Don Luis walk across the floor and read the fury in his steps.

***

CHAPTER 13

THE PRANKSTER

THE PRANKSTER

A faint stirring of cool air cart wheeled lazily across the dusty road. San Ramon stood silent in the starlight, waiting on the gentle wind, its only relief from the day's punishing sun. The haze, which had hung oppressively above the town's solitary road, dissipated in the night air, heavier particles settling on the earth, its lighter elements spared to ride the currents of the wind.

Seeking freedom from their confines, the wind spirits abandoned the village to explore the path leading to the Valenzuela hacienda. A cavorting tumbleweed, possessed by an errant breeze, flailed the dirt and danced erratically off into the desert.

Coyote looked out from his lonely citadel, down the slope now bathed in moonlight, to the town and ranches of San Ramon. His scruffy hide bristled in the restless air and his large ears twitched apprehensively. The strumming guitars had stopped, their mesmeric strains replaced with the airborne sound of human voices. Men and women were departing the place of brilliant light, and the lone sentry watched curiously as they and their horse-drawn buggies joined him in the dark.

There seemed to be no immediate danger. Coyote settled onto the rock ledge, his wariness receding, his attention fully focused on the scene below. With a subconscious need to express his solitary vigil, the coyote lifted his head and called to the moon. The night belonged to him.

***

Chano and Chuey peered out from the barn's loft and watched the soldiers approach. Moonlight spilled across the ground, its soft patina of light glistening on the men's scabbards and dancing off their uniforms' braid and shiny medals. The scene imitated the blue-white light of winter, leaving the boys with an unseasonable chill. Just when their world appeared convincingly turned to frost, a warm nimble breeze lifted from the earth and carried the scent of jasmine through the loft's open window.

"You are familiar with the goatherd's cabin at the river?" asked Lt. McGiver.

"Yes, he trades in horses. Is that correct?" a soldier asked.

"That's the one. We'll stay there the night. The old coot will provide us with clothing and horses, which will disguise our identity. If we are seen and thought to be Comancheros, so much the better!"

The ball was over and all of the guests except the soldiers had withdrawn from the hacienda's gates. Chano and Chuey had thought their work finished when the last carriage left and were exploring the loft with its sweet-smelling hay when they heard the voices of the approaching men.

The three soldiers entered the barn door and stood just out of the light's circumference. It was obvious they thought this a safe place to continue their conversation, removed from the eyes and ears of anyone still milling about the hacienda. With quiet restraint, Chuey placed his hand on his brother's shoulder. It was too late for them to announce their presence. The men were below them now and the brothers held their breath, repressing a desire to look lest they be seen.

"How are we going to explain our absence to Captain Sedlow?"

The voice of the third man was clear and alarmingly close. The Indian boys hunched down to make their profiles small and hopefully invisible.

"That should be no problem," McGiver chuckled. "I've my orders to lead a mapping expedition into the Sangre de Cristo Mountains. And these things take time, right?"

The men laughed easily as they moved back outdoors, their voices quickly fading in the night. Chano felt his brother's hand release its grip, and he shrugged circulation back into his aching shoulder.

"They're talking about Tito's half brother, aren't they?" he asked Chuey.

"Yeah! The goatherd's hut is the last chance to water horses before crossing the river and riding into Santa Fe. This must have something to do with the raid McGiver is planning!"

"Hush, someone is coming!" Chano whispered. He pulled back into the darkness and out of reach of his brother's hand.

"Chuey! Chano! Are you here?" Carlotta stepped into the barn and immediately fastened her eyes on the moving shadow in the loft.

"Come on down!" she scolded. "Cuenta has fixed us something to eat!"

The boys scrambled down the ladder, the thought of food suddenly more important than the soldiers' plans.

"How did you know we were up there?" asked Chuey.

"Oh, that's easy. I would be there, too, if I wasn't needed in the casa," Carlotta answered.

The children ran from the barn across the moonlit ground, oblivious to the owl's shadow that raced ahead.

***

Cuenta's cocina was a glowing room, rich with cooking smells and alive with the voices of los niños. The long table, which normally served as her work area, was the center of the children's attention. Seated on long benches at either side, they were devouring the remains of the marvelous dishes served earlier in the main dining room, and scarcely noticed the return of Carlotta with the twins.

Excited chatter resumed as Cuenta hurriedly departed to visit Pedro, a basket filled with food on her arm. Joaquin was seated beside his friends, and Diego raised a questioning eyebrow.

"It's all right. My father is talking with the governor and Captain Sedlow," Joaquin said, answering Diego's implied concern. "So what have we found out tonight?"

"I know what ordnance means!" Carlotta offered. "Don Luis told me that it means weapons!"

"That answers one of our questions," said Jean Paul, matter-of-factly. "It probably means a shipment of guns or maybe a cannon!" He pulled out the log from underneath his shirt and began busily scratching in the new information.

"We can tell you where," said Chano. "We overheard McGiver and two of his men talking. They said they were going to visit the old goatherd by the river, where they'll exchange their horses and clothes for those of the Comancheros."

"This has to be part of the plan in the log, don't you agree?" Chuey directed the question to the room at large.

The children were encouraged by the new information and fell into an intense discussion. Even Virginia's eyes were bright with the renewed comprehension of possibilities. The soldiers were obviously planning to steal an incoming shipment of weapons. The caravan was probably due in Santa Fe or Fort Granger on August third. Wouldn't Tito Sanchez be the final destination for the weapons, at least until he sold them? The children tried to place themselves in the enemies' shoes, imagining their motives and guessing the next turn of events. And even when they agreed as to the soldiers' plans, they still came to the inevitable point of confronting their own inadequacy. How were they to stop the soldiers? They were children, after all.

The circle of niños hummed with questions and ideas, a noticeable exception being Miguel, who sat looking dreamily into space. The boy's elbows were propped on the table, his open palms cradling his head as if it were a weary load.

"Are you with us?" Jean Paul asked, visibly aggravated.

"I'm dreaming of the future," answered Miguel.

His reply, though understood by the others around the table to mean their friend was deep in thought, perturbed Jean Paul.

"This is no time for dreaming, Miguel!" Jean Paul protested. "I must record the facts!"

Miguel raised his head sleepily. With no malice in his voice, he replied simply, "Don't bother me."

The others, who had learned to overlook Jean Paul's rancor, ignored the two, but Carlotta's head snapped with recollection. This scene had happened before, and like a rock she had plucked from the water of a stream bed, she felt the edges begin to take shape as she drew it closer.

"Shhhh. Listen," Diego said.

They felt an icy chill as the frenzied laughter of a coyote coursed through the open doorway. The loud yipping was unidentifiable at first, then surreal, but just at the moment of recognition they heard a horse scream in the paddock.

The coyote's hideous voice was forgotten with the new disturbance among the horses. Joaquin and Diego were the first ones through the door, and before the others had left the table, they heard Diego call out that El Norte had broken out of his corral. The children rushed outside to discover the wooden railing separating the black stallion from the governor's white horse in shambles. Both stallions were on their hind legs, menacing hooves slicing the air between them, their eyes wild with fear. The boys ran to the paddock and vaulted the corral's railing. Moving slowly toward the frantic steeds, Diego spoke calmly, his words a soothing balm on El Norte's spirit. The stallion's forelegs dropped to the earth, and Diego affectionately rubbed his head. The governor's horse still wore his bridle and Joaquin easily brought him under control.

"I'll put him in the barn with the soldiers' horses," Joaquin said. "They shouldn't be much longer."

Once the white stallion was led from the corral, El Norte responded enthusiastically to his increased territory. The black threw his head from side to side, whinnied, and trotted away from Diego to explore the paddock's new borders. There was no point in moving El Norte tonight, thought Diego. He left the horse and followed Joaquin to the barn.

Diego lit the oil lamp so that Joaquin could find his way to stall the governor's horse. In the shadows the soldiers' mounts moved restlessly, and Diego watched the lamp's glow flicker off their flanks. Down the row to the last horse, each animal carried the U.S. brand.

"That's it!" cried Diego.

"What?" asked Joaquin, returning to the door.

"We'll steal the horses while the men are in the goatherd's cabin. They won't get far without them!"

Carlotta stopped. The others ran ahead to watch the boys deliver the governor's horse to the barn, but she saw a huge moon hanging on the horizon and a black silhouette looming on a rock in the foreground. Once more, the coyote's heckling yips echoed across the landscape. The powerful memory of the cave returned, and Carlotta knew with a chilling certainty that this mocking, wild dog was the same trickster who had encouraged the warring horses. As she stood transfixed, listening to the coyote's insanity, Carlotta recalled the older memory of the Plaza in Santa Fe.

"Come on kid," Joaquin said, interrupting her thoughts. "The horses are all right now."

When Carlotta looked back, the coyote was gone. She followed the others to the cocina and the table where they had deliberated unsuccessfully. This time, both brother and sister offered an idea that soon inspired a plan.

***

There were only three days until McGiver's raid, and the feelings the children took back to the mission were both exciting and confusing. The orphans' cloistered lives behind the mission's walls had given protection without nourishment. The children's instruction and brief education had prepared them miserably for a secular life. They had not been conscious of these things until recent events revealed their own inadequacies, thrusting them in the unaccustomed role of discoverer. Each child had grown rapidly as he or she learned to think and act independently, but each depended on the other to strengthen his or her valor.

Leaving the Valenzuela hacienda was painful, though no one spoke of it. There was no question that they must return to the source of evil, Friar Alcazar, and, hopefully, set about to undo his harm. The younger children were waiting, innocent and helpless. The task, though beyond their years, fell to them alone; the only truth left undiscovered was their own temerity.

But Alcazar was much too busy to notice that the returning children were doing their best to avoid him. There was the matter of managing the cattle herds, as the friar's new enterprises demanded more of his time. He was exalted with his new standing in the community. Buoyed with self-importance, Alcazar would often walk into San Ramon to meet with accomplices. The poorest villagers would watch their friar stride swiftly, purposely through town, and mistakenly take comfort in the church's presence.

The gossip that had circulated through Valenzuela's great ballroom, only substantiated the talk in town, and now that Alcazar had taken the pulse of Santa Fe's elite, his confidence soared. Laughing Coyote had taken on life, becoming the scapegoat for the silver raid and, most importantly, the attack on Blue Mesa. There was no reason to be concerned with trivial matters such as the lost saddle bag. It was most likely buried with the children, he thought. Just as were his dealings with Lt. McGiver and the bandit, Tito Sanchez.

His duty was to enforce the governor's proclamation. There would be no more trade between the pueblos and the Apache and Navaho; he would see to that. This isolation would bring the pueblo further under his control. Alcazar could imagine Sak-mo-i-si's arrogance wither under these new restrictions, and he foresaw the Sun Priest's boy, Two Bears, become an extension of his own will when the shift to the Church's influence became permanent.

Yes, his goals were clearly blessed and except for an uncomfortable awareness of the children's new friend and ally, Luis Valenzuela, Alcazar felt his success guaranteed.

***

The second of August came and the tension in the orphans' sleeping quarters was almost unbearable. A sudden chorus of frogs announced the setting sun, and the children huddled at the door to wait for the cover of night. They had decided that only six of them would join Joaquin at the hacienda after dark. There had been some argument, but a consensus was finally reached. They had recognized their plan required horsemanship and agreed that Miguel, a boy from the village who had never been on a horse, would stay at the mission. Much to Pilar's chagrin, she and Virginia would stay behind, also. They would be missed if the young Apache children required their care. Once Pilar understood the importance of the two girls remaining at the mission, it became her assignment to action and she accepted it with simple grace. And so Carlotta, the only girl with experience on a horse, left with the boys.

Diego gently latched the gate behind them, and the children made their way through the sleeping village without incident. Joaquin was waiting, as arranged, at the path leading to the hacienda.

"Follow me. We'll go to the north pasture where I've put the horses," Joaquin said.

He quietly led the group down a dark path. A wind came up and softly rustled the leaves of the cottonwoods above them. The children walked into the unknown, a breeze stirring the air around them giving them a feeling of expectation. Carlotta felt her heart beat and realized how fortunate she was that she had no fear for herself or the others, because tonight they had a course of action. She thought this night almost made up for the last few miserable days.

El Norte heard Joaquin's whistle and came thundering to the fence, the other horses behind him.

***

The goatherd's cabin had long surrendered to the earth. Barely adequate to provide shelter, it settled comfortably into the angles of the hillside. The hut, with its falling roof and broken beams, was reduced to a lean-to, while its foundation of rotting wood was decayed to mulch. The shack was an open invitation to the goats, who joined their keeper as he sought relief from inclement weather. Through the winters, they would huddle by the fire, bracing themselves against the howling wind that always managed to find its way inside, despite the many on-going repairs the previous summer. The goatherd no longer counted the years he had lived by the river. They had become no more significant than the days themselves.

As a watering hole for weary travelers and their stock, the goatherd's primitive homestead became the stopover for wagons and coaches on their way up the Santa Fe Trail. These caravans were carrying the hopefuls to their destinations, some no farther than Santa Fe, others on to California and Oregon. But here they rested, all in need of water, the precious commodity that determined every camp and settlement across the frontier.

The old man asked no questions of those who came to refresh themselves before crossing the river into Santa Fe. He simply offered his assistance to the freighters who stopped to unload cargo from a wagon to combine it with another in order to avoid an extra tax. He had learned every man has his story and it was not his business that many were on the wrong side of the law. This code of silence was an asset as important as the water itself.

***

The soldiers from Ft. Granger unsaddled and unbridled their mounts. Noisily slapping their horses' hindquarters, the men drove them into the three-sided corral. The river Rio Santa Fe formed the yard's northern border and the horses plunged their heads into the cold water and drank thirstily.

"You have as many good mounts then?" Lt. McGiver asked.

"I have anything you want," the goatherd answered confidently. "You say you only want my horses for a short time? All right, no problem. You come now and we'll see about la ropa de los Comancheros ... for you and your men."

He turned to lead them to his cabin, laughing huskily.

"Maybe you want some of my beans with cabrito and a little whiskey, huh?"

McGiver was prepared for his company to settle in for the night. The freighter from the ordnance department was expected sometime the next day, and his own arrangements had been made. Their civilian horses and clothing would provide the necessary cover in the morning. They would ride down the Santa Fe Trail to intercept the shipment of weapons and then deliver them to Tito.

Tito Sanchez had made it very clear that this time McGiver was the one to get his hands dirty and had given him a menacing warning if anything went wrong. Twice now the Comanchero had been cheated of his silver. So had McGiver, but his gambling debts were growing, and Tito was not a man to be crossed.

At their last meeting at the Comanchero's hideout, McGiver saw Tito crazed with alcohol. The half-breed had reverted to his Comanche superstitious ways and was talking wildly, incoherently about Laughing Coyote and his women who had run away. Tito had mumbled something about witches and death and even in anger there was a measure of fear in his eyes. McGiver had asked about Tito's half-brother, the goatherd, but the Comanchero became further enraged and so he did not pursue the subject.

The men entered the ramshackled cabin and shooed a nosy goat kid away from the wood stove and a curious smelling pot they suspected was their dinner. The goatherd brought down his jug from the cupboard, and a soldier took out a deck of cards and began shuffling.

***

A waning moon was just rising as Chano and Chuey, with the others behind them, came riding over the crest of the hill. Stretched out before them was the river, a shimmering ribbon of water that marked the boundary of the goatherd's homestead. The cabin was clearly visible, a glowing oil lantern in its only window. The voices of the soldiers carried in the night air, and the children heard their words alarmingly close and intelligible. There was no need for words between themselves, and they sat immovable on their steeds, waiting for Diego's orders.

Diego was seated on El Norte, and as Joaquin had predicted, the black stallion was quietly obedient under his charge.

"Now," Diego whispered to his friend.

Joaquin turned to pass the word down the line.

It was a distance from the cabin to the horses and Diego was reassured to see their plan would work. Slowly, he led them as they walked their horses directly to the corral, altogether bypassing the cabin.

In the light of the moon it was fairly easy to recognize the U.S. brand among the Comancheros' horses. The boys and Carlotta quickly cut the military stock from the herd. When they had bridled and saddled the soldiers' horses they opened the gate to run off the others. There was a soldier's horse for each child and his mount to lead, and they retreated quickly in the night.

Chano and Chuey were excellent horsemen, their bragging legitimate, thought Carlotta. Without a saddle or even a blanket, they leaped over the rump and on to their horses. Once they left the goatherd's camp and had escaped across the river, the children broke their silence. There were several open miles to Santa Fe, free range that harbored no threat, and they ran full out across the high desert, whooping and hollering, every bit as noisy as the coyotes had been several nights earlier.

Carlotta's hair whipped behind her and she laughed exuberantly as she, Joaquin, and Two Bears raced to catch up with the others. Ahead, the twins rode in one fluid motion, horses and boys blending as a team instead of one obedient to the other. Much like Diego and El Norte, Carlotta thought. Her admiration for Joaquin had increased when he bid Diego to ride his horse. There was something very grownup and appealing about his offer.

She realized they were one child short and turned to look for Jean Paul and saw a precarious silhouette laboring on the horizon. Lagging far behind, Jean Paul was bouncing in his saddle and tilting dangerously to one side. Signaling to Two Bears and Joaquin, Carlotta and the boys broke away to rescue the "scribbler," as they had come to call their friend.

Jean Paul and McGiver's log were inseparable as of late, and the boys had teased him about his compulsion to scrutinize and record every detail. "I think he'll work in one of Santa Fe's banks when he grows up," Joaquin had predicted. The others thought Jean Paul a bit odd, but good naturedly accepted his behavior because his preoccupation with this military record frequently proved beneficial to the group.

When the three reached Jean Paul, they saw he was engrossed, again, in McGiver's log and didn't seem a bit upset that the others had gone on ahead.

"Oh, I knew you'd be back. Because you don't really know where you're going, do you?"

Jean Paul's attitude was ridiculously confident, thought Carlotta, but then he leaned out from his horse even farther, almost falling, and poked his book under her nose.

"It's difficult in the dark, but see, there is a map of Santa Fe."

Carlotta drew the reins on her startled horse. Sure enough, she saw the dark lines indicating the roads of Santa Fe.

"You're right, Jean Paul! That's a map and it will be important when we get there," she said.

"Yeah, well, you're not going to get anywhere, if you don't get down and let me tighten the cinch on your saddle."

Joaquin had no sooner uttered his warning, and the children watched as Jean Paul and his saddle slipped to the right and circled under the horse's belly. Dropped the remaining couple of feet onto the crown of his head, Jean Paul crumpled in a pathetic heap.

The boy's even-tempered horse held his composure, and Carlotta quickly took the reins, while the others held their breath. Jean Paul groaned a little, but managed to get to his feet.

"Are you all right?" Two Bears asked.

"I ... guess so," he answered, rubbing his head.

Joaquin tightly re-cinched the saddle, and Two Bears boosted Jean Paul onto the back of his patient horse. They watched as the boy swayed slightly in the saddle.

"Here, let me take the reins of the horse you're leading," Two Bears said. "I can handle two. I don't know whether you can handle the one you're riding."

Diego and the twins were waiting on a hill, and Joaquin encouraged their group to hurry and catch up.

Sobered by Jean Paul's close call, the going was slower from there. But soon they could see the town of Santa Fe. Even in the dark they thought the town immense compared to their own San Ramon. Looking at the map, Carlotta conferred with Jean Paul and they decided it best to circle to the west and come down the street that led directly to the plaza.

It was risky, they agreed, but the fewer houses they would pass, the less chance of being seen. With their heads down in concentration, the children rode their mounts at an even walk, each leading a horse belonging to Lt. McGiver's company. Carlotta found she was willing the group's invisibility and was reminded of the lizard, the old sentry in the mission yard who went unnoticed because of his camouflage.

There was something else about the lizard's presence that actually prevented his detection. Carlotta wasn't quite sure what it was, but it reminded her of Miguel, her friend who watched life through dreamy eyes. Perhaps it was his will she felt. In any case, she felt wondrously protected and safe and thought the soft thuds of their horses' hooves would exist only in the woven pattern of the dreams of those who slept this night in Santa Fe.

CHAPTER 14

THE HARVEST

THE HARVEST

"Sir, some of your horses are over there."

The boy with the pale yellow hair was pointing down the road to the arena across from the governor's palace. As soon as he said it, he blushed and averted his eyes from the captain's stare. His manners forbade that he interrupt an adult's conversation, and he stared at the ground while he sought nerve to support his behavior.

The captain's orders to Sergeant Davis were complete, and he turned his attention to the young fellow in front of him.

"What was that, young man?" Captain Sedlow asked, good naturedly.

"The soldiers' horses, sir," the boy pleaded. "Look!"

Captain Sedlow couldn't detect anything clearly over fifty feet, but hadn't found it necessary to confess his deteriorating eyesight to anyone other than Mrs. Sedlow.

"Why don't you show me, son," he said.

At this mid-morning hour the sun was glaring' and Sedlow decided to indulge his aging body and the boy by taking a closer look. Together, they walked down the street of Santa Fe. Several passersby politely greeted the two, tipping a hat and offering a "Good morning." The captain, whose sandy mustache and hair bore a striking resemblance to the boy's coloring, was easily mistaken for the young man's grandfather and took pleasure in this uncharacteristic role.

Sedlow was in a cheerful mood as they drew closer to the center of town. Then he saw the horses. He was close enough now to recognize Lt. McGiver's favorite mount, a strong-muscled, dapple gray. There were six other horses in the arena with McGiver's, all bearing the brand of the United States Army. A notice of some kind fluttered from the hinge of the gate.

He had little time to marvel at this before an ox-driven supply wagon thundered around the corner, shaking the ground under his feet. Dirt flew from the team's hooves and giant wheels as women pulled their children out of its path and a dog, ears plastered against his head, yelped and ran for cover.

It was the expected munitions shipment and Sedlow was satisfied it had come in on schedule. What was not expected was Lt. McGiver with his men seated conspicuously on top of the high, canvas-covered wagonload.

***

Several days had passed and neither Carlotta nor the other children heard the consequences of their night ride. They knew Joaquin would be their link to gossip and had thought it better to wait for word from him rather than risk creating suspicion by asking questions in town. In their beds, after nightfall, they speculated on the repercussions of the raid.

"Do you suppose McGiver will be court-martialed?" Jean Paul asked. "Certainly, when a soldier has his horses stolen out from under him, he would be shot, wouldn't he?"

"I don't know, Jean Paul," said Diego, doubtfully. "Most likely they would want to shoot Laughing Coyote instead."

"But that was the whole idea, to discredit the lieutenant!" Jean Paul reminded him.

"Oh, I'm sure he'll lose some stripes and command, but remember, no one has learned what we know about him. There isn't anything we can do about that without revealing what Carlotta saw on the mesa or in the courtyard when Friar Alcazar met with Tito Sanchez."

Jean Paul fell silent, mulling over Diego's words.

"So the best we can hope is that they will kill each other?" he asked.

"It's a real possibility," Diego said. "Can you imagine how mad Tito must be? And if we're lucky, McGiver might think Tito Sanchez is Laughing Coyote!"

Carlotta had listened carefully to her brother's reasoning and realized that the issue left unstated was Friar Alcazar's power. It was he, not McGiver or Sanchez, who held their lives in his hands, and there wasn't anything they could do about it without jeopardizing all of the surviving children. Her young heart felt heavy with the burden of being the only witness ... a useless witness ... to the truth.

***

Summer days passed and the children's patience was finally rewarded. They were called to work frequently by the ranchers on the outskirts of town. The haciendados' crops were maturing and in need of regular weeding. In the casas and the fields, slaves and hired help talked about the notorious Laughing Coyote. A network of rumor flowed from hacienda to town, the stories of their folk hero embellished each time they were repeated.

Some of the townspeople secretly applauded Laughing Coyote's actions. They had viewed with suspicion the coming of the United States' military to the region, but fell short of boldly declaring their support for the renegade, lest they be accused of treason.

But the children did hear all about Laughing Coyote's daring ambush on McGiver's company. The rogue Indian and his small band, their numbers confirmed by their bold tracks that led to the arena, were now being sought by the military. Captain Sedlow had placed a bounty on Laughing Coyote's head after reading the scrawled note that flapped brazenly from the arena's post. It seemed everyone had memorized the words.

These horses should serve a better need
than carrying soldiers to their foul deed.
Lafing Coyote

Chuey found modesty almost impossible when he heard his own poem recounted by villagers and ranchers. The idea was awesome that the military would actually post a reward for the capture, dead or alive, of their fictitious character. The children waited to hear that the military had implicated Tito Sanchez, or even that Lt. McGiver was put on report, but weeks went by and the gossip faded. They could only hope the rumors were incomplete.

Summer was fading and the time was near for Two Bears to leave for the pueblo, as each year he returned to help with the harvest and left when the last snow melted. The Indian boy was carefully folding his few belongings into his bedroll when Father Serna stopped in the doorway to address him.

"Father Alcazar wishes to see you, my son."

Two Bears raised his head to see the lines of worry on the friar's pudgy face. The children looked from one to the other, alert and concerned for their friend's welfare.

For some time they waited quietly knowing the die was cast, and when Two Bears finally returned their fears were confirmed. "Alcazar has forbidden me to return to my people," Two Bears said in disbelief. "He told me it is for my protection ... because of the proclamation. What danger is there for me that is not my people's?"

Not one of the children could imagine an answer, and their silence revealed Two Bears' inevitable decision before he spoke again. "I must go," he said finally.

Carlotta carefully tied the piece of frayed rope around Two Bears' bedroll, ignoring the hot tears on her cheeks.

"I'm going to miss you terribly!" she said in a choked whisper.

Carlotta had expressed what they all felt. It was more than the fear they shared, it was the love of siblings. They could not change the circumstance of their lives, but it was the love of brothers and sisters that enabled them to bear it.

"You are my brother," said Diego defiantly.

"And mine," said Miguel.

Each child reached for the hand of the other and again renewed their strength, reinforcing each other's.

***

As Two Bears climbed the hill he looked back to see the sun receding rapidly in the west. Ahead were his people's fields where the sun had surrendered its life force to awakening plants. The crops stirred and came fully awake under the moon that rose quickly and fully. The corn reached heavenward, waiting expectantly for the caresses of the cool evening wind, and Two Bears watched as the ripening stalks danced joyously, announcing the wind's arrival. The fields flowed with their own undulating rhythm, at first intertwining with mother earth and then blending, becoming one. Two Bears felt the universal vibration course through his legs as the earth throbbed with one insistent and joyous pulse.

The early evening breeze flowed through the pumpkin patch, gently lifting the large frond-like leaves and tilting them upward, compelling the pumpkin patch to lift and fall as a single living, breathing force.

The lush green growth had sent oversized tendrils in all directions, anxious to claim as much ground as possible. Sensing its time on earth coming to a close, the long twirling vines withdrew their support from the spreading tendrils. Here the vine's energy of life had focused to feed the rapidly growing pumpkins.

Two Bears stooped to look beneath the huge leaves at a world that duplicated the lessons of the kiva. Incubated deep within the pumpkins were the seeds and the future. The seeds, which slept now, were in the winter of their life, and yet still gathered nourishment from all parts of the plant. The reality of an approaching autumn lay at Two Bears' feet in drying leaves and withering vines. And he knew that creator, one with all, would again plant the seeds for another spring, which would yield yet another summer. He stared long and hard at the evidence, the endless cycle, the proof that the future is in the process of becoming.

He was almost home, where he belonged. Two Bears left his people's field and began running swiftly. His legs stretched before him, his mind leaping ahead to those who had taught him the Great Mystery ... to his father and the Pumpkin Society.

***

The return of Two Bears had always been a happy event. The People thought of him as a fulfillment of their efforts, a harvest of Sak-mo-i-si's seed. They had learned not to begrudge the time the boy spent away at the mission. It was, after all, an investment in understanding the White Man. The Sun Watcher had offered his son, convinced that the future required their ability to learn.

A grateful people welcomed Two Bears home, but this time with more relief than joy. Sak-mo-i-si, Owl Woman, and the elders listened as Two Bears told them of his disobedience.

"My heart has always belonged here, my father. Please don't make me return," he pleaded.

The elders spoke of the proclamation and the troubled times ahead. They supported Two Bears' decision to return home, and cautioned Sak-mo-i-si not to insist on his leaving.

"It grieves me to hear that my son was forbidden to leave. I wonder if this priest of White Man's god considers us to be the enemy. It is not enough that we are told to war with our brothers the Navaho and the Apache. Alcazar teaches my son to put distance between himself and his people."

There was silence, and Sak-mo-i-si looked down on the woman who sat on his blanket, her shiny hair flowing freely on her shoulders. Owl Woman looked up, her lips forming a small smile of encouragement. She had tried to gently warn him, upon returning from delivering her herbs to the medicine man in San Ramon. Her trip to town was only partially fulfilled, as she had intended to see Two Bears. But Friar Alcazar had not allowed her visit. Sak-mo-i-si knew the message she had taken with her was one of great joy, and he had mistakenly thought her disappointment was the reason for her cynicism.

Before Sak-mo-i-si could tell Two Bears of his decision, or of his own marriage in his son's absence, a loud commotion was heard coming from the mesa's southeastern cliff. Children ran toward the elder's circle, excitedly announcing the arrival of the trader Tito Sanchez.

All of The People's present affairs were put aside as the Comanchero and his men, with their wagonload of goods to trade, were accompanied up the steep trail to the pueblo.

A raucous clamor interrupted the quiet on the mesa. Tito's wagon creaked and groaned under the weight of goods, its large wooden wheels straining at the axle. Sak-mo-i-si thought it was an improvement over Tito's ox cart that had labored on irregularly shaped wheels of cottonwood and bounced unruly over the trail.

Tito brought three men with him, all of whom jumped down from the high, laden wagon, eager to offer their goods. They began unloading several butchered goats first, and The People assisted the men in taking the carcasses of chivo to the homes where the meat would be divided among the families and then cooked or hung to be dried. Once the perishable meat was distributed, the men unloaded bolts of cloth and iron pots. Women and young girls who were not involved with the cooking, eagerly pored over the colorful goods and useful items.

Fresh meat was a rarity, and in due time each family would pour out a fair amount of cornmeal into Tito's bag as payment. Onions, squash, melons, and beans might bring a handsome buffalo robe from a Plains tribe, or tanned leather from the Navaho. Their hardy bread made from corn or the bright pumpkins just coming from the fields would be fair exchange for a good knife, a string of beads, or a turquoise stone.

There was a smile on everyone's face as they happily saw to their tasks. There would be no hurry to finalize these trades, as this was a time of relaxed satisfaction. The first harvests were arriving and besides having enough to eat, they had more to offer in trade. The People would savor this time of abundance, knowing the harsher times were always ahead. This acceptance, on the Indians' part, marked the traders' unhurried stay within the pueblo.

Tito Sanchez was no different, and had planned, as usual, that he and his men would join The People's fires that night before retiring to their own camp on the desert floor at the foot of the pueblo.

Two Bears hung back as he watched his father and his new wife Owl Woman approach the wagon with the others. The news he had just heard stunned him and he needed time alone to think.

They had not waited for his return and this upset him in a way he could not identify. Two Bears thought about his feelings and became even more confused. He loved and respected his father, the tribe's Sun Watcher - a fair and wise man. And he knew of his own indebtedness to Owl Woman, the Tuhikya, the one who saved his life. Hadn't he spoken of her to Carlotta as the replacement for the mother who died when he was born? Was he jealous of their happiness? Or did he now feel like an outsider, no longer a part of his own people?

He stood leaning against a wall, immersed in these thoughts, when his eyes fell on Tito Sanchez. Little distinguished the Comanchero's dark, leathery skin from his dirt-covered clothes. A drooping, scurrilous moustache hung over his cowhide vest and the trader's swaggering movements suggested he had been drinking. Two Bears viewed this murderer of children ... his friends ... and felt sickened with confusion. Was nothing as it seemed?

Two of his girl cousins sat down on the wall beside him, begging his attention.

"Why didn't you bring the white girl back with you?" the younger sister asked.

"Carlotta is her name," the older sister corrected.

Feeling his vision blur, Two Bears stumbled forward, searching for the stairway to his home.

***

Sak-mo-i-si allowed the trading to go on uninterrupted throughout the afternoon. He had no proof that Tito Sanchez' band was part of the massacre on Blue Mesa, and so he remained watchful knowing the importance of the trades. The Comanchero was drunk and appeared harmless. In fact, Sak-mo-i-si found pity for the man who was not a man and wondered if coyote was dogging his heels. The Comanchero had surrendered his pride and his soul, and frequently tilted the bottle to his lips, foolishly seeking his true identity in the whiskey.

The afternoon came and fires roared in front of several homes. The sweet, smoky fragrance of cooking meat filled the air and The People who had not enjoyed meat in some time found their mouths watering. Women attended to the preparations while their children, never quite out of sight, remained alert for the announcement that the enticing meal was ready to eat.

It was the elders, the old men and women who spent the heat of the day in the shade of the eastern walls, who first saw the friar advancing up the trail. Sak-mo-i-si looked up from the fine Navaho blanket that he was admiring and Owl Woman saw his countenance darken.

Friar Alcazar's malevolent figure sat erect on the back of his horse, another tethered behind him. The travelers rode over the cliff's rise at a constant pace and onto the mesa. The People, one by one, rose to watch the arrival of the unwanted visitor. It had been a while since the friar had made known the Church's presence and The People's activities suddenly turned somber.

Alcazar slowly rode across the plaza, cutting between the throng of people who had now forsaken their bartering to follow the horses. He proceeded to where Sak-mo-i-si and Owl

Woman stood, drawing up the reins of his horse. The friar's face was set in harsh, determined lines, and his black eyes blazed from under the brim of his dark leather hat. Without a greeting, the priest stated the reason for his visit.

"I have come for your son, Sak-mo-i-si. It is not safe for him to be here and I insist that he return to the mission with me."

His message was addressed to Sak-mo-i-si, but he scrutinized the woman beside him. Alcazar recognized the significance and his eyes betrayed his growing anger.

"Two Bears will not be returning to the mission," Sak-mo-i-si said, his voice devoid of any emotion.

"I see," said Alcazar. "This woman ... this witch ... has a powerful influence on you!"

The accusation was delivered in biting, clipped words.

"You are aware that she has been seen in town with her witch's coven ... her sisters?"

Sak-mo-i-si's face remained placid, except for a taut line drawn over his jaw. His bronzed neck fluttered with his life's pulse, as he struggled to bring anger under control. Owl Woman watched her husband. She was not afraid for him, but was as still and alert as the night bird for which she was named.

When Sak-mo-i-si made no reply, the friar's gaze darted to the plaza, where Tito Sanchez and his Comancheros were leaning against a wagon. They appeared to be only mildly interested in the confrontation, more anxious to return to their barter.

The friar's head snapped back to the man and woman before him.

"There is my proof!" he said, pointing to Sanchez. "This unlicensed trader, what is he doing here? Did I not warn you that you must cease trade with the warring tribes? From here I can see he has brought blankets and leather from the Navahos and Apache.

"And what has he brought for your woman, here? Magic potions from her sisters? Perhaps she has used them on you, si?" A cruel smile lifted the corners of his mouth, transforming Alcazar's face into a grotesque mask.

Owl Woman replied, "It was I who took medicine to the doctor in San Ramon, and to my sisters."

Sak-mo-i-si lifted his hand to still her explanation.

"We have done no harm here," he said.

A loud boisterous laugh spilled across the plaza. Tito Sanchez pushed himself away from the wagon and walked nonchalantly over to the friar. He looked up at the priest with contempt, openly conveying the full meaning of his irreverence.

"The squaw and the Sun Watcher tell the truth, eh Padre? They could not be responsible for the cruel deeds the governor has posted!"

Tito's last statement was said with great fanfare, and Sak-mo-i-si listened curiously.

Several minutes went by without a word from the priest, and Owl Woman and Sak-mo-i-si watched Alcazar unconsciously bite into his lip, a drop of blood showing at the corner of his mouth. The friar, too, was seeking control, but found no peace. Alcazar pulled on the horse's reins and dug his spurs into the poor animal's flanks, finding one at least who would be obedient to his rule.

The People watched the friar depart across the plaza, knowing there was no victory in his retreat. Only Two Bears felt an immediate surge of relief and watched attentively as Alcazar drew closer to the Comanchero's wagon. For a moment the friar hesitated and reached out to run his long fingers across the smooth wood of the handsome rig.

Two Bears felt his breath catch in his throat. He had not recognized, until now, the wagon belonging to Luis Valenzuela. High on the driver's seat, the wood was marked with red paint; the same paint that had stained his trousers on the night he and his friends had replaced the wagon's cargo with rocks.

Two Bears wanted to run. Like a rabbit blinded in a lantern's light, he felt the panic of his own impending fate, and his thoughts lashed out at the woman who had made all things different, the woman who had cast her magic on his father - Owl Woman.

***

CHAPTER 15

THE POWAQAS SPELL

THE POWAQAS SPELL

The sun had journeyed midpoint across the pueblo when Tito Sanchez and his men finally stirred from camp. Inexplicably, they weren't asked to join the Indians at the evening fire as they had expected. There was no drumming or dancing, almost as if The People, generally warm and hospitable, found no reason to celebrate. And so the Comancheros returned to the desert below, where they made their own revelry with the aid of Tito's whiskey.

***

Red-eyed and rumpled from a night of drinking, the scruffy traders groggily broke camp. They were satisfied that their trading had gone well. The harvest was good this year, and the Valenzuela wagon rolled along the road to the Comanchero hideout with its precariously laden burden of colorful melons, pumpkins, and squash.

It was nightfall when they entered the narrow pass into the valley, and Tito willingly gave rein to the team of horses, who hastened their way back to familiar grazing land. Above his head the stars multiplied as the sun deserted the heavens, and Tito heard the first lonely call of the coyote.

The animal was close enough to startle the horses and Tito regained control of the team by yanking on the reins. The first two horses tried to rise on their back legs. Finding the piece of iron biting painfully into their mouths, they bolted for freedom. Veering to the left, away from the bold coyote, the wagon tipped at an unstable angle. Tito reached out to catch the pumpkin rolling toward the edge, knowing if one fell they would all tumble. For a moment Tito was caught in suspension, as if fate wasn't entirely convinced of its role, and then centrifugal force slung the half-breed off the wagon seat and deposited him on the hard ground.

The wagon tore ahead, unmindful of the Comancheros who raced after it. Tito watched the eerie blue mirage as it grew distant and finally disappeared. Alone in the dust of the road,

Tito turned his attention to the cold night that was as quiet as death. A hideous laugh pierced the silence, and Tito yelped in alarm. The coyote was directly in front of him, unafraid and very large. "Vamonos!" he yelled, grabbing his hat and whacking the dirt in front of him with it.

The coyote did not move, but laughed again - a horrendous sound, mocking and personal, Tito thought. Frightened beyond reason, Tito scrambled to his feet shuffling backward as he did so. He had to put distance between himself and the animal whose saliva hung from his jaws in foaming strands.

"Did you enjoy the rocks?" asked coyote, his voice gurgling like those of people Tito had watched struggle to speak just before they died.

Tito fell back on the earth, terrified and unable, this time, to get up.

Coyote lifted his head and laughed again, knowingly.

"You've forgotten," coyote said, disappointed. "The rocks I gave you for the silver?"

The wild dog's eyes, a vacant luminous glow and absence of soul, drove Tito's mind to the brink of an imagined precipice.

"I saved one stone, though," said coyote, slyly lapping at his spittle. His vacant eyes burned red as he continued. "And I threw it in the water. Would you like to see if it sank? Come with me and we'll look over the edge ... and we will see if you will die."

Coyote's hideous long face, with its protruding foolish ears, actually smiled at Tito. The Comanchero screamed in wild terror, and wheeling in the direction of the horses' escape, ran madly down the road in hopes of joining them.

***

The United States Cavalry was in need of good enlisted men, but the low pay and hard work, under the most extreme circumstances, was a deterrent to men who would make the soldier's life their career. John McGiver had been one of those who persevered under hardships on the frontier, following orders without question and demanding the same of those under his command. Because these attributes served the army well, he had moved quickly up the ranks. Thus far he had managed to keep his ambitions hidden from his superior officers, his personal vices in check; the other side to Lt. McGiver that served only him.

Those who carried the terrible secret that could lay to waste the lieutenant's career, were powerless to do so without jeopardizing themselves. Friar Alcazar, Tito Sanchez, and McGiver's own troopers, all accomplices in the incident on Blue Mesa were silent conhorts. McGiver had learned the advantages and the limitations of implication. On one hand his story could always be corroborated by his associates, but on the other hand, there was the worrisome fact that he could be found guilty by association.

It had never occurred to McGiver that his military career might be imperiled because of something as stupid as the theft of his company's horses. He considered the care of army horses, pack mules, and issued weapons a soldier's chief responsibility. His humiliation was almost forgotten now, but not the irony that it was in an area that had almost cost him his command, despite his conscientious efforts.

Capt. Sedlow's wrath, directed toward the lieutenant and displayed in front of the citizens of Santa Fe, was just a fading memory as fall came to the Sangre de Cristo Mountains. The advancing season turned the sycamore leaves dark gold and rust, just as it muted the reality of the past, and McGiver felt the sting of his embarrassment diminish and mercifully lose some of its intensity. What remained, and had begun to eat as worms on the decaying remnants of last summer's memory, was the vision of Laughing Coyote's taunting note dangling from the arena's gate. Here was a mockery meant for him alone, and of all his enemies, one in particular rose to haunt McGiver.

As time went by, the lieutenant became more certain that Tito Sanchez was Laughing Coyote, and he set about to plan his revenge on the Comanchero. The officer called on all the tact necessary during a campaign. Biding his time, he studied his enemy's strengths and weaknesses. In late October he thought he was finally rewarded as a situation presented itself.

McGiver was pleased that good weather had prevailed, allowing for early completion of his mapping expedition in the Jemez Mountains. In a celebratory mood, he and his men stopped at the saloon in San Ramon for a drink before continuing east to Fort Granger. They took a table in the corner of the room, out of the way of regulars at the bar and gamblers sitting at game tables in deep concentration.

McGiver was determined to refrain from gambling, the obvious reason for the deplorable risks he had taken with his career. He was cold sober that afternoon when he glanced up from his glass to see the two Indian witches enter through the saloon's swinging doors. The witches paused and nervously searched the room. When their black eyes settled on McGiver and his men, they self-consciously approached his table.

"What can I do for you?" McGiver asked half annoyed.

He was certain the girls were going to try and hawk their potions, and was surprised when they relayed their tale of fear.

"We are here to beg the help of soldiers," said the older girl, peering anxiously from beneath her lowered brow.

She hesitated a moment, looking again across the room in the direction of the door. The younger girl clutched her sister's skirt, as if to deny her escape unless she fled with her.

"And why would you need the help of the United States Army?" asked McGiver, sarcastically. The men at the table snickered, openly confident in their superiority.

"Tito Sanchez is going to kill us," she said, unmistakably. "The Comanchero is loco ... and is looking for us ... to make dead."

McGiver laughed. "Whatever did you do to the poor man ... for him to make you dead?"

His men laughed out loud.

The two girls were silent, obviously reluctant to go on.

"Come on, you can tell me," McGiver encouraged.

"He says that we cast a spell on him, and that Laughing Coyote is going to kill him."

"You can ask the doctor," said the younger sister. "Tito was looking for us at the doctor's!"

"All right," he conceded. "I'll look for the trader and see what I can do. In the meantime, both of you go to your rooms upstairs and bar the door."

All of the conclusions Lt. John McGiver had reached regarding Tito Sanchez were in question, once again. This was a curious development and he wasn't sure what to make of it. McGiver had looked into the eyes of the Indian girls noting their fear. Had Tito's affinity for Taos lightning been his final undoing? Could he be losing his mind? The lieutenant knew he wouldn't find the answers sitting in the saloon and decided to pay Dr. Gentry a visit.

***

"That's right, the trader Sanchez was here ... looking for the Indian girls," said the doctor. "And by the look in his eye, I could tell he wasn't up to any good. So I told him they weren't in town. Didn't need to start up any more trouble. Fortunately, he believed me ... and rode out the way he came."

Gentry walked over to the window and yanked the curtains closed.

"Damn sunlight! It's blinding this time of the afternoon."

The doctor returned to his chair, rubbing his chin thoughtfully. Lt. McGiver waited patiently, his eyes following the young girl who was cleaning the doctor's office. She was standing on a stool, reaching with a feather duster the large volumes on the bookcase, seemingly unaware of their presence.

"That man is a scary one!" the doctor continued. "But, you know ... I didn't smell any liquor on him."

That was apparently all the doctor had to say, and McGiver rose from his chair, thanking him for his time.

The lieutenant removed his hat from the rack by the door and as he placed it on his head asked, "Did he say anything else that you remember?"

"Well ... yes, come to think of it. He wasn't coherent, mind you. But he mumbled something about that confounded Laughing Coyote and the Church. A strange combination, don't you think?"

McGiver acknowledged that it was and said good day.

The lieutenant stepped into the street and felt the warmth of the autumn sun. Down the road the mission's walls glowed pink and gold against the western sky. He thought about Tito's reference to the Church. What did it have to do with Laughing Coyote? It wouldn't hurt to question Friar Alcazar. Tito's sanity was as much a threat to the friar as himself. Perhaps he would learn something there.

***

The sun, following a low southern path across the sky, entered the open doorway of the church and stretched languidly across the adobe floor. Its light, only a filtered, vague memory of last summer's intensity, fell on the empty crude benches assigned the villagers, and ended abruptly before three carved pews belonging to San Ramon's gentility. Alcazar felt a shiver in the church's dark, cold recesses as he smoothed the gold-embroidered mantle on the altar. The shudder, which involuntarily flowed through the friar's body, was caused not so much by autumn's chill as by the parishioner who had just departed.

At first the friar had not noticed the dark figure kneeling at the bench with the sunlight at his back, as he had just entered the church from the vestibule and was preoccupied with the preparations for evening mass. When Alcazar did become aware, he paid no mind to the eclipsed face shrouded in common clothing. The man was deep in prayer and obviously content to be alone. Although his physical presence was obscure, his prayers were not. In the tomblike stillness of the adobe walls, the voice of the anonymous parishioner called out his repentance in one soulful outburst.

"I vow to return the chalices, mi Dios, but I beg you, remove the Powaqas curse and send the sick dog away!"

The voice was distorted with emotion, a full octave above its normal range, but Alcazar thought it vaguely familiar. He looked up to see the man grovel, his back bent and head almost touching the floor in supplication. And then the dark figure rose, meekly bowing as it retreated hurriedly from the church.

Alcazar stood still, the lingering memory of the man causing his skin to crawl. When at last the friar had attended to his duties and stepped down from the altar and into the sunlight, there was a new visitor standing in the open doorway.

McGiver entered, hat in hand, awkward with the strange formality of the unfamiliar. "We have to talk," he said.

Before McGiver told him of the reason for his visit, Alcazar understood. The peon who begged before the altar was ... as incredulous as it seemed ... Tito Sanchez.

The friar directed the lieutenant into his rectory rather than risk another visitor, and was amused to see McGiver's confidence instantly improve. He recalled the burial on Blue

Mesa and thought McGiver more vulnerable to matters of the Church than the young lieutenant would care to admit.

Lt. McGiver stared at Friar Alcazar. The friar's slight smile was disconcerting, but he asked his questions, knowing both of their futures hung in the balance.

"Tito has threatened the witches from the pueblo. Doc Gentry thought he might have come here. Have you seen him?"

Alcazar felt a convenient gaffe in McGiver's words. He had preceded his question with information, which inadvertently gave the friar opportunity to better prepare his answer.

"And why would the unfaithful come to the Lord's house?" Alcazar asked with righteous anger.

"I don't know," answered McGiver, "but there is some question about his sanity ... and that might be trouble for both of us."

McGiver wasn't about to be put on the defensive again.

"Tito Sanchez has always been a superstitious man ... appealing to the black arts and the devil's ways. If he has threatened the witches it is because he has made a pact with the devil! The trouble is not mine, or even yours. It is his!"

The lieutenant watched the friar disengage himself from Tito's plight, as skillfully as he had removed himself from the Blue Mesa affair. And why not, he thought. Perhaps it was time he did the same. If Tito was crazy, he should put distance between himself and the trader.

"Well, all right then," he answered, somewhat consoled. "We'll let this Laughing Coyote take care of him."

McGiver laughed, relieved in discovering the solution had been there all the time, but Alcazar's face had turned to stone. McGiver encouraged him to see the humor in their situation.

"Tito has accused the witches of putting 'Laughing Coyote' on his trail. They claim Coyote is going to kill him!"

***

Tito had managed, with the utmost effort, to function as best his fragile mind would allow. He left the church in San Ramon concerned for his life and even more fearful for his soul. Crossing himself every few moments, he felt the deep, inexpressible sorrow of one who has not been forgiven.

Mounting his horse, Tito left the village intent on discovering his own redemption, but his ability to concentrate was disrupted with frequent waves of panic and he fought the extreme anxiety that washed away all reason. He labored to focus on a practical solution to the curse placed on him by the Powaqas, but each time the incongruity of this thought brought him closer to the edge.

The coyote was the Powaqas' doing. Tito knew the witches had conjured coyote to haunt him as their implement of revenge. To undo the curse ... to find a way to placate the Indian sisters ... these were Tito's prayers, but beneath the surface lay the hapless knowledge of his own incorrigible evil. He relived the scenes, the Indian sisters cowering before his open fist, and the haunting memory of children falling like broken flowers under thundering hooves. But then his mind retreated to an earlier time, to the place by the spring where he found the Indian girls living, unaccountably, without shelter.

The girls had paid twice for their survival. The first time had been their banishment from the tribe for stealing the silver chalices, and the second when they turned them over to Tito. And he knew the chalices had changed hands before that, for they were clearly vessels of the church. It was God to whom he owed repentance. Tito's mind clasped onto this thought, and his own salvation. He would return the silver chalices to the church and buy back his soul. It was evening when Tito's hard ride returned him to the valley of the Comancheros. He released his lathered, weary horse and immediately saddled a fresh mount. It never occurred to him that he, too, was exhausted. There would be no rest or escape from the vision of the hideous coyote, not until he had kept his promise. A man possessed by demons, Tito gathered up the bundle of silver, long coveted, beneath the rickety floor boards of his cabin. Mounting his horse, he returned to the entrance of the valley.

Tito headed west, traveling north of the pueblo and Blue Mesa and the old trail where coyote had confronted him. He spurred his horse on to breakneck speed, hoping that he could outrun time itself. Certainly an apparition would first claim his body in order to overwhelm his mind, Tito thought, and so he urged his horse to race across the high prairie, willing his escape from destiny.

Hours passed and the night grew black and thick, filling Tito with dread. From across the hills Tito felt, or heard ... he wasn't certain which ... a drumming beat that seemed to feed the earth its life. It echoed, surrounding the rider and his horse with pulsating waves of blue. The Comanchero disregarded his perceptions, verification of senses he could no longer trust, and fled the known path in hopes of eluding coyote.

For some time Tito rode west thinking he had escaped. Frequently, he looked over his shoulder and was relieved to see his phantom fading in the distance. He could return to the trail to San Ramon when he reached the Rio del Norte. The river had come alive this time of year, its roily waters spilling through gorges and canyons, filling its banks with late summer rains. Ordinarily, travelers would be warned of danger by the steady roar as they drew closer to the impassable chasm, but this night, one lone rider was caught in his own fearful world, oblivious to the danger that lay ahead.

And then, in spite of Tito's denial of his fears, he heard the coyote's laughter. It grew louder, overpowering his senses with a barrage of sound. His body turned cold and clammy in the night wind. The horse, too, was spooked by the voice of the unearthly coyote and struggled to throw his imaginary demon. Rather than risk being thrown, Tito dismounted, clutching the bundle that meant his salvation.

"Is that for me?" asked coyote.

"Aiyeee!" Tito screamed.

He jumped back from the slobbering animal, whose sudden presence was incomprehensible.

"Give the silver to me," coyote urged, his voice as smooth as silk, "and I will give you this last stone."

Tito gazed into the vacuous eyes of the dog, bereft of soul. He watched the animal's sly, beseeching gestures and knew that, if he were to obey, this would be his final undoing. The exchange would be death ... the silver chalices for his own death.

Holding tight to the silver, he turned on his heels and fled into the night. Running blind with terror, he never again looked over his shoulder and was oblivious to what lay ahead. Tito's last leap from earth propelled his body into an arch over the river, his legs and arms thrashing to no avail. He plummeted into the river, and coyote's laughter fell on him like a shroud.

***

Cuenta had set a vase of red and gold leaves in the center of the table, and Luis wistfully realized that fall was here and another year almost gone. He pulled out the chair and Rebecca gracefully swooped her skirts aside and took the seat to his right.

"It has been some time, Governor ... since the ball, I believe," Luis said.

Luis Valenzuela acknowledged his detachment from Santa Fe's society without apology. His guests were here tonight, not for the social occasion they supposed, but because of his own troubled mind.

"Well, I know you're a busy man, Luis, but the doctor here has said you haven't been seen even in San Ramon!"

Governor Maxwell sat back in the chair Luis had offered and smiled magnanimously.

Rebecca noticed Luis seemed unaware of her uncle's remarks. The governor and Dr. Gentry were silent, the graciousness at the Valenzuela table turning slightly awkward with their host's absent-mindedness.

"Tell me, Luis, did your housekeeper ... Cuenta, isn't that her name ... get married this summer?" Rebecca asked, changing the subject.

Rebecca's chestnut hair fell in soft tendrils on her white shoulders and dark green gown. Her beauty, and her sincere bright eyes, brought Luis back and reminded him of his duties as host.

"Pardona me," he said. "Yes, Cuenta and Pedro are married, at last."

Luis looked around the table at the small gathering. There were only his three guests, the governor, Rebecca, and Dr. Gentry, as he had instructed Joaquin to eat in the cocina this evening. An informal group he must place at ease, in order to learn the answers to his questions. Deliberately, Luis picked up the silver knife at the edge of his plate and laid it across his fork as an invitation to his guests to speak openly about affairs of the Church.

Cuenta entered the dining room with a tureen of steaming soup, and there was a discreet silence while she ladled the broth into their bowls. When she withdrew, Luis continued.

"There was a small wedding in our chapel the week after my dinner party, and Friar Alcazar conceded to hear their vows.

"But tell me, Gentry, that recent business in town is much more newsworthy. I understand you were at the church when they brought in the body of the Comanchero."

Luis picked up the linen napkin and smoothed it in his lap. The skilled direction of his conversation did not go unnoticed, and Rebecca looked up, her eyes locking with those of her host.

"It was a strange affair," said the doctor.

"Tito Sanchez had come to me looking for Owl Woman's sisters and when he didn't find them at my office he went over to the mission. I decided the next day to talk with the friar about it, and Alcazar admitted that Tito had come to the church begging the mercy of Jesus, Mother Mary, and the Holy Ghost. He was frightened of the Powaqas and swore that their spell had put Laughing Coyote on to him.

"It was while I was there ... while Alcazar was telling me of the trader's involvement with witchcraft ... that the rancher brought in Tito."

Gentry shook his head sadly. "It was a ghastly sight," he said, unwilling to recall the scene at the dinner table.

"The friar was terribly upset. Angry, actually. He discovered Tito had the holy relics from the church. It appears he recognized, from stories told at the abbey, that these were silver pieces stolen by the Indians during the revolt.

"I listened while he went on about those 'savages.' Years ago, he said, the Indians allowed the priests into their pueblo, took their gifts, and pretended to accept religious instruction, all the while harboring their heathen beliefs and worshipping their idols in hiding.

"One day, while the priest was giving mass at the pueblo, he said the savages turned on his holiness and threw him from the pueblo's cliffs to his death. His body was never found and neither were the silver chalices.

"Well now, he claimed, he had the proof! Apparently, Alcazar had gone to the pueblo to fetch a runaway child when he discovered Tito trading illegally with the tribe. He said Tito had obviously traded for the stolen booty, the silver."

"That certainly makes sense," agreed Governor Maxwell.

Luis wasn't all that certain, but felt no closer to the truth.

"Governor, did you bring the note Laughing Coyote left on the arena's gate?" asked Luis.

"Why, yes, I did," answered the governor.

John Maxwell fumbled through the pockets of his vest searching for the piece of paper. Finding it, he handed it to Luis.

Luis unfolded the note and stared at the signature's misspelling.

"I would say that's enough proof, wouldn't you?" asked Maxwell. "Our Laughing Coyote is an uneducated red man. He probably never hesitated to victimize even those with whom he traded!"

"Oh Uncle, you don't mean that!" Rebecca was aghast at this circumstantial indictment.

Dr. Gentry interrupted. "I believe it was reported a Mexican burned out the Fletchers. So, do we really know?"

"We can be assured," answered Maxwell, "that Friar Alcazar was correct when he said that other Indians beside the Jicarilla are a danger to the settlements."

"Excuse me, Governor. Who made the initial suggestion that led to the proclamation?" Luis was following a hunch, a feeling he had previously not allowed himself to explore.

"Why ... the good friar, of course. He's in position to know, having worked so long to help the Indians."

"But, Uncle, that's the same kind of thinking that caused the witch hunts back in Salem!" Rebecca protested.

"Hmmm. It's strange that you should say that, my dear," said the doctor. "Alcazar said that witches had been hung in Santa Fe in the past ... and could be again."

Rebecca's eyes flashed alarm and she looked to Luis for support.

But Luis thought it too soon to state his beliefs, recognizing the scope of danger to be larger than he had first believed.

They had finished dinner and retired to the library and the stone fireplace with its crackling fire when Dr. Gentry added to his story.

"It was interesting ... the condition of Tito's body. I would have thought he drowned, having been pulled from the Rio del

Norte. But his body was ravaged with rents and tears. I've only witnessed those kinds of wounds from an animal mauling."

The doctor was silent and the others, too, tried to imagine the horror.

"It could have been wild dogs. Yes, it was probably coyotes," he said.

***

CHAPTER 16

EL IDOLO

EL IDOLO

The cottonwoods were bare, their delicate frame of branches strangely familiar to Virginia. She sat on the wall beside Carlotta, neither girl conscious of the cold wind whipping about their naked legs. Carlotta had told the tale again about the Kachinas, the magical spirit-people she had seen dance on the pueblo's mesa. Both girls were caught in the dream world Carlotta was able to envision, one of color, the warmth of summer, and nurturing love. Neither child felt winter advance with its need to purge and cleanse, a process of renewal that indiscriminately made victims of all life.

They had wished their thoughts away from fear, and sought the niche in the decaying sandstone wall where they could live the freedom of their dreams. This unspoken truth bonded the two girls. Their need to communicate was pushed beyond Carlotta's chatter ... beyond the scene she set before her friend. Like children everywhere, they imagined ... thereby invented ... their own measures for survival. In Virginia's mute world lay the means. Carlotta said the words that inspired, and Virginia intuitively coaxed her into the place where they were real.

The girls left behind the specters that haunted the people of San Ramon, the tales told at the mercantile's counter, and the solemn conversations in the cantina. The stories of Tito Sanchez' death had reached everyone's ears, from the old men who slept through the afternoons sitting in the sun, to the town's young mothers who walked hurriedly through town, clasping tight their children's hands while suspiciously eyeing the dogs lying beside the road.

The villagers were familiar with death. Life was hard and the frontier took its toll, but the sight of the body brought in on the rancher's wagon caused the strongest to have nightmares. It was not just the evidence of gnawing, which everyone supposed was the result of a pack of coyotes, but also Tito's face that was still recognizable though frozen in a perpetual scream of terror.

Laughing Coyote was no longer just a rumor altering with each description. He had become more than a renegade Indian and perhaps even more than man. Against all logic, Laughing Coyote was just that ... a beast who dared to flaunt his evil, leaving as evidence a mauled victim and hideous laughter echoing across the hills.

As winter approached, the superstitious and afraid townspeople sought refuge in their church, while Friar Alcazar and Friar Serna found the pews and benches filled at every mass. But for the children of the mission there was no comfort in the church, for the beast lived within their adobe walls.

Virginia encouraged Carlotta, her eagerness burning through deep blue eyes. Now was the time. The corridor was empty, everyone about their business or chores. Carlotta reached behind the wall, as she had done so often in companionship with her friend, to the secret place where her Kachina doll was hidden. She withdrew the bundle and carefully unfolded Diego's shirt. A spider ran across the sleeve and over the wall, searching for asylum elsewhere.

The girls gazed in quiet admiration at the Kachina, the beautiful little wooden figure cushioned in soft feathers. Virginia remembered other real-life figures, similarly dressed with feathers and painted bodies. Men who wore elaborate wooden headdresses that floated above their heads like the branches of the cottonwoods, as they danced around a fire in the night.

"Gan," she said.

Carlotta looked sharply at her friend.

"Gan. Yes. Did you have a doll like this?" Carlotta asked.

"No," Virginia answered. "Th .. they ... were...The People."

"The People?"

Carlotta had forgotten the miracle of Virginia's voice, her attention fixed instead on her words.

"Have you been to the pueblo to see The People?"

Virginia, too, was unaware, as memories of her forgotten past begged to be examined.

"No," she said. "I lived with the ones they call the enemy ... the Apache. They ... called themselves ... The People."

Virginia's mouth turned upward in a knowing smile.

Carlotta laughed and Virginia joined her, a delightful bell-like sound that rang down the corridor.

"The People are everywhere, I guess!" Carlotta said.

Into the cloister, a heavy wooden door creaked open and Friar Alcazar entered, towering over them.

The girls jumped with fright, too alarmed to hide the doll.

"What have we here! Have you nothing else to do, but ..." said the friar, scowling.

Alcazar's eyes looked at the Kachina lying in Carlotta's lap. He did not see its beauty. He saw only *el idolo*, just one of many worshipped by the savages. He saw his word disobeyed, and he felt his power slip from his control.

Angrily, he reached out for the little figure and threw it to the ground. Shards of wood flew as the doll hit the adobe tile. Carlotta and Virginia watched, paralyzed, as small feather crescents floated downward slowly to join the remains of the broken gift.

"Thou shalt hold no other gods before me!" thundered Alcazar.

Ignoring the mute child Virginia, Alcazar directed his wrath at Carlotta.

"You are forbidden contact with the pueblo and the Indians! It is providence that Two Bears has gone back to his heathen tribe, because I will no longer tolerate any contact with Owl Woman and her sister witches! I can see that their influence has jeopardized your soul, child. Your Uncle, ... your benefactor, expects you and your brother to be raised in the Church."

Alcazar saw the shock on Carlotta's face, but misunderstood the reason.

"You have strayed from the Church, Carlotta. Go and kneel at the altar in your room. Pray to the Virgin Mary for forgiveness ... and understanding."

The girls fled down the corridor, their bodies shivering in absolute recognition of winter's arrival.

***

As he left the cloister for the rectory, Alcazar's anger followed him like an unwanted companion. He reasoned, reminding himself that the proclamation was working to his advantage and the Indians were under his control.

Certainly, the Church had fared well lately. Tito's death and the circumstances surrounding it had brought the people back to the Church. The fear of witchcraft pricked the consciences of the villagers, revealing their discomfort with their own evil inclinations. Alcazar remembered his discovery during his years at the abbey ... that good required evil by way of contrast ... the dichotomy of the fallen angel. Tito Sanchez' death had ultimately served the Church, and Alcazar knew he should grant absolution to his parishioners, dispensing generously the Church's forgiveness.

But this time his own instincts betrayed him and Alcazar was bothered, even haunted, by Tito's death. The confidence with which he had told the doctor about the history of the stolen chalices belied his horror when he saw the condition of Tito's body. Just as Tito feared, he had been attacked by a "sick dog", and his vow to return the chalices had not earned God's mercy. The similarity between the "sick dog" and Laughing Coyote was unsettling. For the first time in the friar's life he felt vulnerable in the area in which he had always known strength ... moral superiority. It was not the logic of his mind that told him so, but the irrational fear deep within his heart. Alcazar found his anger unreasonably give way to this fear and recognized he had more in common with his parishioners than he dared believe.

The Kachina doll was not a threat, he told himself. But there was something else, a larger threat. Though Alcazar had thundered the word and the wrath of God, he felt more removed from Him than the child felt from the Kachina that he had destroyed. It was the shock of witnessing the child's intimacy ... her embrace of this false idol, which had gauged his own distance from God.

***

The afternoon's sun brought little warmth and the cold white light flowing through the room's high windows fell cheerlessly upon the girls. Virginia sat on her cot, hands resting in her lap, and watched her friend pray before the small statue of the Virgin Mary. The unstated emptiness within their hearts gave little hope for understanding.

Carlotta tried hard to focus her thoughts on God ... the God who jealously wanted her complete, undivided devotion. She repeated, methodically, the prayers she had learned. Reciting the words over and over, she hoped to act as God expected.

Even in Carlotta's great desire to sacrifice her own will to that of God's, the dream of the pueblo would not leave the edges of her mind. Just beyond the cold adobe walls she felt the warmth and color of another world. One where she was loved because she was a child of the world ... and not shunned or made guilty because of the adult she would become one day.

Carlotta was still too young, not yet able to name the impossible contradiction she was expected to accept, to give complete obedience, trust, and love to a God who spoke through the person Friar Alcazar, the murderer of children. But because she was young, Carlotta was still hopelessly unable to deny her heart, and so she cried not so much for her repentance but for her lost Kachina doll.

***

The girls kept their secret. The entire day was set aside, its meaning unfathomable. They spoke no more about the Kachina or the encounter with Friar Alcazar, as to do so would leave no hope in their lives. Part of their silence was due to Virginia's choice not to speak aloud except in Carlotta's company. It was only within this secret covenant that Virginia became increasingly familiar with her own voice.

Diego forgot about Carlotta's doll and so did the Indian babies who were consoled by it upon their arrival at the mission. The mission became a darker place, one with no laughter, just haunting reminders of those who would not return.

Carlotta desperately missed Two Bears. She dreamed of sunny days and foot races with her Indian friend, and then she would hear Miguel's voice call her back and the spell was broken. Again, she was sitting on the wall, merely one of the mission's abandoned children. At other times Carlotta dreamed of the Valenzuela hacienda. She could see Joaquin and his father, in the same kind of relationship she had witnessed with Two Bears and Sak-mo-i-si ... a relationship filled with love and honor. These were examples in her life, painful to remember, impossible to forget.

There was Carlotta's own memory of love, Owl Woman. Was this a child's love for her mother? Was this the wonder of being loved? She felt it to be the same, and now that she knew, how could she forget it?

Friar Alcazar's reference to Diego's and her benefactor made her curious. She had not known of the arrangement. Was this uncle someone who cared for her, but had, for some reason she was too young to understand, assigned her upbringing to the friar? It was hard to accept the possibility of being loved and denied in one breath. Still, the knowledge of a living relative offered hope.

Carlotta wanted and needed love, but she had learned the only unconditional love was that of God. Longingly, she went to the chapel and gazed at the figurine of the baby Jesus in Mary's arms. If she could not feel the arms of a mother around her, couldn't she hold love in her arms? Father Alcazar had said her love was false, because it was not for God. She thought she was beginning to understand why he objected to the Kachina; it was not Jesus.

These thoughts were on the child's mind as the days grew colder. The first snow flurries blew into the courtyard, reflecting shiny black puddles as they lay melting on the last leaves of summer. Carlotta began to eye the barren cottonwood in the courtyard. She thought of her Kachina doll, remembering what she had learned at the pueblo ... that the dolls were carved from los alamos. She waited and one day the idea spoke to her. A limb of the mission's tree, twisted and weakened from the winds, finally fell to the ground. Once she shortened the branch it would be the right size.

Carlotta didn't tell Diego the reason she needed the limb, but she worried her brother until he finally agreed to use his knife, a present from Señor Valenzuela. She watched as Diego whittled a groove in the wood and bent the branch back and forth until it gave way.

"Now, what do you want with this?" Diego asked.

"I want to learn how to whittle, too!" Carlotta said, seeing a way to extend her brother's aid.

Anxious to show Carlotta his skill, Diego took another section of the branch and began to wield his knife. Carlotta watched attentively. Diego was encouraged and worked with the wood throughout the afternoon until a crude, but recognizable, horse emerged from the limb.

It pleased his sister and she expressed her delight.

"May I try it now?" Carlotta asked.

There was little Diego could say, and so he handed the knife to her, admonishing her to be very careful with the sharp blade.

She seemed to catch on right away, just as she had with the horses, Diego thought.

Every afternoon Carlotta spent time alone chipping away at the chunk of wood. It began to take a human shape and she was encouraged by her progress. When she was finally satisfied that the carving halfway resembled the Christ child, she wrapped it carefully in an old blanket, and returned the knife to her brother.

"Show me what you made, little sister," Diego prompted.

"No," Carlotta said, shyly. "It is a gift ... para Feliz Navidad."

Diego shrugged his shoulders in resignation. His sister's secret was evidently important to her and he decided not to pry.

Carlotta didn't realize until the words came spilling from her mouth what she had intended to do with the doll. The need to make the little carving was her own need to shower love on an acceptable doll, but even as she whittled away the wood from the tiny round face, she knew her real joy would be to give the baby Jesus to someone who loved him as much as she did.

There was no doubt in her mind who would be that person. That gift of love had already helped her friend to speak. It was the sight of the Kachina that triggered the memory of the Gan. Surely, the baby Jesus would make Virginia as happy as she. Folding the blanket tenderly around the carving, Carlotta dropped down from the wall and walked gingerly along the corridor. She picked her way around the drifts of new snow and over the treacherous sheet of invisible ice. The cold was stimulating and Carlotta felt her body warm with the anticipation of presenting her gift.

Virginia would be returning from the doctor's office soon, and Carlotta would wait at the gate and watch her friend gasp with surprise as she unfolded the blanket. Carlotta was spellbound, her vision clear and profound as she imagined

Virginia's smile and tears of happiness. Her eyes were lost within the dream, her arms wrapped protectively around her gift, and she didn't hear the footsteps coming toward her.

Her eyes followed the hem of the friar's robe, up the dark folds to Alcazar's stoic face. His black eyes burned and the muscles in his jaws clenched reflexively, but he didn't say a word. Carlotta knew at that moment she was doomed. Her explanation, that this was a carving of the baby Jesus, the son of God and the Virgin Mary, was futile. Her plea for understanding, from a priest who had no compassion, fell on deaf ears.

It was not his forgiveness she sought but his love, and the friar had no love. Carlotta's eyes sprung hot tears and she blinked, denying her emotions the ability to erase the truth. Alcazar reached for her hand and cruelly yanked her to his side. Then he pulled, half dragged her along the corridor, her feet sliding out from beneath her. The friar's long stride dragged her past the school room and the work rooms, her burning, scraped knees leaving a trail of blood on the melting ice.

They entered the storage area at the end of the work room. The cold and dark cubicle was used to store grains, vegetables, and fruits through the winter. The friar roughly pushed the child into the room where she fell against the wall. A large rodent scurried out from under a burlap sack and ran across the floor, but Alcazar never took his eyes off the frightened child.

He regarded the child, who sat huddled still clinging to her primitive representation of the Christ child. Her circumvention of the Church had been his undoing. This is what had turned his anger into fear. Carlotta, this wisp of a child, had no need of the friar's intervention on her behalf. Religion would not save this child's soul. She was lost ... not to God, but to the church...and therefore to Alcazar. He felt his power slip away and yet reminded himself that she was here, the one who had supposedly defeated his reign, at his feet, weeping submissively, fearfully.

He needed desperately to feel a larger sense of this power, to feed on this like a wild animal would feed on a rotting carcass.

"I will bend your will! You will remain here until you beg forgiveness for this sin of idolatry!" Alcazar's voice trembled in spite of his discipline.

"God is unattainable to man. You must pray ... and ask to accept your own unworthiness!"

Carlotta watched as the friar left the small room and closed the door on all light. For several moments she felt lost, disoriented, as if in a dream without color. She nurtured the last scene, freezing the visual frame onto her brain, for she knew Alcazar intended to hold her as a prisoner. There was absolutely no doubt. For him to win, she must lose.

She would leave. She would go home to The People, those who understood that all life was one life. Carlotta's intensity was so deep that she found herself drawn to another world, one where she could imagine the black cold room transformed into the cave.

There was a part of her that knew she was locked away and that no one was likely to find her here. Maria had her pantry in the cocina and wouldn't have a need to visit this storeroom until late winter, when her supplies dwindled. If Carlotta called out no one would hear her through the thick adobe walls or the heavy wooden door. This part of Carlotta was logical and served her well, but it was not all of her. It was not the only means to know and it was certainly not the only means to solve problems.

Somewhere she heard the measured drip of melting snow as drops fell on the floor's clay tiles. It was still quiet and a little frightening, but the other world became the place within, the fertile ground for creativity. This time Carlotta deliberately chose the path into the deep recesses of her mind, willingly succumbing to her imagination.

She thought about the white owl's gift, the ability to see the truth, and she was thankful. The pain of acquiring knowledge fell away from her like a garment no longer needed. The truth was everything. She trusted it implicitly and this left her mind free to explore beyond the confines of her prison.

Following the white owl, Carlotta heard the rustling of mouse, and she allowed herself to be led farther into the black tunnel. Though all was darkness, she began to see. Again, she felt the dizzying pull of the golden light, and with the trust of a butterfly allowed for her own transformation.

Deliberately, Carlotta looked for her brother out on the meadow with its blowing grass. The white horse, with the raven, hovering above his shimmering mane, recognized her and came flying to her side.

***

Diego was anxious. He had left Maria in the cocina, not certain where to look next for Carlotta. Maria hadn't seen his sister and something deep inside troubled him about her absence. Besides, it was getting dark and the corridor was thick with scary shadows. The gate rattled and Diego jumped with alarm, but he saw it was only Virginia returning from Dr. Gentry's.

Diego unlatched the gate and Virginia entered, shivering.

"I wonder why Friar Alcazar isn't here?" Diego questioned out loud.

When was the last time the friar wasn't there, his hand out in expectation of their wages? Virginia, too, seemed concerned, but turned to face the dark corridor. Suddenly, she knelt down, and Diego thought she had lost something in the frozen snow along the wall.

Drops of red ... blood, Diego thought. There was a thin broken line, a trail of some poor wounded animal. Here and there the flecks of blood were almost erased as they faded in the melting ice. Virginia took Diego's hand and lifted her head, as if to sniff the air. Diego felt an energizing current pass through Virginia's hand to his own, and an immediate understanding of what they must do.

The two children followed the erratic drops of blood down the walkway leading to the stable, but as they passed the school room, the trail stopped at the doorway to the workroom. Diego felt his heart pound. He knew with complete certainty this was the blood of his sister. What would he do if something happened to her? She was all he really had. Even the horse he held so dear belonged to another. El Norte would forgive him his allegiance to his only known relative, his own blood! With his heart, Diego thanked his horse for understanding and sensed his own courage begin to grow.

Tentatively, Diego pushed open the door. At least it wasn't locked. Quietly, he and Virginia entered the large room.

It was here that all the livery repairs were made. Broken equipment, wagon wheels, and axles were strewn across the floor. The light was fading quickly, and Diego's eyes skirted the room, seeking any evidence of Carlotta. At the far end was the storeroom and he felt drawn to its wooden door.

As Diego approached with Virginia close behind, he heard his sister's voice. This door was locked.

"Diego? Is that you?" Carlotta asked.

"Yes! Are you all right, Carlotta?"

A heavy iron lock hung from the door's latch and Diego realized that its key was one of many hanging on a chain from Alcazar's waist. Diego's heart sank. "Did Alcazar put you in here? Did he hurt you?" he asked, remembering the blood.

"It doesn't matter anymore. You just have to get me out of here."

His sister's voice was resolved. Diego didn't think he had ever heard her sound so grown up, which only heightened his own feelings of inadequacy.

"How am I ever going to get you out of here?" Diego anguished. "I think Alcazar has the only key, Carlotta."

"You and Virginia go back to our room and get Jean Paul. He has the patience ... he'll find a way to pick the lock."

As Diego trudged across the courtyard he wondered how Carlotta had known Virginia was with him, but he didn't have time to think of these things now. He knew his sister was right. Jean Paul had a way with small things and their intricate workings. It was just so sensible to use his talents. The "whys" weren't important anymore, only the results.

They found Jean Paul where Carlotta had said they would. He and Miguel were sitting on the floor bent over the compass from McGiver's pack. The other children, Pilar, Chano, and Chuey were in the cocina with Maria, Jean Paul said.

Diego quickly told Jean Paul of his sister's imprisonment and asked if he could open the lock.

"Certainly," answered Jean Paul, with the calm of one who spent hours unlocking the puzzles of mechanical objects.

The two boys jumped to their feet, ready to follow Diego and Virginia back to the room. Virginia eyed the forgotten compass and retrieved it from the floor. She hurried out after them.

Miguel carried the candle, sheltered with his hand, and Jean Paul felt along the floor of the workroom for anything of the proper shape to pick the lock. His hand settled on a large rusty nail and he excitedly reported his discovery.

The four hovered at the door, their shadows falling behind them on the floor. Jean Paul went to work, meticulously probing the lock with his nail.

"We'll have you out of there soon, Carlotta," Diego encouraged his sister, who was all too quiet.

"Diego ... I am running away," Carlotta said. "I don't belong here."

Diego found he wasn't really surprised at her words, but asked, "Where would you go?"

"Home ... to the pueblo," she answered.

"Well, you're not going anywhere without me!" said Diego.

"Miguel ... you're in my light!" said Jean Paul, slightly ruffled by the conversation going on around him.

"You don't belong here," said Miguel, dreamily. He was thinking of Carlotta's future and was convinced. "Your future is in a different place," he said.

"Well ... I belong here ... and you are in my light!" repeated Jean Paul. "Can't you wait until I get her out of here before you say goodbye?"

***

CHAPTER 17

THE RETURN OF THE KACHINAS

THE RETURN OF THE KACHINAS

It was Jean Paul's way to hide his emotions under a flurry of busy detail, but after a time of concentrated probing with the iron nail, he heard the lock audibly click and the door swung ajar. Jean Paul was thoughtful, as the others whispered their concerns for Carlotta. He heard Diego say that he had come with his sister and he would leave with her if she was determined to run away. The slight boy who mustered a grand bravado when occupied with the particulars of life, found himself unable to cope with his own rush of feelings.

Once back in the room with the other children, Jean Paul began to cry, and in the lengthening shadows of evening his soft sobs were finally recognized.

Miguel clasped an arm around his smaller friend's shoulder and said, "Don't worry, Jean Paul. We will see each other again. In a dream I saw us all in a circle again."

Pilar returned from the cocina with a soothing balm for Carlotta's knees and she and Virginia huddled around their friend as they helped her nurse her wounds.

"You're going to need a horse, Diego," said Chano, "There is snow on the ground and you might lose your way."

"I've been thinking about that. Joaquin will let me ride El Norte and I can return him after I leave Carlotta at the pueblo."

Virginia left Carlotta's side and extended her hand to Diego.

"The compass, Diego. It will guide you when the raven returns," Virginia said.

In Virginia's open palm lay McGiver's compass, but the children stared at the face of the girl they knew as mute.

"You can speak!" cried Diego.

"Yes, Carlotta and I have kept it a secret ... until now. But listen, please. The raven is my friend and he will lead you for a while, but then he must return. Use the compass and travel in a northeasterly direction and you will reach the pueblo."

The children no longer questioned one another's wisdom. It felt more natural to trust their own innocent intent, now that they could see the deception that surrounded them.

Diego decided they should leave quickly, before Alcazar visited the storeroom and found Carlotta gone, but first Diego had to go to the hacienda for El Norte. He said his goodbyes and went out into the cold night.

***

The small pebbles pelted the bedroom window, and Joaquin woke instantly. He knew without a doubt it was his friend Diego. Joaquin shivered, his nightshirt providing no protection from the freezing air as he opened the door onto the balcony.

"Take him, Diego," Joaquin called down. "I will think of something to tell my father. You'll never make it without El Norte."

"Gracias, mi amigo ..."

"Via con Dios ..." Joaquin called after him.

El Norte trembled with the excitement of the boy's presence. Diego felt the horse's quivering flesh as he heaved the saddle onto his back and whispered calming words of praise and reassurance into El Norte's ear. Slowly, Diego led the black out of the barn where they both carefully chose their footing on the rutted icy path. It was only after he had closed the hacienda's gate and was out of view that Diego mounted the stallion.

Avoiding town, Diego and El Norte picked their way over the snow-patched landscape and arrived at the back gate to the mission's courtyard. Carlotta was waiting for him as planned. Diego looked down at his little sister and felt a moment of doubt. He saw the little girl, so shabbily dressed in her torn coat, holding fast to a bundle of their belongings. She had even remembered his guitar, which was slung over her back.

It would be up to Diego now; it would be his strength that could protect his sister. He knew that to accept this fact was tantamount to accepting the responsibility of manhood.

"Help me, El Norte," Diego called softly.

Diego slung McGiver's saddle bags onto the horse's back and cinched them snugly. Then he boosted his sister up to sit between him and the pack.

"Did you bring everything belonging to the lieutenant?" Diego asked.

"No ... it was just a good place to carry our clothes and to put some food that I ... stole ... from the cocina," Carlotta said, "Do you have the compass?"

"Yes, but look!" Diego pointed to the top of a tree.

Silhouetted against the deep blue sky a large raven looked down on them from a tangle of cottonwood branches. The bird cawed, a rakish sound that harshly accentuated the cold night. Satisfied that he had their attention, the cumbrous bird unfurled his expansive wings and lifted heavily into the air.

Diego gently nudged El Norte, who turned in the bird's direction, and the three proceeded into the night.

Mounds of snow spotted the frozen earth, glowing blue beneath the evening sky. Ice crystals glistened softly like the stars on a winter carpet rolling out to meet the horizon. It was a still world, peaceful and non threatening. It was a world untouched by any human, though occasionally the children would see the tracks of a small animal snaking across a white dune, and they wondered about the secret purpose of mice and rabbits.

As Virginia warned, the raven soon left them. Circling once, the bird called his farewell and disappeared. Diego clasped the compass securely in his hand and watched the trembling silver arrow point its way into the north. Slightly to the right, just a few degrees, Diego traced an imaginary line out and over the hill. This is where they would find The People.

The land was unrecognizable from their summer visit. Drifts of snow obliterated old landmarks, sometimes treacherously disguising the depths of terrain, but El Norte picked his way carefully over icy banks, seeking solid ground wherever possible. Hours went by and the children were comforted, even mesmerized, by the horse's rhythmic muscles that rippled warm and vibrant beneath them.

Dawn came, and Diego and Carlotta saw the hills off to their right become distinct, their shapes clearly edged against the morning sky. Straight ahead they beheld the blush of the sandstone cliffs rising dramatically from the desert floor. As El Norte brought them closer, they saw the white blanket of snow that cloaked, gently molding, the tiered walls, and draped the steep cliffs of the pueblo.

The drowsy state in which Carlotta had ridden all night, vanished with the first light and the realization that she was home. Excited, she thought of her first journey to the pueblo ... was it, also, a dreamlike voyage?

El Norte carried them forward. Up the worn path they climbed, rising just as the brilliant sun ascended to illuminate the eastern walls of the pueblo. Above them stood Owl Woman and Two Bears waving their greeting, almost as if they had been expecting them.

Carlotta nuzzled her head into the blanket that enveloped Owl Woman's body, and the Indian woman clasped the child warmly, as if she were her own. Lifting her face, Carlotta's eyes met those of the woman who was like a mother.

"I know the truth...I belong here," Carlotta said.

Owl Woman smiled.

"Of course, child. But when you know the truth, you belong anywhere that the truth will be heard."

Two Bears welcomed his friends and excitedly explained that they had arrived at the last possible moment.

"How can this be true?" asked Diego. "You didn't know we were coming, did you?"

"No," Two Bears laughed, "but the two paths entering the pueblo will be closed this evening. It is part of the Wuwuchim ceremony."

He turned more serious as he explained.

"At sundown a member of the One Horn Society will draw lines across the paths with sacred cornmeal, keeping out any evil that might come. If you had arrived this evening you would die."

Diego was shocked. "Do you mean that someone here would kill us?"

"No, but you would die within the next four years. I don't know how," he said simply.

Two Bears was grave in his certainty, and Diego, having learned to accept his friend's behavior, said nothing more.

The two children were brought up into the plaza where others greeted them, as well. The light that had followed them up the trail splashed across the mesa, simulating warmth, and Carlotta yawned with new contentment.

Sak-mo-i-si and the elders approached. Though the Sun Watcher was genuinely happy to see the two children from the mission, he seemed preoccupied. Owl Woman admitted to the children that her new husband was concerned for the safety of

The People, particularly during this most important time of the year.

Wouldn't the priests from the mission come looking for the children, some asked? It was not an issue that could be avoided since the ceremonies were forbidden, but the danger did not seem imminent either. Certainly, there was enough time to complete the initiation rites, ceremonies, and dance of Wuwuchim, said Sak-mo-i-si. After that, Owl Woman told the children, the Soyal Kachina would appear and, finally in the night sky, the Pleiades and the three stars of Orion would appear to mark the winter solstice.

It was decided that in two days' time The People would make their decision, and until then the children would be confined to Owl Woman's home. This would be the day the first Kachina appeared and a respite from the more serious ceremonies taking place in the kiva.

The children were famished, but their sleepy eyes indicated they could not stay awake long enough to satisfy their hunger. Owl Woman intervened, and said that she would take them to rest. The elders agreed, and Two Bears led El Norte to the corral on a lower ledge of the mesa, while Owl Woman ushered the children from the plaza.

Sister and brother did manage to eat some piki bread before they retreated to the warm buffalo skin lying in the corner of the room. As soon as their eyes closed, they fell asleep.

While the children slept throughout the afternoon, the people of the pueblo continued with their preparations for the ceremonies, and when evening came everyone's position was fixed. The initiates had entered the kiva, where their solemn prayers prepared them to symbolically transcend the previous underworld, by way of the ladder and the One-Way Trail through the roof opening into the present world.

Carlotta and Diego woke to the clacking of turtle-shell rattles and the clear sound of clay bells. Owl Woman explained that the pueblo was closed tonight and members of the Two Horn and One Horn societies were patrolling the terraces of the mesa searching for intruders. No one was allowed outside because this would contaminate the ceremony with evil and would mean death for all those in the kiva.

For the next two days Carlotta busied herself grinding corn, while they listened to the stories Owl Woman told about the tribe. Diego became restless. He worried about El Norte, concerned whether he would find enough to eat. But Two Bears assured him that he had taken the horse off the mesa to a southern canyon protected from the coming snows. There was dried grass there, enough to keep the horse alive.

It began to snow softly, steadily, and now it was the weather that prevented the children from returning to the plaza, or to the terraces to play. The second phase of creation began ... Soyal. Owl Woman explained that Wuwuchim had laid out the pattern of life development for the coming year, and now during Soyal it would be accepted, and during the third phase Powamu would purify it.

Carlotta was worried that Alcazar would be looking for them, but Two Bears was certain that no one was traveling during the storms, for he said the snows had arrived early this year. At first there was little alarm. The People were well prepared with a bountiful harvest. Two Bears had forgotten his usual modesty when he told of the wonderful stores of corn, squash, and pumpkins laid away in the cool dark adobe rooms.

One day, as if to prove their bounty, he descended the ladder with a watermelon. The children gasped in disbelief. While they greedily devoured their broken share, sweet red juice dripping off their chins, Two Bears explained that the tribe preserved the melons in sand and frequently had them to eat all through the winter.

With the arrival of the new moon the people congregated more often for story-telling. Carlotta and Diego learned from Sak-mo-i-si and the visitors to his home about the progression of the ceremonies. They reported on the careful observations of the stars and spoke of the four powerful forces to which the tribe appealed during Soyal and Powamu ... the power of germination, heat, moisture, and the magnetic forces in the air. And they were ever thankful for the answered prayers of a harvest that now filled their bellies.

Finally, it was reported that all of those events were complete, the special dances and songs so carefully performed, the changing position of the three stars. The great turn of the winter solstice had been made, and now The People opened the kiva to the return of the Kachinas.

Carlotta and Diego were allowed to watch the first returning Kachinas distribute gifts to the children, and then they watched the men disappear into the blinding snow as they departed for a rabbit hunt. When they returned the women came out to throw water on the Soyal men so that rain and snow would bless the crops, and everyone felt confident it would be so because the snow was still falling. Later, huddling around the coals for warmth, the children relived the return of the first Kachinas. Every detail was recounted, each mask and costume depicted once more in order to leave their snow-white world for one of color. Owl Woman stirred a pot of rabbit stew, its enticing smell causing her husband's stomach to announce his hunger.

In the corner Two Bears was painting an imaginary picture of the Coyote Kachina to Carlotta.

"Remember the right side of his forehead was painted green and the left side was white?"

Two Bears pointed to his own face, tracing imaginary stars and crosses. He squinted, pulling the corners of his eyes into slits.

Carlotta giggled.

"He had parrot feathers on the top of his head and eagle feathers down his back, like this," Two Bears said, holding a string of dried chilies from the top of his head.

He continued, describing Coyote's protruding jaw by fiercely jutting his own in front of him. Carlotta shrieked, pretending fear, and the three children howled with laughter.

The plank covering the rooftop opening was pulled aside and several older members of Sak-mo-i-si's clan and friends descended, stomping their feet free of ice as they entered the room. The snow was coming down harder, an uncle said, and briskly rubbed his hands together in front of the fire.

Sak-mo-i-si, who was eager to hold on to his family's more lighthearted mood, pointed to his cousin and teasingly said that this was the man who prowled the mesa looking for someone else's dinner.

"Not so, Sak-mo-i-si," the man protested. "My wife was ill...and I was needed in the ... den," he added, laughing.

All of those in the room laughed with him, except Sak-mo-i-si, who turned serious.

"How can this be? Who was our Coyote Kachina?" he asked.

No one seemed to have a satisfactory explanation.

"Perhaps someone of another clan?" offered the brother to Sak-mo-i-si's mother.

But it was now much too cold to go and ask, and as they listened to the wind whistle along the pueblo's walls, the members of Sak-mo-i-si's extended family drew closer, seeking comfort in the hot bowls of rabbit stew that Owl Woman set before each of them.

When they had finished eating, the clan's eldest member, an old and wrinkled man, said that the mystery of the Coyote Kachina reminded him of a story. The elders encouraged him to tell his tale for everyone's benefit. This grandfather was very learned and practiced in the ways of storytelling and it would be through his careful repetition that they, too, would learn the history and the stories of the tribe.

The grandfather made himself comfortable, and with one twisted leg tucked under his bony body, he gratefully accepted a cup of warm tea from the Tuhikya, Sak-mo-i-si's new wife. He then began his story.

Coyote lived with his wife and children near the springs south of the pueblo.

Diego and Carlotta's eyes opened wide at this humanlike reference to coyote's family. The old man continued in a raspy voice.

Early one evening, when the sun had finished its journey, Coyote decided to go for a walk. Coyote wrapped his blanket tightly around his shoulders, for there was snow on the ground.

The grandfather pulled his own blanket closer as the wind outside began to howl. He continued with his story, his sentences carefully metered for effect.

Coyote told his wife that he would not be gone long. As he walked along he noticed that one by one the men were leaving their homes and entering the great kiva in the plaza. The men were laughing and talking. Then he saw Spirit

People coming from all directions. He watched them descend into the kiva. Some of the Spirit People were dressed like clouds, some looked like the sun, others appeared like animals.

Coyote paid strict attention to all the Spirit Animals entering the kiva, and he noticed that there were no Coyote People entering. Then he saw the brothers of the Flute Clan standing at the kiva entrance. The brothers had spotted Coyote, and the older brother asked, "I wonder what the old boy's up to now?"

"Probably no good as usual; he always thinks he has to know what's going on," replied the younger brother.

Coyote waited, hoping the brothers would go inside the kiva, but they showed no signs of leaving. Coyote trotted past the kiva, ignoring the brothers, and walked down one of the paths, pretending to leave. Every so often, he turned his head and looked behind him, as coyotes often do.

Carlotta giggled, as the picture the elder presented was in some ways more real than the truth. Diego immediately hushed his sister, but the corner of the grandfather's mouth lifted with amusement as he continued.

When the brothers saw coyote leave, they, too, descended the ladder into the kiva.

But Coyote returned down a side alley. The brothers were nowhere in sight. He heard thunder and saw lightning flashes coming from the kiva, and wondered what kind of magic was occurring. Looking around, he saw that he was alone in the plaza. Curiosity getting the better of him, coyote sneaked up onto the roof of the kiva. Peeking into the kiva hole, coyote saw only blackness. This just made him more curious. Now coyote wanted to go inside the kiva and see for himself just what was happening. How could he get inside the kiva? Coyote needed time to think ... Coyote always needs time to think; he thinks his way into trouble.

Pulling his blanket tighter around him, Coyote headed for home. Just before he entered his house, coyote realized what he could do to get into the kiva. His wife was waiting for him, and he was so excited about his idea that his words kept tripping over one another. Coyote told his wife that she must help him make a mask, just like the Spirit People wore.

In the flickering light of the fire, the children's eyes shone with bright interest. Spellbound, they did not hear the mounting wind, and the driving force of a blizzard sweeping the roof above them.

All day, the coyote and his mate worked on the mask. He sent his sons to collect feathers and pitch from the piñon pine. His mask resembled the sun. Using the pitch, Coyote placed the feathers all around the sun. Coyote stepped back and admired his work.

Carlotta remembered the Coyote Kachina she had seen earlier and another that had looked like the sun. Recalling her own struggle to make a Kachina doll, she felt some sympathy for poor Coyote and his foolish effort.

As it became dark, Coyote's wife helped him on with his mask. Coyote, proud of his new mask, walked quickly back to the pueblo. He thought his mask looked so good, that some of the Spirit People might envy him.

The brothers of the Flute Clan were standing by the entrance to the kiva. Coyote waited until the Spirit People started coming and joined several who were making their way to the kiva entrance.

The older brother leaned over and said, "Here he comes again, what must he be planning this time?"

The brother replied, "Look at that ridiculous mask, how can he possibly think we can't spot that. If that mask isn't bad enough, look, his tail is sticking out! We would have to be blind not to see it."

Coyote approached the Spirit People, but the brothers stepped in front of him. The younger brother quietly pointed to the Coyote's tail that was twitching nervously, and he shook his head. Coyote turned and saw his tail dragging behind him. Coyote picked up his tail and brushed it gently with his other hand.

The grandfather had mimed the movements of Coyote, his wrinkled hands picking up an imaginary tail and softly stroking it. The children could almost believe it was Coyote sitting at their fire.

Coyote greeted the brothers and commented on what a nice night it was for a walk. Then he turned and quickly trotted down the plaza. Coyote was so mad that he didn't even feel the cold. He disappeared from sight and the brothers descended into the kiva. Coyote returned and headed for the plaza. As he approached the kiva, he heard singing. He waited a while and when he didn't see anyone, he crept up onto the kiva roof. The Spirit People made beautiful music and Coyote, forgetting how mad he was, placed one oversized ear over the kiva hole. And that is how he spent most of the night. When he heard The People begin to stir inside the kiva he jumped up and ran home.

The next morning Coyote was quickly at work on his next idea. He carefully molded clay over a form and when he finally finished, he thought he had created the most perfect human mask. Coyote spent the rest of the day painting it. The only problem arose when his wife helped him put on the mask. It didn't fit over his snout. His *wife helped him make the nose bigger. They tried again, but still it wasn't big enough. Coyote's wife made the snout even bigger. Coyote thought he looked very nice. His wife didn't say anything. She helped him tuck in his ears. His ears were so long that they didn't fit under the mask. Finally, she tucked them flat against his head. As Coyote started out the door, his wife grabbed him by the tail. Coyote, not wanting to make the same mistake twice, as coyotes are known to do, tucked in his tail.*

The children laughed heartily at the vision of such an immodest creature. But there were humans like this, Carlotta thought. She remembered several guests at the Valenzuela ball who revealed their vanity as they sought a glimpse of their reflection in the silver she had polished.

Coyote congratulated himself on his cleverness. In his eagerness Coyote had arrived early. There wasn't anyone there, not even those dumb brothers of the Flute Clan. They always gave him a hard time, but this time he would sneak past them into the kiva. Coyote began to pace nervously. No one came. Coyote began to wear a path around the kiva. Then he decided to wait around the corner. People emerged from their homes, and soon the Spirit People began arriving. Coyote saw the Rainbow Spirit, the Stone Spirit, and the Star Kachina.

The brothers followed the Spirit People. The older brother nudged the younger one. "Look down, Coyote's tracks are everywhere. I can hardly wait to see how he's going to disguise himself tonight."

The younger one said, "You won't have to wait long, look at that large nose on the person coming. Does that look like anyone you know?"

"That's the worst yet!" The brothers started laughing so hard that tears came to their eyes.

Coyote walked up to the brothers, who by now were doubled with laughter. The closer he got, the more they howled. Coyote couldn't figure out how the brothers recognized him. Someone must have told them. Didn't they have anything else to do but hang around bothering him? Coyote didn't acknowledge them, he just turned and left. He didn't remember ever being this angry.

Coyote turned down a side alley and headed to the plaza. This time he smelled the most delicious scent coming from the kiva. Slowly he crawled up to the kiva hole. Coyote stuck his nose into the hole so he could enjoy the enticing smell. Breathing deeply, he filled himself with the delicious aroma. Hearing a noise, Coyote thought it might be those troublemakers, the Flute Clan brothers, sneaking up behind him. He jerked up his head, but nothing happened. His snout was stuck in the hole. He placed his hands on both sides of the hole and pushed with all his might. Coyote couldn't pull himself free. He could feel his nose swelling from the pulling. He could do nothing else but wait until the cold diminished the swelling. He stayed there in that silly position all night. Shortly before dawn he found he could pull his snout free.

Rubbing his sore nose, he walked home nearly frozen from his time spent on the kiva roof. His wife greeted him at the door and helped pull the mask from his head. His ears were hopelessly flat and his nose seemed to have grown a bit, she thought ... which explains why, today, Coyote's large ears flop over and he has such a big snout. And here the story ends.

The grandfather said no more. Children and adults were a little disappointed to find this was the end of the story. The tale the grandfather told, for a time, had transported those sitting on the earthen floor to an animal world where the creature's motives and tribulations were as real as their own.

Gradually, their attention focused on other sounds, and they began to consider the frozen reality outside the kiva.

CHAPTER 18

THE PEOPLE OF THE PLAINS

THE PEOPLE OF THE PLAINS

The room began to lose its warmth, and Owl Woman returned to the fire pot to ladle boiling tea into several bowls. The grandfather held out his bowl for more and eagerly inhaled the steam's sweet vapors as she filled it. Poking a bony finger into Owl Woman's face, he said, "Tell the story of the Llanero to the children."

Owl Woman finished serving the elders and sat beside the old man. Her eyes were distant as she recalled the hardships of the Jicarilla band.

"The Indians of the Plains, the Llanero Jicarilla, came to the mesa during the last Soyal. They were very hungry and wanted to trade with The People. But they had so very little to trade."

The Tuhikya's eyes mirrored the pain she had witnessed. In honor of those of whom she spoke, Owl Woman lifted her head and told their story.

"We welcomed them into the plaza and were struck with the terrible condition of their people. They were mostly women and children, weak with hunger and freezing in the cold. And most of all, terribly sad, for many of their men had died in battles with the soldiers. The only males who came with them were the ancient ones and small children.

"I remember very well one woman. She had three children and no food. She wanted to trade the pitch-coated bowl that she had made for food to give her children. We opened our homes to the Llanero, doing our best to fill the bellies of their children and the older members of their tribe.

"When it was time for them to leave they were very grateful, humbly pledging their allegiance forever to our people. I had made up a bundle containing bread and pumpkin for them to take, for they were leaving even as the snow fell. The woman with the small children removed her shawl to give to me. She stood shivering, while the wind tore at her thin dress, telling me repeatedly of her appreciation for all that we had given them.

"Of course, I could not accept her shawl, her only protection from the cold. But, I looked in her eyes and saw the return of her pride, and I knew that I could not take that either."

Owl Woman smiled through glistening eyes.

"What did you do?" whispered Carlotta, not able to bear this terrible ending.

"I traded her a blanket for the shawl."

***

Above, they heard the wind groan and the roof door slam shut. The room began to fill with smoke and Sak-mo-i-si climbed the ladder to secure the door so that it would allow the smoke to escape and still protect them from the storm.

The storm blew fiercely, and Sak-mo-i-si's relatives and friends left the comfort of the fire to secure their own homes. Through the blinding snow they clung closely to the walls of the pueblo, tracing their route down the ladders and narrow walkways, lest they be swept off the terraces.

The People of the pueblo settled in for the duration of the storm, resigned to life indoors. They were well prepared; the storage rooms were stocked and their adobe dwellings secure shelter from the biting cold winds. They turned to the chores of winter, the women to the endless task of grinding corn and the men to the making and mending of tools and weaving. Days passed with no let up in the storm, and the elders began to review their ceremonies for miscalculations and misdeeds. It was suspected that Soyal had been betrayed, and the rumor among The People was the unexplained presence of the Coyote Kachina. Was the Trickster close? Stories abounded in the pueblo's dark dwellings, as The People spoke of other times when the discipline and order of the ceremonies had been violated. Droughts and famine were remembered history, and in the past even witchcraft had been suspect.

Two Bears' fears were given sustenance. All things were different since he had come home to the pueblo, but he knew he would never voluntarily return to the mission. There was no one he feared more than the evil priest Alcazar, and yet he remembered the friar's accusation of witchcraft and wondered if others remembered, too.

The winds died to an eerie whistle that explored the mesa like a sightless visitor. The People, oppressed from being days on end confined to the dark rooms of their homes, spilled forth onto the mesa and were greeted by a world turned white against a slate gray sky. Deep drifts of snow flanked the adobe walls and reached the doorways of the keyhole openings. Women scooped away the snow, clearing passages from the terraces, while the men gathered corn cobs for fuel. The children were instructed to sweep the snow into the rock cisterns where it would melt and replenish their stores of water.

They went solemnly about their tasks, hurrying beneath a sky turning darker by the moment. The ominous mood of the mesa intimidated speech, and the few words that were spoken were whispered nervously.

Two Bears and Diego were sent to check on the animals, and Sak-mo-i-si cautioned them.

"It will be dangerous on the snow covered trail," he said. "Uncertain footing might mean your fall from the cliffs."

Carlotta stood beside Owl Woman and watched her brother descend the trail to the animal pens. She lifted her gaze to the southern sky where, on the horizon, she saw a line of detached tiny clouds break away from the earth below and drift lazily until they became a smear on the darker clouds.

"Is there a fire?" Carlotta asked.

Owl Woman followed Carlotta's gaze and intently studied the smoke. After a time she explained.

"This is the sky language of the Red Man, a way of sending thoughts through the sky. It is a plea for help from The People of the plains - the Llanero Jicarilla. Their smoke signals say that they are starving," she said.

Others had gathered beside Owl Woman and the child to read the message in the sky. There was uneasy talk as The People discussed the White Man's order not to trade with the Jicarilla Apache.

"Aren't they the same people of your story?" asked Carlotta, "Isn't she the woman who wanted to give you her shawl?"

Owl Woman sadly nodded her head.

"Can we help them?" Carlotta asked.

Sak-mo-i-si had joined them and his arm fell comfortingly around his wife's shoulder.

"I must go to them," she said. "Please don't protest, my husband. It is best that I go alone. If I am caught by the White Man it will not be so bad for The People. The government people will let me go because I bring my herbs to the doctor, and they know me as a trader in the town."

Sak-mo-i-si did not give a hurried answer. It was not an easy decision. The lives of The People came first. But which people? Their red brothers were on the snow- covered Plains, without food or shelter. The People of the pueblo had never turned their back on a cry for help, how could they now?

"Please," Carlotta begged. "Diego and I can go with you. El Norte will be a big help!"

The Sun Watcher was about to object, when Owl Woman said, "It might be wise, husband. If we are caught, I am taking the children back to San Ramon."

The Indian woman smiled and squeezed Carlotta's hand.

Sak-mo-i-si searched his wife's face and found the confidence of a Tuhikya.

"Then I will call to the boys to bring up the horse and a mule," he said, resigned.

"We'll pack food supplies onto a travois," he added, and left to prepare for their trip.

"No!" cried Carlotta, when the Sun Watcher was out of hearing range. "I am never going back to the mission! There is evil there ..."

Recalling the pact that she had made with los niños, and afraid that she had already said too much, Carlotta let her words trail off uselessly. She could not endanger the lives of her friends, no matter what decision she had made for herself. Even though Tito Sanchez was dead, the children couldn't defend themselves, not against the soldiers and Alcazar. The evil and lies were everywhere, and she could not bear the thought of The People's betrayal.

Owl Woman knelt down beside the child and clasped her face with two gentle brown hands. Their eyes met and she said,

"Would you deny what you know with your heart, One Who Traveled Far? If you see clearly the evil, you must see the good - and learn to trust it."

Stunned with the memory of the name Owl Woman had first called her, Carlotta thought about its meaning.

"I will not betray you and neither will The People."

Rising to her feet, Owl Woman brushed the snow from her skirt.

"Come," she said briskly. "I must get my medicine bundle and we must hurry."

***

Though it was still morning when they left, the sky was bleak and promised snow. Sak-mo-i-si saw that the travelers were delivered safely to the bottom of the mesa. For a moment, unabashedly, he held his new wife close with his blanket wrapped around them. Reluctantly he left Owl Woman and approached Diego and his mule. Holding out his rifle and several bullets, Sak-mo-i-si counseled the boy to use the weapon wisely, then he turned and walked back up the trail.

Carlotta and Owl Woman mounted El Norte, and Diego followed, the travois dragging behind his mule. The animals moved slowly through the deep snow and their riders did their best to seek shallow drifts.

The newborn snow lay like a blanket on the land. Not a hoof print or a blade of grass broke the white landscape. Owl Woman and the children looked ahead and navigated their mounts on a course as straight as possible to the source of smoke, the unseen fire with its cry for help rising into the sky. The path stretched across the Plains, leading them over hills where stands of naked aspen stood in sharp contrast to the green gnarled piñon.

The travelers moved with difficulty across the snow-covered fields and eventually came to a frozen pond. The watering hole lay bleak and lifeless, water fowl having long since migrated south searching for food and warmth. Close now were the messages in smoke, which carried the smell of burning wood. Owl Woman and the children heard the caw of raven and looked up in time to see the huge bird swoop out of a cloud of smoke and drop swiftly from the sky. Huge jet black wings silently swept the snow as raven came to rest on the drag marks of the travois.

Carlotta gasped. Up close, the bird was even more magnificent than in the air. Iridescent blue washed his wings, and his shiny black feathers rippled as he gingerly picked his way across the trail. Raven presented one piercing yellow eye,

- 257 -

then, turning his head, he offered the other. The raven appeared unafraid and openly curious as he inspected the travelers.

"Cr-r-ruck."

El Norte and the mule held still as Owl Woman and the children studied the bird's heavy head and bill and listened to the harsh sound, which came from its shaggy, feathered throat.

"Prayers have traveled on the smoke," said Owl Woman. "The raven has brought us his magic."

"I think that is my friend Virginia's raven," whispered Carlotta. "He put us on the trail to the pueblo."

Diego reached out and touched Carlotta's shoulder. "Look," he said, pointing.

Raven bent his head stiffly toward the snow-covered ground. There lay several bright yellow kernels of corn that had fallen from one of the baskets they were carrying to The People of the Plains. With a scooping motion, raven caught one golden kernel in his beak, and lifting his gigantic wings, soared into the air.

Returning to the smoke, he disappeared.

"The message of our intent has been delivered. Let us hurry, The People of the Plains are hungry." Owl Woman lifted her arms to the gray skies and murmured words barely audible to the children.

"What do "tuawta" and "poko" mean, Owl Woman?" asked Carlotta.

"I was thanking Great Spirit for the magic we have seen and the animal who does things for us."

***

The small party of mercy moved across the snow. To their left the terrain became more rugged, visibly completing a barrier between the travelers and the smoke. Jutting rocks protruded from a snow-banked mountain, creating ledges sculptured in white. The trail, necessarily, led the horse and mule around the stone abutments, crossing the long shadows on the snow. Owl Woman and the children climbed steadily amongst the rocks, often ducking beneath a low-hanging shelf that threatened their progress.

As they rounded a particularly large out-cropping of rock, they were startled to see a slim gray figure, standing barefoot in the snow. It was an Indian woman. She was dressed in drab rags and held an emaciated child, who hung limply from her arms. The woman's position in their path seemed to indicate that she had expected them, and her eyes, the one exception in her futile demeanor, flashed a spark of hope. Owl Woman spoke to the woman softly and when she received a reply she instructed the children to dismount. Approaching the woman slowly, Owl Woman held her hands out to take the child.

Carlotta watched the thin arms tremble as the woman surrendered her child to Owl Woman, all the while one fist was clenched tightly on a secret treasure. As she weakly dropped to her knees, her hand opened to reveal the bright yellow kernel of corn laying in her palm. Diego rushed to the woman's side and helped her rise from unsteady feet. Leaning heavily on Diego's shoulder, the woman turned to lead them down the path.

Against the mountain side, the overhanging rock offered The People of the Plains protection from the weather. In the blue recesses of the cave like shelter the woman's clan members were lying on the stone floor. Weakened from starvation, they offered their feeble bodies to the western sun, and stared dully at the approaching visitors. There were five women and seven children, two of whom were infants. The eldest of the children was approximately Carlotta's age.

Several yards from the shallow cave sat two elders, apparently the tribe's only men. One man was naked to the waist and coughing profusely, while the other poked at the remains of a fire. A wet blanket, its steam rising in the air, was laying on the snow beside it. This was obviously the source of the smoke signals and yet their fire was dying for lack of fuel.

Owl Woman sent Diego in search of dried grass, twigs, and animal dung, anything that would burn to warm The People and cook their food. She and Carlotta began the task of unloading the travois.

Obediently, Carlotta helped. She first distributed the blankets to the elders. The sickly old man placed his withered, skeletal hand over hers, and though his dried-up body seemed to have lost all moisture, the child saw tears well in the corners of his eyes.

The travelers lost all sense of cold as they began to help The People. Diego returned with kindling, and soon Owl woman had a pot of lamb stew bubbling on the fire. Carlotta held the weakest child, wrapped warmly in her arms, and offered him tiny sips of the meat broth.

Hunger and cold were The People's worst enemies, but also, from these came illness. The Tuhikya opened her bundle to find the herbs that restored health. She made a poultice for the old man, smearing his chest with the aromatic herbs and then bundling him tightly. Owl Woman insisted that he drink a special tea and after several servings, and little protest, he began to perspire. The People quickly realized her abilities and called her by her earned title, medicine woman.

As night fell, so did the snow begin to fall. The skies opened to discharge a steady white sheet, which floated down silently, adding to the depth of earth's blanket. The coals of the fire were brought in under the stone ledge and nurtured during the night with the fuel Diego had gathered. They huddled together, warm and receptive to hope, now that their stomachs were full.

Carlotta and her brother learned of The People's plight as Owl Woman gently asked them questions. They told of relatives, an entire clan that were annihilated by the soldiers. When The People had returned to camp from tilling a plot of corn they found their bodies. All but three children, who had been taken captive.

"They are at the mission!" Carlotta blurted out excitedly. "We heard the children the night they were brought. Virginia, Pilar, and I tried to comfort them. They are my friends," she explained.

A woman came closer to where Carlotta was sitting and with hopeful eyes, asked if it were true.

"My boy, he saw only three summers when they took him. Are you saying he is alive?"

Carlotta remembered how it cheered the children when she brought out her Kachina doll. She pictured the shy little boy who hid behind Maria's skirts.

"Did he say the word Hactcin?" she asked the woman.

The woman gasped. "Oh, yes! His father sang for the Hactcin ceremony. He made the masks and kept them safe. My boy, he liked to touch them."

"Yes!" cried Carlotta, "When I showed him my Kachina doll, with its costume, he said Hactcin!"

The woman's eager eyes searched for more and Carlotta hastened to assure her.

"My friends will take care of them," she said, not all together convinced that this were possible.

A soulful howl pierced the quiet of the night, and the children looked up, concerned.   "It is wolf," said one of the old men. "They are hungry, too."

Others in the pack joined the chorus, and Carlotta felt her spine turn to ice.

The People explained that the wolves had come in closer as their own hunger had made them more desperate. They told the children not to be afraid, because the fire would keep them away.   And besides, the Tuhikya would protect them now. Friendly smiles reflected The People's confidence, and they drew the new blankets close about them as they prepared to go to sleep.

Carlotta lay close to her brother and listened to the wolves. As she grew drowsy, their voices mingled with the pitiful cries of humans, an expression of all the suffering that she had seen this day. The mournful plea reached deep within her, touching and then dislodging something, which even in her dreamlike state, she knew to be her will. And then white owl was before her, whispering, "Know that you are safe, and with that knowledge allow your heart to see ..."

As Carlotta dreamed, unafraid, she allowed this inner self freedom to explore. She knew that she was awake as she recognized a slumbering power stir deep inside, and she saw that the power's other name was Truth.

***

For three days the storm raged. Sometimes the north wind whirled and blew into the cave, in spite of the opening to the west. Humans and animals would huddle, seeking warmth close to one another, bracing for the next fierce thrust of nature. El Norte and the mule became their only warmth, blocking the brunt of the storm. Diego lovingly stroked his faithful horse and stubbornly saw that the animals received a share of the corn.

Daylight fell bright on to the new snow. Glaring brilliant sun rays penetrated the shelter under the rocks, and Carlotta woke with a sense of the morning almost gone. The others were already up, and Owl Woman told her that Diego was just returning from a hunt.

Carlotta scrambled to her feet, her heart full of an excitement she could only hope no one would see and ask her to explain. Her body resonated a vibration, a high-pitched quickening that placed her on the edge of an unnamed discovery. Nothing seemed different and yet everything was forever different.

She noticed then that indeed El Norte and the mule were gone. They had ventured out into the sunshine, instinctively seeking grass, she thought.

Carlotta saw them, her brother and the other children. They were laughing, their happiness impossible to contain. Standing in the children's midst was Diego, mounted on El Norte, magnificently white against a blue sky. Carlotta rubbed her eyes in disbelief and walked out into the snow.

"Los niños painted El Norte. He looks beautiful, don't you think?" Diego said, admiringly.

"They say that they painted my horse and me to protect us, because they see we are good friends that came from the north."

Diego's face was also painted with white lines, and Carlotta thought her brother looked very handsome straddling El Norte, dressed in the rawhide shirt Two Bears had given him.

"And look at the good fortune it has brought us. See what I've shot this morning?" Diego asked.

Across El Norte's rump was a slain antelope, its sleek body steaming in the cold air.

Carlotta reached out and touched the antelope's graceful small head. Her fingers traced the animal's slender horns, and back down his fawn-colored neck until it came to the bullet's entry. Standing on her toes, Carlotta gently placed a kiss between his eyes.

"Thank you for your gift ... so that the children may live," she said.

CHAPTER 19

RABBIT'S SNARE

RABBIT'S SNARE

Capt. Sedlow's ears still burned from the friar's scathing attack. He was uncomfortably aware of his blood flowing through capillaries and a queer sensation of heat radiating from the sides of his head. The captain wondered if another New Mexican would have affected him so.

Friar Alcazar had reproached the military for their lack of support and accused Sedlow of not dealing with the Indian problem. It was the friar's religious self-righteousness, his disdain for the military as an evil necessity, which deflated more than defeated Sedlow's authority. He had the feeling that no matter what he did, he would always be guilty in the friar's eyes, and so the captain was left contemplating an ill-defined enemy. It was all vaguely reminiscent of his childhood, when the adults in his life were automatically right because they held the power.

There was only one way to prevent this insidious desertion of self-worth, this leaking of efficacy - which Captain Sedlow would confess only to himself as a lack of courage - and that was to take action. The weather finally broke, and though it would be difficult traveling, there were blue skies above and justification in his hand. He waved the paper, the friar's signed account of the abduction, in McGiver's face.

"I want you to find the Medina children and bring in their abductors, every last one of the Indians involved with this kidnapping ... and the murders on Blue Mesa! Alcazar has accused this Owl Woman of witchcraft and the teaching of idolatry. Apparently he has good reason."

"Yes sir!" snapped Lt. McGiver.

Lt. John McGiver was pleased with his assignment. It could have gone to Sgt. Davis, thereby circumventing his control, but obviously Capt. Sedlow was willing to place his trust in him again. Here was an opportunity to bring the Jicarilla Apache to trial for the Blue Mesa massacre and remove the possibility of his involvement being revealed. His moment of satisfaction evaporated as he heard the captain speak.

"Lieutenant," the captain leaned conspiratorially across the desk, "the friar specifically asked that you search for the children. He said that he had confidence in your compassion and ability to return the orphans safely to the mission."

Sedlow glared over the rim of his glasses.

"Don't disappoint him ... or me!" he warned.

***

He planned to bivouac one night on the Plains. The men were exhausted from their slow trek through the deep snow, and were already grumbling about the wisdom of making this campaign in such freezing weather. As they neared the mountains, McGiver saw the smoke. It was not from the pueblo but from the hills to his left. His instincts told him that this would be an Indian camp, probably Jicarilla looking to trade with the pueblo Indians. Half his objective would be met in finding the Jicarilla Apache.

Breathing into his gloved hands, the lieutenant felt the short gusts of air warm his face and he heard a crackling sound as his beard began to thaw. The weather was treacherous. He thought of the warm fire ahead and knew that they could make it to the camp before nightfall. Pulling up the collar of his woolen coat against the cold wind, McGiver yelled to his men to keep moving.

The snow had turned blue in the last light of a sinking sun when the soldiers saw the campfire. They were almost upon the people huddled around the glowing fire, before they were seen. The succulent aroma wafted through the air, and the cold and hungry men barely restrained themselves as they viewed the feast before them. The Indians were roasting an antelope and its juices dripped, splashing fire-fly sparks over the red coals.

Alarmed, Owl Woman turned in their direction, and Diego lunged for the rifle hanging from El Norte's saddle.

"No!" Carlotta screamed.

At the moment she heard the clicking sounds, the soldiers' cocking their guns, Carlotta saw, again, the boy on Blue Mesa and the volley of shots that followed. She felt an arm reach for her and a hand cover her mouth. It was Owl Woman's. Carlotta heard her own scream smother and die beneath the Tuhikya's hand.

"Hush," Owl Woman whispered.

McGiver held up his hand to stop his men.

"Put the gun down, boy," he ordered. "We're not here to hurt you or your sister."

At the mention of his sister, Diego stopped in his tracks. He suddenly saw the situation and all of its implications. If he were fortunate and got off one shot, it would be his last and everyone would die, including Carlotta.

Slowly, Diego lifted his hands to show he was not armed.

One of the soldiers took the rifle and affectionately ruffled Diego's thick black hair. Diego instinctively whipped his head back and away from the soldier's hand, as he struggled to regain control of his anger.

There was the sound of laughter and the moment's tension broke.

The lieutenant quickly assessed the threat and saw that there were only women and children and two sickly old men. They were the survivors of the Llanero Jicarilla, The People of the Plains, pathetic and harmless. The two Spanish children were the missing orphans, and obviously the Indians' hostages.

McGiver dismounted his horse and walked over to the woman who was clasping the girl, keeping the child from speaking.

"You are Owl Woman, aren't you?" he demanded.

The Indian woman's hand dropped to her side, but she didn't reply.

"Answer me!" McGiver yelled. His gloved hand struck her cheek, but Owl Woman only gasped.

Carlotta struggled free, fiercely kicking the lieutenant in the shin.

"Leave her alone!" she screamed.

McGiver held the child out at arm's length while her leg thrashed ineffectively in his direction. One of the soldiers took away the feisty girl and the lieutenant rubbed his injured leg. There was no point in attempting to enlighten the Indian woman. She would learn soon enough, when the charges against her were read in court.

The company took over the camp, shooing the women, children, and old men back into the cave. McGiver ordered his men to set up the tents, while a couple of soldiers tended the fire and finished cooking the meat. No one offered meat to the Indians, but Carlotta and Diego were ordered to the campfire where they were served a slice on a tin plate.

Where only moments before the tempting smells of the roasting antelope had made her salivate, Carlotta found she had lost her appetite. She was terrified to the point of nausea. What was going to happen to Owl Woman? and to the People? She and Diego sat apart from the vulgar soldiers, who were eating greedily, their greasy hands glowing in the fire light. They seemed completely oblivious to the hungry children who peered out from the dark cave.

Carlotta couldn't risk talking to her brother out loud, and so she tried to imagine what was going to happen to them all. When her imagination became vivid, she retched futilely into the snow.

From the time that Lt. McGiver and his men arrived, the children were kept apart from the Indians. Denied any communication or contact, Carlotta and Diego were assigned their own small tent. There, they remained awake long into the night, fearing for their future.

The company broke camp early the next morning and Carlotta overheard McGiver discuss their destination to San Ramon, as an intended detour in their route to Ft. Granger. They were going to deliver the Medina children to Friar Alcazar and take the Indians on to the fort.

McGiver reviewed the pack animals and his regiment as they prepared to depart from the Indians' stronghold.

The People of the Plains stood huddled together, dressed in the rags of all their worldly goods. A woman and two of the children had no leggings or even moccasins, but were preparing to walk between the mounted soldiers as they rode across the snow.

McGiver, seemingly oblivious to their plight, admired the black stallion Diego was saddling.

"You two, get on the black," he ordered Diego and Carlotta. "I wonder where the Indians stole him from?" the lieutenant asked, absently.

"Sir, please, I borrowed El Norte with permission. Would you let someone who doesn't have shoes ride him?" Diego pleaded.

Diego hoped that no one would be accused of horse theft, but more urgently, he didn't believe several of the Indians would make it if they had to walk barefoot.

"It doesn't matter to me, but you'd better not fall behind." McGiver turned his back and rode to the head of the procession.

Diego helped the resisting Indian woman onto El Norte's back and then he boosted up the children, one to ride in front and one to ride behind her. The mule they had brought from the pueblo would carry the ill old man and the weakened child.

McGiver ordered them to move out, and the scraggly group of women and children, both Indians and orphans, began the miserable pilgrimage through the snow.

Despite the sun, the cold air stung Carlotta's face. It seemed no more unnatural nor contradictory than the soldiers' raid on the gentle People of the Plains.

***

Two Bears and his father walked the narrow terrace, a treacherous sheet of ice cracking beneath their feet. Sak-mo-i-si's face was stern with worry, and he said nothing as he looked over the plains. It was useless. There wasn't a sign of Owl Woman or the children, and worse, not a wisp of smoke rising in the sky to indicate there was life on the frozen prairie.

The sun's rays glinted off a piece of turquoise stone embedded in the adobe above a doorway, just one of many The People placed to guard their homes from witchcraft. But Two Bears felt far from secure. He remembered the children who had gone to the corn fields never to return, and he recalled an anguished mother's cries at discovering her son and daughter had vanished. He had heard the elders speak of witchcraft and wondered why they didn't say anything now? The empty saddle bags Diego had left hanging in his father's home were the painful reminder of other missing children, and he was curious as to what knowledge the Tuhikya had of their disappearance.

The woman who had married his father had special powers. Two Bears had seen how Owl Woman used her powers on Sak-mo-i-si. The Sun Watcher had stared too long into her black eyes, he thought. She had blinded him to his duties to The People. The People of the pueblo required his care and protection from Alcazar and the soldiers, but especially from the Coyote Kachina, who had mysteriously appeared during the Soyal ceremonies and caused the fierce turn in weather. His father was hopelessly under Owl Woman's spell now and could not think of anything except her safety.

Reluctantly, Two Bears followed his father's orders and the two departed from the pueblo. They journeyed in the direction they had last seen Owl Woman and the children, and for a while Two Bears rode quietly by his father's side. He felt the trust, which he had always had for the adults in his life, weakened by his fears, which grew larger as they approached the mountains. What would they find? Did Owl Woman abduct his friends or worse? Two Bears' imagination loomed menacingly and he was sickened by his own suspicions.

Sak-mo-i-si led their horses over the rocks, seeking what others before him sought, a shelter from the cold wind. For there were two ways to hunt prey or find a man, and with all tracks erased by three days of snowfall, he knew that he must put himself in their place if he were to find The People of the Plains.

They came upon fresh hoof tracks and saw that they were the prints of the soldiers' heavier, saddled ponies. Sak-mo-i-si and his son quickened their pace, enabled by the trail of clear depressions on new snow. The tracks brought them directly to The People's camp, a recess under the mountain's stone ledge. But they were too late, The People had left. Descending from their horses, father and son studied the evidence before them.

Owl Woman, Carlotta, and Diego had been here. Their footprints were everywhere on the floor of the cave, which had protected The People from the weather, but also in the snow and leading away with those of The People and the soldiers. Two Bears recognized the heel prints of Diego's boots and Carlotta's shoes. He was horrified to learn that his friends and Owl Woman were on foot, while others rode the horse, El Norte, and his father's mule. Two Bears could feel his father's tension as he prowled about the cave searching for clues.

"The soldiers are a day's ride ahead of us and they have taken your mother. We will ride directly to Santa Fe and talk to the White Man's governor," said Sak-mo-i-si.

Two Bears did not protest, it was pointless. Besides, how else would they find Carlotta and Diego?

***

"You asked for me, Father?" Joaquin entered the library and softly closed the door behind him.

Don Luis looked up from his desk, where he had been reviewing schedules of imports. His eyes were red and weary from strain, but he gave his son his full attention.

"Did you honestly think, Joaquin, that I wouldn't notice that your horse was missing?"

Though he had known this question was inevitable, Joaquin did not answer. He was still not prepared with a story, and he stood before his father aware that he must appear as stupid as he felt.

"It is, also, time that you told me about these notes from "Lafing Coyote".

"You are thirteen years old, son, accountable now for your actions. I expect an explanation."

Joaquin waited expectantly for his father to volunteer information about the officer he had just seen leave the hacienda. When he saw that he would not, he became genuinely worried.

The officer had ridden to the house with El Norte tethered behind him, and Joaquin's father had motioned for him to take the horse's reins. He had obediently led El Norte to the barn and out of earshot of their conversation.

Joaquin's heart was in his mouth as he considered what might have happened to his friends. He stammered, seeking the right words, ones that would not betray but instead coax the answers from his father.

"I loaned El Norte to Diego. I knew that he would take good care of him, Father!" Joaquin added hurriedly.

"That doesn't worry or concern me. I know the boy, I know his character.

"What does concern me is your character! You have never lied to me, Joaquin. Why must you begin now?"

Joaquin tried to deny his father's accusation, feebly protesting, but Luis cut him off.

"No," he said firmly. "Your lie is one of omission but a lie nonetheless!

"Now, why did you not tell me?"

The boy had no answer, no answer that would not break his solemn promise to his friend.

There was a soft tap on the door and it opened slightly.

"Señor, pardona me. The soldier, he say they have taken the Llanero to the fort?" Cuenta asked.

Her expression was one of alarm. In fact, Joaquin had never seen the Indian woman appear so anxious. It had been her composure that had calmed Joaquin more than once during his childhood. It was incomprehensible that the adults in his life could lose their serenity.

"Those are your people, aren't they, Cuenta? Yes, they are being held at the fort. But you mustn't worry, I will inquire as to the exact charges," said Luis, dismissing her concern.

"... The children, are they all right?" Cuenta asked.

Joaquin's head snapped at the mention of children. He studied his father's face, hoping to find the answer.

"They are in good care. The lieutenant took them back to the mission," Luis answered.

"Diego ... Carlotta?" Joaquin could not restrain himself.

Luis waited till Cuenta closed the door.

"Yes," he said. "They were with the Indians, most likely against their will."

"Oh no, father ..." Joaquin caught himself. His head dropped and he said no more.

It was then that Luis saw. A glimpse of the anguish on his son's face, and a brief moment of intuition explained the boy's behavior. Joaquin was covering for his friends. He was afraid for their safety, perhaps their lives.

Luis dismissed his son. He felt useless, ill-equipped to deal with the boy's stubbornness, and attempting to re-establish his parental role, ordered him to his room.

Alone, Luis reviewed the growing mystery. On one hand he had made up his mind to inquire how he could aid Cuenta's people, and decided to see Governor Maxwell immediately. On the other hand he was determined to get to the bottom of this business about Laughing Coyote. Luis could no longer pass off the disappearing and reappearing silver as a childish prank. But most of all, he was alarmed at his own conviction that the children were in danger.

An instinctive sense of predator led Luis to think of Friar Alcazar. What were the friar's motives in this roundup of Indians? Ever since he had asked the governor who had been the first to suggest the proclamation, Luis had thought about the profits that Alcazar stood to gain. When the new fort was built ... which, he reminded himself, was also encouraged by Alcazar ... how would the friar benefit?

For some time Luis had wrestled with his conscience. The suspicion that a man of the Church would value profit over the welfare of his parish was disturbing. But despite his desire to hold the Church above reproach, during the last few months suspicions had arisen. The friar was not a comfort to Luis or his family, nor to Cuenta and Pedro ... not even to the orphans who he had robbed of their small earnings.

Luis' eyes narrowed as he pushed himself to see things as they were truly. Friar Alcazar was first a man, he thought. A man, like all others, able to choose the unearned. Because Alcazar was so adept at gaining and accepting the unearned, did he think that he could cheat God, as well?

***

Lt. McGiver remembered the captain's reference to Alcazar's words, his trust that the children would be returned safely to the mission. McGiver understood the message with its implied warning. Impatiently, the soldiers had lifted the two from the snow, snatched from where they had fallen too weak to continue, and sat the children behind them on their horses.

The company arrived at the mission and handed over the Medina children as Sedlow had instructed, but McGiver wasted no time and left for the fort, eager to escape Alcazar's formidable presence. Friar Alcazar saw that the children were locked into the rectory, telling Friar Serna that this was for their own protection. This would prevent their recapture by the Indians of the pueblo. He explained, as well, that Carlotta and Diego had obviously been instilled with the ways of witchcraft and taught idol worship. The Medina children were an evil influence on the others, and must be kept separate, their only contact to be Friar Serna and himself.

For the first twenty-four hours, Carlotta and Diego were unaware of their new imprisonment. Lying on the rug beside Alcazar's bed, the children slept. The long walk through deep snow had overwhelmed their youth and their intent to ease the Indians' pain.

Friar Serna was diligent to his duty. He felt sympathy for the exhausted orphans and checked on them often until they woke. He attributed the children's silence to the suffering they had experienced during the abduction, and hoped to nurture their spirit and bodies, cheering the two with steaming bowls of beans and tortillas. When nothing the friar said brought life back to their faces, he left, convinced they had been deeply traumatized by the abduction.

Serna passed the gate leading to the street and heard the bell announce a visitor to the mission. He recognized Don Luis Valenzuela, the wealthy haciendado, and politely offered him entrance. The don was not in a cordial mood. His mouth was fixed in a grim line and his mind seemed to be elsewhere. "Would you take me to Friar Alcazar, Father?" he asked.

Serna was relieved to find useful service and led his guest to the chapel's door.

"He has spent much time here, as of late. The children are a big worry ... and I'm certain he seeks solace with our Lord."

Serna's plump body bowed quaintly, a small movement that bid Luis Valenzuela's leave. He left Luis and pattered down the corridor.

Luis opened the chapel door and entered the room.

"Señor Valenzuela, it is good to see you again. I've been expecting you!"

Alcazar looked up from the silver chalice that he was polishing, and Luis saw that he indeed was not surprised at the visit.

"Good day, Friar. But how is it that you were expecting me?" asked Luis.

Alcazar smiled. "The Medina children, it is obvious that you care for them, no?"

Luis saw the feigned compassion in the friar's smile. The mechanical adjustments to his face came a little too quickly, Luis thought. His cold eyes were at odds with his words. Luis was, suddenly, keenly aware, his perception that of a skillful hunter.

"As a matter of fact, that is why I am here. I would like to take the children back with me to the hacienda. Their ordeal has had an effect on them, and on my son and me. We will do our best to make them content ..."

"I am sure you would," Alcazar interrupted, "but it is not quite that simple. They have been used most brutally, their very Christian upbringing, shall we say ... challenged."

Luis gazed, long and searchingly into Alcazar's face.

"What do you mean, Friar, exactly?"

"Don Luis, surely you are aware that they have been influenced, if not outright kidnapped by the Indians. They were made to worship false idols, and their very souls are in jeopardy."

"In jeopardy?" Luis was astonished, in spite of his suspicions. He had other questions, hard questions, but stopped himself. He was beginning to see this was not the place nor the time to ask how this were possible because the children had borrowed his son's horse.

"I see," Luis answered, doing his best to keep any negative inflection from his voice. "Well, perhaps we will see them when they are well..."

***

Two Bears walked with his father to the horses. They were miraculously free. The White Man's captain soldier had released them, and he felt his heart pound with both fear and relief. They would not release Owl Woman, and were charging the Tuhikya with the kidnapping of Carlotta and Diego, and the practice of witchcraft. The White Man's law said they were to appear in Santa Fe in two days for the trial. A stiff warning had accompanied the order. Any communication with the warring tribes, or with those who practiced witchcraft would be severely punished.

This new definition of the enemy jarred Two Bears. The White Man had given voice to his suspicions. Worse, they were going to find Owl Woman guilty and make her accountable for witchcraft. The Indians of the Plains would also stand trial, and how would they defend the charge of murder? How had the suspicions of the townspeople grown unchecked? How did the imagined become the truth? Two Bears felt trapped, as if he were caught in a rabbit's snare. His very fears had materialized.

***

CHAPTER 20

THE PEOPLE ARE EVERYWHERE

THE PEOPLE ARE EVERYWHERE

The morning was cold and dark. Joaquin looked out across the snow-dotted hacienda to Volcan Mountain, looming blue and hazy in the distance. Outside the window of his mother's room the world looked bleak, yet here he felt the promise of the day. He shivered as he imagined the wolf pack running down the trail, returning to their dens before the first light filtered through the pines. He could see the wolves loping, crouched and low on the mist-filled path, hurrying to return to the refuge and comfort of family after a night of lonely vigil. The portrait of Señora Valenzuela smiled down benevolently from its place on the bedroom wall. Joaquin felt his mother's happiness and love for the horse depicted in the painting, the one who looked so much like El Norte, and he was filled with her warmth.

They would be leaving momentarily for Santa Fe, his father, Cuenta, and he. Soon he would hear his name called, and then the three would depart for the courtroom, where his father would defend the Indians against the charges of murder, kidnapping, and witchcraft, and where the fate of his friends, the children of the mission, would be determined.

Joaquin saw his own path stretch before him, a long and winding journey into adulthood, and he felt a glimpse of understanding. He understood the desire of the wolf to learn so that he might return to the clan and teach, just as his father had created the freedom necessary for his own education. At this moment Joaquin never loved his father more, nor had he ever been more proud of him. But here in the sanctuary of his mother's room, he allowed himself to miss her terribly.

"Cuenta, what in the world is all of this?" asked Luis, referring to the large basket brimming with food.

He had already explained to her that they would be staying in Santa Fe until the trial was over. They would take their meals at the hotel, and it was certainly unnecessary for her to prepare food.

The Indian woman folded her arms resolutely across her midsection. Luis saw her familiar gesture as one of stubborn defiance and decidedly altered his tactic.

"I respect your judgment, Cuenta. I would just like to understand," he encouraged reasonably.

Joaquin joined them and casually picked a red apple from the basket.

"No," Cuenta said firmly. "This food is for The People of the Plains."

***

The visitor was impatiently rattling the gate. Friar Serna shuffled down the corridor as quickly as his plump body could manage. Mumbling platitudes, which beseeched patience of the anonymous presence on the other side, Serna opened the gate to a large man, splendidly dressed in military uniform. In the officer's hand was an official-looking communiqué.

"I have an order from the court in Santa Fe," the officer said urgently.

Before Serna could offer the explanation that Friar Alcazar had already departed for Santa Fe, and unfortunately there was no one about with the friar's authority, the officer began to read from the letter.

"From the United States of America, Territory of New Mexico, County of Santa Fe." He cleared his throat in an effort to emphasize the solemnity of the occasion.

"The Honorable Judge Robert Lawrence Beckworth of the District Court for the First Judicial District of said Territory, County of Santa Fe, on this day January Seventeenth A.D. 1851, hereby requests the presence of Diego and Carlotta Montoya de Medina. They are to appear at the trial of the United States versus the Llanero Jicarilla, a tribe of Apache Indians, and the Pueblo Indian woman known as Owl Woman."

Beads of perspiration sprouted on Serna's brow. This was most irregular, and he knew Alcazar would not approve. And how were the children to be delivered? He sighed heavily, conceding the inevitable to himself. It would fall on him, as Maria was needed at the mission to care for the younger children.

The officer expressed the speed required to have the children there in time. "It is most important that you follow the order of the court," he said sternly. "Do you have transportation? A carriage or wagon?"

"Yes, yes," answered Serna nervously. "But, I must get them ready ..."

The friar accepted the document and hurriedly turned to leave, flustered but resigned to oblige the United States Government, when the officer called him back.

"Wait. Here is another letter." He scrutinized the envelope. "It is addressed to Friar Alcazar from a Señor Carlos Montoya, postmarked Madrid, Spain," he added.

He handed the letter to Friar Serna and smiled. The friar did his best to return the smile and closed the gate.

Entering the rectory, Serna absently laid the letter on Alcazar's table, and clapped his hands together as if he were calling school.

"Come, come, children! We must leave for Santa Fe! I want you to wash and dress quickly while I inform Maria. There is no time to waste!"

Without explanation, Serna left Diego and Carlotta stunned and alone. From imprisonment in Alcazar's quarters they would suddenly be traveling to Santa Fe.

"What do you think, Diego?" whispered Carlotta. "Are we going to jail with The People of the Plains?"

Diego handed her the crude bar of soap and said cynically, "Could it be any worse than this?"

Carlotta approached the basin reluctantly. Dutifully, she splashed water on her face and began to scrub. The burning soap filled her eyes, despite her efforts to blink it away. Reaching blindly for the towel on the table, Carlotta's hand fell, instead, on the letter. The stinging blur finally cleared and she read the formal handwriting. From its swirls and flourishes emerged the written name, Carlos Montoya of Madrid, Spain.

She slipped the letter into the pocket of her dress just as Friar Serna entered the room.

Serna hurried the children off to the stable, instructing Diego to help him hitch up the team. Carlotta climbed into the wagon ahead of her brother just as a raucous noise spilled across the courtyard. She looked out of the barn to see their friends running toward them.

Word had spread that the prisoners were released, and Maria had no power in this world to stop the six orphans who ran to find them.

Carlotta looked down at the sunny smiles of Virginia, Miguel, and the others and felt the love of the only family she had ever known. The twins clambered noisily over the wagon sides and Miguel and the others followed.

Friar Serna shrugged his shoulders. He was not accustomed to his new authority, but no longer felt a desire to enforce Alcazar's rule of segregation. Besides, it just seemed right that they should be kept together. The friar bundled the children in blankets, fussing as he tucked them in against the cold, dark ride ahead of them.

He was concerned that it might begin to snow before they arrived in Santa Fe, but they had no choice, he reasoned to himself. Friar Alcazar had taken the carriage. Serna struggled into the driver's seat and took the reins.

The team of horses lurched forward. With the mission gates behind them, Diego asked his sister to hand over the letter.

***

The muddy streets of Santa Fe had begun to fill with carts and carriages, as the wagon from San Ramon's mission arrived. The wheels tore deep ruts into the sticky clay and wobbled uncertainly as they sought the grooves of those that had passed. There was an electric quality to the air, much the same as before a thunderstorm, as New Mexicans from far and wide drew closer to the plaza, the common center of their lives.

They had heard: the town's merchants and residents, the outlying farmers, together with the wealthy haciendados and their hired hands. Whole families came, dressed in their very best, some grand and others more drab, drawn by the excitement of Santa Fe's most social affair. Ordinary routines and the monotonous lives of long winter days were suspended, willingly placed on hold for the duration of the trial.

The trial itself, with its accusations of the prosecution and the defense of the accused, was mostly obscure to the good citizens of New Mexico. There was, of course, the story of Blue Mesa. Rumors of the horrendous massacre by the monstrous Indian known as Laughing Coyote had drifted into their homes this fall and winter, finding their way through the cracks in mortared timber, and weighting the air like smoke from a blocked flue. Then there were the tales of witchcraft.

The mysterious Indian woman from the pueblo, whose skirts glided unobtrusively through the streets as she sought her way to Dr. Gentry's bearing baskets of herbs, she was a suspicious one, they said. It was becoming increasingly obvious that they had been affected by her and those of her kind. From their neighbors, the Fletchers, who were burned out, and the Indian raids that terrorized the countryside, to the dark skies that pummeled storm after storm on them, their very lives were caught in a death grip. It was their duty to bear witness, to seek God's justice here on earth.

Don Luis Valenzuela stepped out of the hotel's doorway. The cold air struck his face and he turned his head against the wind, drawing up the collar on his coat. From the porch, Luis and Joaquin watched Father Serna shepherd the children from the wagon into the courthouse. Luis was relieved that they had arrived in time.

Luis watched his son's response at the recognition of his friends and stopped him just before he descended the porch.

"No, Joaquin. The children may be called to testify. It would be improper, in the eyes of the court, that the son of counsel for the defense be seen talking with them."

Joaquin looked hopelessly into his father's eyes and Luis turned away. Farther down the busy road, past a crowd of citizens, Luis caught a glimpse of silver hair and recognized the governor and his niece walking toward the courthouse. For the same reasons he had given his son, Luis suppressed his desire to greet Rebecca. Instead, his eyes patiently followed the lovely young woman dressed in green velvet. Even from here, he could imagine the softness of her blushing cheek above the gold-braided trim of her traveling suit. Luis watched as Rebecca collapsed her parasol, and taking the governor's arm entered the massive doors, disappearing into the courthouse.

"Yoo-hoo, Don Luis ..."

A woman was frantically waving her handkerchief, attempting to gain Luis' attention from across the street.

It was Señora Juan Quiros, a guest at Luis' summer ball. As he and Joaquin approached the courthouse, Luis felt himself stalked, as if by a very large social butterfly. There was apparently no way to evade her insistence on his attention, and so Luis surrendered.

"Buenos dias, Señora Quiros," Luis greeted her in his most formal manner.

Out of breath and flushed, the Señora plucked at Luis' fine coat and gushed,

"Oh, Luis, you look so handsome! You really must visit us some evening ... with the lovely Señorita Rebecca Maxwell, no?"

Leaning closer to Luis, Señora Quiros whispered secretively, "Did you hear?" Her eyes gleamed bright, and Luis braced himself for her latest gossip.

"Friar Alcazar has just received a shipment of exquisite furniture from Spain! Oh, but of course you know! How silly of me, you must have made the arrangements for the delivery to his ranch!"

***

The courtroom was large and in the past had easily accommodated the major trials for the territory of Santa Fe, but as people filed through the large doors, eager to escape the cold, it was soon obvious that not everyone would find seating. There were noisy conversations and much stomping of muddied boots, as the good citizens of New Mexico looked for a vantage point from which to view the most celebrated case in the history of their lives.

Dark oak bookcases and benches graced the old adobe walls, a yellowish glow reflecting off its wood, a cheerless offering from the pale winter light that streamed through the windows. The banister railing, which separated members of the actual trial from the growing throng who would bear witness, fairly groaned under the crowd's assault. Luis left his son on the other side and found his place at the table for the defense.

At the table for the prosecution sat Alcazar, serene and dark in simple robes. In striking contrast beside him, sat an officer impeccably dressed in military uniform. Luis surveyed the room and saw the military's presence everywhere. There was a brief commotion as people turned their attention to the doors where Indians were entering to quietly stand against the back wall. Luis scanned the gathering crowd and recognized many of the merchants who used his freighting business, the wealthy New Mexicans who had prospered from the flow of goods, besides the unmentioned migration of human flesh that passed over territorial lines, seeking a better way of life.

Governor John Maxwell, too, examined those who were filing into the courtroom, but with deep satisfaction. The fulfillment of his proclamation had brought the authority and even the glory for which he had yearned. The citizens of New Mexico would witness, for the first time, the law of American government in action. He, personally, had little tolerance for the silly superstitions of the New Mexicans, but admitted to himself a great admiration for Alcazar's ability to manipulate their fears to serve his own purpose. He watched carefully the demeanor of the man beyond the railing. Alcazar's pious, though noble, figure was quite effective in support of his own cause. If it had not worked so well for the United States' Government, Maxwell thought, the friar could be a formidable adversary.

Diego gave a small tug to his sister's hand and Carlotta stumbled forward. He had brought her attention back to where they were walking. Friar Serna was leading the children, singlefile, to the first row behind the railing. Carlotta tried to pay attention, but her eyes kept lifting to search the room. The chairs and benches were filling with those of all manner of society. The people were everywhere. She had seen some of their faces in town at the mercantile, others at the great Valenzuela ball. Yet, those of the pueblo, like Sak-mo-i-si, who accompanied Two Bears, and was now standing against the wall, were seldom seen by anyone but her. Even on this cold winter day the air was warmed by their life breath: Indian, Mexican, Spaniard, and American.

She shivered. What was expected of them? she wondered. Carlotta looked up and saw Luis Valenzuela approach the table directly in front of her and her friends. Don Luis gave her a quick, open smile and then his countenance became more sober. Carlotta supposed he was immensely more familiar than she with this building and all of these people.

Carlotta squeezed Diego's hand and Jean Paul's, who was seated on her right. They, too, must recognize one of the town's few adults who had befriended los niños. To the left of Luis Valenzuela, Carlotta saw Alcazar. Involuntarily, she trembled and ducked her head from his view. She reminded herself that if the friar was here, he was not at the mission with the little ones.

When she dared to look again, Carlotta saw that she had hidden too late. Alcazar had recognized her, and his glare revealed that for a moment he was taken off guard. Reaching over to the officer seated beside him, she watched as they conspired.

Suddenly, a man's voice rose and overrode the chatter and chair noises of the room.

"Please stand," he ordered.

There was a noisy scuffle, as chairs were pushed back and boots and shoes found their places on the muddy floor.

"Judge Beckworth of the First Judicial District of the Territory of New Mexico, County of Santa Fe, presiding."

A small older man, dressed in dark robes of finer cloth than Alcazar's, swept across the far side of the room and climbed the steps to a chair more grand than any Carlotta had seen. From this vantage point, Judge Beckworth could see the entire room.

"Bailiff, are the accused here?" he asked.

At that moment, doors to the side of the podium opened, and a soldier led Owl Woman into the room by a thin chain linked to her wrists. She was brought to the table where Luis was sitting and given a chair with her back to the children.

"Your Honor, the Jicarilla Apache are retained at the fort. They have willingly placed their defense in the hands of Señor Luis Valenzuela, who has agreed to plead their case along with the case of the Indian woman, Owl Woman.

There was a commotion as both counsels for the prosecution and the defense protested until Judge Beckworth asked them to approach the bench. Huddled closely, the judge leaned toward them and spoke quietly with the officer and Luis.

The room settled down again, and the bailiff read the charges.

Carlotta's eyes opened wide. This was the first time she had heard the accusations against Owl Woman and the Indians of the Plains. The full understanding of the threat presented in the courtroom filled Carlotta with dread. She was too young to comprehend the workings of a court, but she was to learn.

On her right, behind a railing just like the one in front of her, sat the jury. In this box, there were seated twelve men who would judge the case against her friends. Curiously, she looked into their faces. They seemed harsh and yet each held a hint of fear. Stiff and awkward in their unaccustomed finest clothes, they, too, looked out warily at the room. It seemed to Carlotta that they suspected that something beyond their ken - their understanding - would be expected of each of them.

As she viewed the roles of others in the trial, Carlotta began to interpret what had seemed to be excitement, as a tension of wills. The last shreds of her own childhood naivety dropped away.

Rising from his chair, Capt. Banning sauntered to the center of the well...an area directly in front of the judge, bordered by the jury, and the tables for the prosecution and defense.

"You have heard the charges. Now, you will hear from various witnesses who I will call to testify, the evidence of those who know firsthand the horror and the evil of the accused.

"Your neighbors - farmers...humble people ... who have lost all of their earthly possessions, their very lives, to the Indian heathens! Those who've suffered for years in their attempts to settle this territory, were finally given protection this summer. Your new American governor, Governor Maxwell, with his deep compassion for our plight, read in late July from his proclamation to the Indians ... at the very home of Señor Luis Valenzuela, the appointed counsel for defense!" the officer ended emphatically.

A murmur rose from the room like a drone of angry bees.

***

CHAPTER 21

TRUTH AND DECEPTION

TRUTH AND DECEPTION

Luis' opening remarks were not as stirring as he had hoped. He walked, slowly, deliberately over to the jurors, where he stood for several moments with his arms folded in thoughtful silence. When he spoke, he tried to appeal to his fellow New Mexicans' reason, their ability to detect truth from sham. He would attempt to disclose, he said, through the testimony of witnesses, the concocted inventions and lies of those egged on by their own hysteria.

He returned to the table where Owl Woman was seated, the woman he had not met until this very morning. Luis tried to read her face, searching for some sign that she was eager to participate in his struggle for her defense, and instead, found her expression to be one of incomprehensible detachment and even peace.

The first witness for the prosecution was Lt. John McGiver.

Luis inhaled deeply. He was only one of many, he reminded himself.

"Tell me, McGiver, in your own words, what you know about the massacre of Blue Mesa on that fateful day of June twenty-sixth." Capt. Banning commanded.

McGiver shifted his weight in the witness chair.

"We were returning to the fort ... my company and I ... from an assignment, and we ... we saw the children. Several were still breathing ... we did our best, but to no avail."

"How many children died that summer day, lieutenant?"

The captain's voice had lowered and those in the courtroom strained to hear the lieutenant's answer.

"Sixteen, sir."

"And did you identify, or try to find the perpetrators?" encouraged the captain.

"Oh, yes. They were Indian. Jicarilla, according to the arrows. We tracked them for some distance, but eventually we lost their trail and returned to report the incident to Friar Alcazar ... and then we assisted him ... in the burial."

"This must have been a difficult assignment, Lieutenant." Banning's voice was soothing, gently prodding further details.

McGiver lifted his head, straining for control, and found his response to be surprisingly genuine. Emotion filled his voice, and he apologized, hoarsely, for his inability to continue.

It was an easy matter to recall the wistful young bodies strewn amongst the wild flowers. Jolted back by the captain's question, McGiver dropped his head and found himself gazing directly into the riveting black eyes of Alcazar. He then recalled the search for those same bodies in the dark, by lantern light, and trembled visibly.

The people carefully followed the young soldier's reactions, quick to note and sympathize with his sincere display of compassion.

The moment of endured suffering hung in the air, as the prosecutor returned to his table and Luis Valenzuela rose from his chair.

"Lieutenant McGiver ... It is lieutenant, am I correct?" Luis smiled warmly.

"Yes, sir."

"Well ... I wasn't sure. You seem to be so young for such a commission. Quite an honor, wouldn't you say?"

"I suppose so." McGiver seemed a little confused at this unexpected flattery.

"You needn't be so modest, Lieutenant. Your position is one of great responsibility. There are many of us who are in great debt to the United States Army and its many fine officers ... such as yourself." Luis looked steadily into McGiver's face, apparently eager to give credit where it was due.

"Certainly, this was a most-difficult assignment. Not only had you accidentally come upon the dying children and with good conscience offered your help in their burial, but you came face to face and actually pursued their murderer, Laughing Coyote!"

McGiver squirmed nervously. "We didn't actually see him ..."

"Excuse me ..." Luis turned suddenly and faced the lieutenant.

"You didn't see Laughing Coyote?" Luis asked, astonished.

"No. The war party of Indians had all left before we arrived."

"You are certain, though, that the Indian Laughing Coyote was one of them."

"Not exactly," answered McGiver. "He was involved in so many crimes this summer and always managed to stay just ahead of me and my men."

"But you saw him ... you know what he looks like?" Luis's head nodded agreeably.

Moments went by. Someone coughed, but in unison everyone else held their breath expectantly, waiting for McGiver's reply.

Lt. McGiver was silent. Luis restrained himself, resisting the temptation to fill in the pause.

"I didn't actually see him," McGiver answered reluctantly. Suddenly aware of the attention his reply had drawn, he added hastily, "but, I certainly saw his handiwork!"

"Thank you, Lieutenant McGiver. I believe that will be all."

***

Several townspeople of San Ramon were called to testify for the prosecution, victims of the scattered raids that had taken place during the previous year. The room fell quiet as Joseph Fletcher told his personal story, the burning of his ranch and his family's subsequent financial ruin.

Capt. Banning next called Dr. William Harold Gentry to the stand. Without hesitation the doctor climbed the steps into the witness box and took his seat. From this vantage point Gentry could see the mission orphans, and in particular the familiar blonde head of Virginia seated in a row behind Luis' table. A smile broke across the doctor's face and he flashed a mischievous wink.

"Doctor Gentry, you probably, more than anyone in the village of San Ramon, have seen first-hand the terrible handiwork to which Lieutenant McGiver has alluded. Am I correct?"

"And what handiwork would you be speaking of, Officer?" asked the doctor.

"The handiwork of the Apaches and Laughing Coyote, of course!" cried Banning.

"Objection, your honor," Luis interrupted, rising from his chair. "We cannot expect the good doctor to answer in specifics, if we are made to guess at Captain Banning's intent."

Judge Beckworth waved a hand in an impatient gesture of dismissal. "I believe his line of questioning is on course now. Please continue, Captain."

Banning's eyes fixed Luis with a glare and then returned to his witness.

"Did you, Doctor, on July fourth of this year, tend to a soldier that Sergeant Davis brought into town with an arrow in his leg?"

"Yes, I did. And I might add that it was a hunting arrow, not an arrow belonging to a war party!"

"Well, of course it was, Doctor," Banning's words caressed the air like a soothing balm. "Remember, Sergeant Davis actually caught the Jicarilla by surprise.

"But, enough about this incident. Tell us about the witches, Owl Woman and her sisters."

***

Carlotta had listened mesmerized, as first Lt. McGiver answered Luis Valenzuela's questions, and then the doctor. The courtroom drama swept past her eyes, barely allowing her time for comprehension, much less judgment.

She found she almost wanted to believe McGiver's account of Blue Mesa, as it relieved her from such painful memories. How simple it would all be, if only the truth could become a lie so that McGiver's lie could become the truth.

And Laughing Coyote, he had become real. He was more than just the whisperings in town, the haunting stories that had drifted over the mission's walls that day she and Virginia had tried so desperately to bring light and joy back into their lives playing with the Kachina doll. These people had made him real ... as an answer to their problems. Carlotta's head fell in shame. Hadn't she and los niños done the same?

Dr. Gentry was telling the captain about the healing herbs that Owl Woman brought to town each year. Carlotta listened, as he explained the value of these herbs, which had long been known to the people of San Ramon, but whose source had obviously been overlooked.

"Certainly, Doctor, you are aware that Owl Woman and her sisters had been banished from their own tribe for practicing witchcraft, and that many of those herbs have been used for unholy purposes?"

"I'm not aware of any such thing!" Gentry answered adamantly.

Gentry's testimony was bantered about pretty much as the captain wished to direct it, and when Luis had at last the opportunity to cross-examine, he read the faces of the jurors and saw that the damage had already been done.

They loved the doctor, but they knew him as a congenial old coot who was attempting to deal with things beyond his professional knowledge. This was an area that surpassed his understanding of medicine, and besides, you could not live in, or close to, the town of San Ramon and not hear things about the Indian witches.

Luis did his best to rehabilitate the doctor's credibility, and returned to his chair to wait on Capt. Banning's next surprise.

"Your honor, I wish to call Owl Woman to the stand," said Banning.

So, this was it ... the last witness for the prosecution, Luis thought. Perhaps, he would see the light at the end of the tunnel after all.

Sak-mo-i-si stood straight, his vision unobstructed, his figure tall above the mostly seated crowd. Two Bears strained to see over the heads of those in front, and was troubled when his father seemed unaware of his struggle. Quietly, he crept away to the edge of the aisle to peer at the woman the entire town knew as a witch and who was married to his father.

Alcazar leaned over to conspire with the captain, and then Banning rose. In a fatherly tone he began his line of questioning of Owl Woman.

"Is this true, Owl Woman? Were you and your sisters driven from your pueblo by the elders?"

"Yes," she answered.

"What were the charges?"

"The theft of the silver chalices and witchcraft." Owl Woman answered. The object of her gaze was indiscernible to those who pressed curiously forward in their chairs.

"I see," said Banning. "So this is not the first time that you have been accused of witchcraft.

"Tell me," Banning continued, "do I understand correctly that you have recently married the pueblo's Sun Watcher?"

"Yes, this is true." Owl Woman's lips betrayed just a hint of her smile.

"And would his name be Laughing Coyote?"

"Your honor, I must object ..." Luis protested.

A flurry of speculations ran through the courtroom, and Judge Beckworth pounded his gavel to resume order.

"Let the woman answer," ordered the judge.

"My husband...he is Sak-mo-i-si. He is not Laughing Coyote," Owl Woman answered.

"Do you know who is Laughing Coyote?" the captain asked.

"No," answered Owl Woman.

"But, he exists?" he urged.

"Oh, yes, he exists."

"Just two more questions, ma'am, and then we'll be done," the captain smiled condescendingly.

"Why were you the only sister who was allowed to return to your people?"

"Because the Great Spirit has given me the power to heal."

"Oh, really. I'm curious, is Owl Woman your given name?"

"No ... as a child it was Blue Corn."

"And when and why was your name changed?"

"When we lived in the cave, my sisters and I, the white owl came and befriended me."

"Thank you, Owl Woman. I believe that will be all."

With a flourish, the captain faced Luis and added, "Unless the defense has some questions?"

Luis felt the stinging smugness of the prosecution. Alcazar's face was frozen with an expression of stoic acceptance of the legal process, just a trace of disdain marring the face of a martyr. Luis breathed deeply, hoping to clear his head of angry reprisals waiting to sabotage his need to focus on an uncooperative witness.

"Yes, thank you counselor," Luis answered, his voice barren of emotion.

"Owl Woman, Captain Banning has asked you why you were banished from your people's pueblo, but he failed to ask if the charges were true. Would you please tell the court ... did you ever steal anything from the pueblo?"

"No," answered Owl Woman.

"And so, even though you heal with the same herbs that you bring to Gentry...you are not a thief?"

"That is true."

Luis smiled. "And your husband is not Laughing Coyote?"

"That is true, also," answered Owl Woman.

"What proof then, do you have that there is a Laughing Coyote?"

"The same proof that tells me there is a White Owl. The power of the animal speaks to those who listen with their heart."

"What is this power of Laughing Coyote ... can you tell us about it?" Luis asked.

For several moments Owl Woman was silent, and Luis wasn't certain that she had heard.

"I don't think White Man can listen with his heart," she said finally with disappointment. Her eyes followed Luis, as he paced in front of her.

"Try me," he said, softly.

"Indians know Coyote as the Trickster. In many ways he is like man, in that he has the ability to trick himself. There is a tale among Indian people, about the beginning of time."

"Would you tell it to us?" asked Luis.

"Objection, your honor," cried Banning. "Fairy tales serve no purpose here!"

"But, your honor, that seems to be the very point Owl Woman is trying to illustrate," Luis countered.

"Objection over-ruled!"

Owl Woman scanned the rows of people until her eyes settled on the Indian standing in the back and the boy at his side. Taking as much strength from them as they were from her words, she continued.

"Coyote threw a stone into the water and said that, if it sank, living beings would experience physical death. It is said that the stone did sink, and so man was put on the path of life and death.

"The old ones say that if man's eyes had followed the ripples caused by the stone, and saw things as they were, instead of studying man's own reflection ... the part of himself made of earth - the stone - he would not have plummeted to his death. Instead, the elders say, man would have escaped the need to repeat the lessons.

"We look at him – Coyote - and we are reminded of our own foolishness. We, too, sometimes break with the truth and believe our own lies. But we are caught up in our own trap ... eventually."

The courtroom was hushed during the time Owl Woman told her story, but now that she had finished, Alcazar could be heard insisting, vehemently, on some point with counsel.

***

"Your honor, I would like to briefly re-cross-examine the witness," stated Captain Banning.

"An amusing story, Owl Woman, but beside the point, eh?

"Now, is it not true," he asked, "that you lured the children, Carlotta and Diego Montoya de Medina, to the pueblo and corrupted them with your Indian idols?"

Again, there was a low rumble throughout the courtroom, and Judge Beckworth intervened, banging his gavel insistently on the podium.

"Answer the question, Owl Woman," directed the judge.

The Indian girl looked hopelessly to Luis and then back to Banning.

"I don't understand this ... lured?" she asked, seemingly confused.

"It means to trap!" said Banning.

"No, I could not trap them. Especially, The One Who Traveled Far ... Carlotta. I was there to reveal to her the truth of what she had seen."

Friar Alcazar began to rise from his chair, and Capt. Banning motioned him to be seated.

Turning to Judge Beckworth, Banning said, "I would like to excuse this witness, your honor, and call my last witness, Friar Alcazar."

It was apparent that Alcazar was eager to refute the previous testimony. He walked swiftly, arrogantly to the stand.

"Friar, for those here today who might not know, would you please tell us what really happened on Blue Mesa?" asked Capt. Banning.

"Yes," Alcazar breathed deeply, obviously struggling with his emotions. "I had allowed the orphans to go to Blue Mesa to play. They loved to play there, in the sunshine ..."

"I realize this is difficult for you, Friar. Take your time ..."

"No, no, this is much too important. As Lieutenant McGiver said ... it was a slaughter. The children's bodies were everywhere ... cut down unmercifully by Indians!"

"This must have been very difficult for you and ... Friar Serna, is it?"

"Yes, Serna," answered Alcazar. "But we took solace in our Lord and the children who had escaped harm. We accepted God's will."

Carlotta felt Jean Paul tug on her arm.

"Here's McGiver's log ... it's all here!" he whispered.

Carlotta quietly took the book into her lap. It was a miracle. With all that they had been through, Jean Paul still had the log. Her excitement overwhelmed her. Reaching across the railing, she tugged at Luis Valenzuela's sleeve.

"Please, Señor ... look!"

Luis could not abide the distraction. Absently, he took the open book from the child's hands, placed it on the desk in front of him, and returned his attention to Banning's witness.

Banning's line of questioning had left the massacre and its grizzly detail and moved on to Owl Woman.

"She has taught these children heathen ways!" Alcazar claimed. "Not only did the child, Carlotta, return from the pueblo with one of the Indian's idols, but when I took it away from her, she attempted to make one disguised as Jesus!" Alcazar was pointing at Owl Woman, and all eyes in the room followed his accusing hand.

"By her own testimony, she and her sisters had in their possession the holy chalices that were stolen from the Church! What more proof do we need? Owl Woman is an idolater, a practicing witch, doing the work of the devil!"

Raising his hand still further, Alcazar pointed directly at Sak-mo-i-si. "Tito Sanchez, the trader, was gruesomely killed by

Laughing Coyote because he dared to return the sacred vessels! Sixteen innocent children have their blood on this Indian's hands. How many more must die?"

Alcazar's eyes burned as he searched the crowd, many of them his parishioners, for their answer. His voice dropped to a whisper as he asked, "How many more will lose their very souls to this Indian witch?"

People were on their feet, their anguished cries repeating the friar's words.

"Witch, witch!" the words spread through the room.

Fear and anger intermingled until the room took on a caustic, fetid odor, such as that surrounding an animal caught within a trap.

Luis' stared at the book in front of him. In the midst of chaos, the handwritten words penetrated some part of his mind ... still rational, still accepting. It was Lieutenant John McGiver's log.

***

"Friar, we are acquainted, correct?" Luis asked, approaching the witness box.

"Yes, don Luis. I have administered chapel at your hacienda, and we have met socially, as well."

"You were, also, a guest at my dinner party and ball last summer, is that right?"

"I am surprised that you remember me among your many guests," Alcazar answered, humbly.

"Of course I do! Besides, from time to time I have employed several of the mission children at the ranch. Isn't that right?"

Alcazar nodded slowly.

"Please answer the question, Friar," Beckworth instructed.

"Yes," Alcazar said.

"And when I pay for their services, Friar, may I ask what happens to their money?"

"Well, the children contribute to their welfare at the mission."

"I see. Oh, one more question, Friar. I understand that you own a cattle ranch?"

"The mission owns a cattle ranch," Alcazar clarified.

"A very successful ranch, I might add," Luis said, flatteringly. "Didn't you just receive a shipment of fine furniture from Spain?"

Alcazar was taken off guard.

"That is true," he answered, struggling to regain composure.

"And won't you pay for it with the proceeds from your beef contract with the military ... when they build the new Fort Union ... its purpose will be to war against the Indians?"

"Your honor, I must protest! Señor Valenzuela refuses to allow the friar to answer one question before he asks another!"

"I apologize, your honor," Luis smiled, graciously, "and I withdraw my questions, both of them, and thank the friar for his testimony.

If this is prosecution's last witness, and if it pleases the court, I would like to call the child known as Carlotta Montoya de Medina to the witness stand."

Carlotta heard Luis call her name and she felt the world stop. It was no longer the courtroom and it was no longer a trial. She stepped over her brother's long legs, and unconsciously followed the instructions Luis Valenzuela was giving her.

She climbed the steps meant for an adult world, and sat uncomfortably in the hard witness chair.

"Carlotta Montoya de Medina," Luis softened her name with a smile. "Do you understand what is the truth?"

"Si, Señor," Carlotta answered.

"Good! You are like a breath of fresh air here today," he added.

"Did you just hand me, a few minutes ago, this?" Luis swept the log off his table and held it in the air for everyone to see.

"Yes, sir."

"Would you please tell all of us how you came to find the log of Lieutenant John McGiver?"

Carlotta began her story, visually striving for a strength she alone seemed aware she had.

She recalled Maria's instruction to her to leave for Blue Mesa and find the small child, Felicia. She slowly recounted the scene of soldiers and Comancheros, and under the gentle direction of Luis Valenzuela, relived the horror of a day she had so wanted to forget.

The courtroom was absolutely quiet, as Carlotta told how she had hidden, frozen in terror, and watched the guns cut down her friends, the orphans of San Ramon. She relived her tear-blinded escape to the cave, and the comfort she had found in the dark when her hand slipped easily into the shallow stone indentions that matched the shape of hers.

Magically, she found it easy to talk to Señor Luis, and soon forgot about the others in the room.

"Owl Woman found me and took me to the pueblo, where I met The People," Carlotta's voice was filled with awe.

"Is this where you received the Kachina doll, Carlotta?"

"Yes! It was a special present at the ceremony. It's not a bad thing, you know?" she said, hopefully.

She went on to tell Luis about her brother's and her return to Blue Mesa to look for reasons for the killing. They found the log and brought it back to the mission, where she and los niños read how Lt. McGiver, Tito Sanchez, and Friar Alcazar were all in it together. Carlotta barely heard the humming drone rise from the courtroom, or Alcazar's voice imploring the court to recognize and end the evil influence of Owl Woman on the poor child.

When she was through with the story of Blue Mesa, Luis allowed her several moments and then gently asked,

"Carlotta ... who is Laughing Coyote?"

"We. los niños and me ...we invented him," she whispered.

"Would you please explain to everyone here?" he asked.

Carlotta looked out at the people in the room, as if for the first time. "We didn't want to do bad things, but we had to undo their plans - the soldiers' and Tito's."

"So, he was your scapegoat?"

"What's a scapegoat?" Carlotta asked.

"He is the one you blame when no one takes responsibility."

"Yes, I guess Laughing Coyote was a scapegoat," she answered, matter-of-factly.

Carlotta's eyes settled on her brother, and for a moment she saw his power as the horse, strong and heroic like El Norte. Two seats over she saw Jean Paul, the mouse, whose ability to scrutinize the facts had brought their evidence to court. There was Virginia, who understood the magic of the raven, and Pilar, whose gift of action was so like the antelope. And she saw Miguel, her sleepy-eyed, dreaming lizard, and, of course, the twins, Chano and Chuey, who had given life to Laughing Coyote. Carlotta turned, seeking out the others in the circle of los niños, those who had found their power in unlikely places. Two Bears smiled from across the room, his rabbit fear met and conquered. And there was Joaquin, the wolf, who would learn to teach what he had learned this day. But, there at the table for the defense, sat Owl Woman, and Carlotta knew the lesson that was hers. She had received the medicine of the white owl. It was the Indian woman's gift to her.

***

"Laughing Coyote has served us well," said Luis. He reached over the railing to enlist the jurors' participation in the discovery.

"You have heard from Owl Woman ... how the Indians have understood his power, which is a lesson about ourselves. It is fitting that the Comanche twins were the children who wrote his poems. Are the twins the symbol of man's choice? The representation of man's dual nature? The choice to see or not to see? When I think about the story of the coyote and the rock thrown into the water, I wonder ... Is it a story about ourselves? When we have broken contract with our own integrity, when we have broken faith or trust, and we refuse to look at the truth, don't we become the victim of our delusions - apparitions, hallucinations, ghosts, and yes, even Laughing Coyote?

"These are the witches of Santa Fe ... and San Ramon. Our very fears, personified! "So, now you know the real villains of this case: our fear of the unknown, in this case, the people and their customs, who've lived here peacefully long before we came to determine their future, by erasing their past! The villains of church and state, yes, but more importantly, our ability to sabotage our own minds ... to deny our own hearts ... to deny reality. But reality exists, regardless of whim, lie, a government's proclamation, or the Church's cleverly placed guilt. A child has reminded us."

Judge Beckworth rose to address the jurors. He stated that the prosecution had failed to produce evidence, and ordered the case to be dismissed. The mood of the room changed irrevocably as the people saw the case for the prosecution disintegrate, and they clamored angrily, calling for new charges to be brought against several of the prosecution's witnesses.

Lt. John McGiver was stripped of his sword and sat looking out dismally at the crowd, his wrists bound, waiting for Judge Beckworth and Capt. Sedlow to determine his fate.

The people began milling about, discussing the inevitable verdict, reviewing remembered incidents, reassuring one another with a clap on a neighbor's back or an encouraging handshake that they were not one of those riddled with fear, of whom Luis Valenzuela had spoken.

In the bustle and confusion, no one noticed Friar Alcazar slip through the back door and out of their lives.

For the most part, the Indians present quietly retreated from the White Man's justice, eager to remove themselves from their loud and raucous ways.

Sak-mo-i-si and Two Bears stood and watched proudly from the back of the room, as the woman who had blessed their lives walked unobtrusively, yet eagerly, toward them.

The bishop and Dr. Gentry joined Luis, Carlotta, and Joaquin at the table for the defense, a circle of eager mission children surrounding them. Carlotta reached into the pocket of her dress and withdrew the letter from Spain.

Handing it tentatively to the bishop, she confessed, "I'm sorry, the letter was not mine to read, but I read it. My brother and I both read it. It is from our uncle, Carlos Montoya!" she said proudly.

The bishop smiled warmly. "Well then child, tell us what it says."

"He is coming to America to make arrangements for our lives!" Carlotta's voice had fallen to an incredulous whisper.

"With your permission, Bishop, I would like the children to live with me and my son until Señor Montoya's arrival."

Luis' hand rested lightly on Carlotta's shoulder, and she lifted her face to reveal a delighted grin.

"That is very gracious of you, Señor Valenzuela, and certainly helps minimize the immediate dilemma, the care of the children at the mission school until the sisters come. Of course, the Indian children ... those with families ... will return to their tribes, but there are others ..."

"Bishop, I believe you are aware that the child, Virginia, has worked for me," said Dr. Gentry.

"She has been mute until recently, and probably suffered some event in her brief life that has left her that way. I don't wish to see her lose that progress, Bishop. You know I have plenty of room above my office, I guess. What I'm trying to say is that I have grown quite fond of Virginia and would like to adopt her."

"That is wonderful, Doctor!" exclaimed the bishop, obviously moved.

"There may be others, Bishop, who will find a home in San Ramon," Luis suggested, as he turned to face the watchful circle of los niños.

The End

EPILOGUE

Indian Agent, James Calhoun, succeeded in signing a treaty with the Jicarilla that established a permanent home for them, but upon forwarding the treaty to Washington it was not acted on and nothing came of it. Hungry beyond that which they could bear, the tribe eked out their survival through raids and warfare.

In 1851, Fort Union was built to provide for the control of the Jicarilla. In 1852, the Jicarilla joined with the Navaho and the Ute for a war party against the Kiowa and Arapaho, but instead raided the farmers. Continued raids brought complaints, and the Jicarilla were assigned to the Albiquiu Agency. Crops were poor. They were fed wormy meat and given meager rations. Again, they were destitute and resorted to theft.

In 1853, Kit Carson, under General Kerny, advocated an agricultural school for the Apache. He gained influence with the Jicarilla, and in time became a peace maker between the warring factions.

In 1854, the Jicarilla and Ute destroyed a settlement on the Arkansas River.

In 1855, troops surprised the Jicarilla and Ute in the midst of a war dance, killing 40 Indians and capturing 6 children. In a second battle, the Indians lost 13 warriors plus all their possessions. Shortly afterwards, the Jicarilla sought out an agent and begged for peace, explaining that they had stolen because of need, and they promised to change their ways. They withdrew to the mountains to regroup their forces and resume their raids. When 24 soldiers were killed in a battle, the governor of New Mexico declared a state of war between the United States and the Jicarilla.

The Llanero Jicarilla - the "Plains People," whose name (pronounced "hick-ah-reel-yah") came from the Spanish word meaning "little basket" - today live on a reservation and occupy the territory east of the Rio Grande, where they still explore their beloved Sangre de Cristo Mountains.

***

Author's Biography

Wendy Padilla

Born in Chicago, Illinois, Wendy has lived most of her life in her beloved Southwest. For the last 27 years she has lived on a small ranch in Alpine, California. Wendy has raised 4 children, has 9 grandchildren, managed a herd of dairy goats, and has written articles for magazines, commentary for newspapers, poetry, and two books, "Dog Society and "Valley Fever". She presently assists writing technical papers with her scientist husband, Ralph Fenner.

A strong interest in Native American culture and beliefs has been the inspiration in Wendy's writing as well as contributing to her life style. The Pa-Gotzin-Kay ranch, "The place to go" has drawn spiritual leaders to its inipi (sweat lodge ceremonies) and it has also drawn those people most important in her life, including her friend and collaborator, Donna Simko, in writing their present book.

Author's Biography

Donna Simko

Donna, a native of San Diego, grew up fascinated with the history and beauty of the Southwest. She raised two boys who, later in life, would become her good friends. The family has expanded in recent years with the addition of a daughter in law and two charming and very active granddaughters.

Donna's love of the creative process has expressed itself through her writing. Inspiration for her writing comes from her love of art, nature, science and philosophy. Much of her life has been spent studying various belief systems, searching for their common denominators. Tibetan Buddhism and Native American spirituality have greatly influenced her. Understanding the science behind the spirituality has led her to explore the nature of consciousness and the limitless possibilities it suggests.

Researching and writing Medicine of the White Owl with Wendy Padilla provided an extraordinary backdrop to a rare friendship already filled with shared ideas and dreams.

Donna has written a children's story and is currently researching and writing another book.

www.ingramcontent.com/pod-product-compliance
Lightning Source LLC
Chambersburg PA
CBHW031108030726
47496CB00002BA/438